FOR ALL THE HORSES

STRAWBERRY SKY

PART THREE OF MIDNIGHT SKY

JAN RUTH

Acknowledgements:

My Son; for his patience with all matters technical.

John Hudspith Editing Services;
for super sharp crossing and dotting.

JD Smith Design; for beautiful insides and outs.

Contents

Prologue - Maggie   1

Chapter One - Laura   17

Chapter Two - Laura   33

Chapter Three - Maggie   49

Chapter Four - Laura   65

Chapter Five - Maggie   81

Chapter Six - Laura   97

Chapter Seven - Maggie   115

Chapter Eight - Laura   131

Chapter Nine - Laura   149

Chapter Ten - Maggie   167

Chapter Eleven - Laura   183

Chapter Twelve - Laura   201

Chapter Thirteen - Maggie   217

Chapter Fourteen - Laura   231

Chapter Fifteen - Laura   249

Chapter Sixteen - Laura   265

About Jan Ruth   283

PROLOGUE

Maggie

Her sister's wedding day, finally. And it was a breathless kind of spring morning, filled with racing white clouds and soaring birds full of song.

So why did something feel inexplicably wrong? Oh, it was nothing to do with the weather, or the outfits. Thank goodness it wasn't too warm for her black and white ensemble after all, even though it would have been so much better suited to the original Christmas date but that couldn't be helped, and it wasn't as if anyone would even see it. From Laura's point of view, it was no doubt disappointing that there were to be no guests at her long-awaited wedding. It was rather typical of James though, and got him out of socialising on a grander scale. Although who could blame him, barely able to walk without assistance thanks to Maggie's daughter's ex-boyfriend. Callum Armstrong might not be her daughter's partner anymore, but he was still the father of her child whether anyone liked it or not. So taking everything into consideration, the intimacy of a small gathering which excluded Jess and indeed all those silly friends of Laura's from Cheshire, would result in a lot less stress for her sister and anyway, who needed all that fuss and expense?

No, the tension in the house was something to do with

Jess, as usual. It was something to do with the way she whispered into her phone at odd hours of the day and night. Maggie tried not to listen, not daring to hope that it was Sam she was speaking to. Good, upstanding Sam. The perfect boyfriend for her wild child. Oh, *why* did he have to live in America? Her daughter had gone through a remarkable transformation during the time he'd spent with them over Christmas. She felt sure they were still in touch though, and despite the awkward historical connections to the bride and groom, Maggie couldn't help thinking that more time spent with Sam would be good for Jess. Sam's mother had even suggested the perfect escape with a job at her ranch in New Hampshire, but Pete had put his foot down. Maggie didn't agree with his reasoning, not in totality. The American adventure would get Jess away from the scene of destruction she'd been dragged into with Armstrong, and allow her to be a teenager again. Get her head straight. Currently, she could barely leave the house for fear of getting ambushed and coerced – it wasn't right she was hassled like this. If Jess was absent for a few weeks it would give everyone else some headspace too and with support from Sam, Jess would surely bond with baby Krystal and return in a better state of mind.

Of course, the huge sticking point in this plan was the actual baby. Jess made no secret of the fact that Krystal hadn't been planned or wanted – except by Armstrong – and Pete fretted about the baby's future, and her welfare. If it wasn't for this, Maggie would be tempted to buy Jess and Krystal a ticket and put them on a plane anyway, although she'd never dare say as much to Pete. Her husband already had his suspicions about a possible conspiracy and laid the law down at every opportunity.

'Once your sister's married, we'll have a talk about this Armstrong fella,' Pete said. 'It's not right him shirking his responsibilities. He needs to be on that birth certificate, so he's made to pay. And if he wants contact he'll have to see the baby on neutral ground so he can be monitored by the authorities.'

'Jess doesn't want that.'

'It's not her sole decision to make! We're trying to run a respectable business here, in case you'd forgotten? Bloody arguments every night on the phone, and the baby crying for hours, I'm tired of it! There's already three reviews on Trip Advisor marking us down for noise, and another cancellation this morning.'

'I know, I know that,' she said, hustling him towards the front door. 'Go on, go to the Cash and Carry and leave us women to it.'

'And stop helping her with the baby, otherwise she'll never learn.'

'Yes, alright, you've run through your usual bullet list for the day.'

He was almost at the car when he stopped and came back, this time with a stabbing finger. 'And keep the doors locked. It's your sister's day today and I wouldn't put it past that lowlife to cause trouble.'

'He doesn't know anything about James and Laura getting wed. And why would he be interested?'

'He's interested in anything he can mess up, that's why.'

She watched him reverse off the drive and closed the front door firmly, then went to check that the back door was actually locked. Pete was right about one thing; they couldn't live like this. No one wanted Armstrong hanging about, especially not Laura and James and *especially* not today. On the upside, the spontaneous wedding preparations put a stop to any disturbing speculation. Jess even gave Laura a dress, a floaty silken thing, the colours of tropical fish and azure skies.

'That's kind of you,' Maggie said, poised at her daughter's bedroom door. 'And you've done Laura's nails beautifully.'

Her grandchild was lying on the messy bed, grizzling

and begging to be picked up while Jess blow-waved her hair, but Maggie restrained herself from interfering. The room was a tip. A plethora of beauty equipment was piled on the dressing table too, but there was no offer of a manicure for her mother.

'Krystal will need another bottle soon, shall I warm one through?'

'Shouldn't you be on your way?'

'Oh, there's a while yet. Laura won't want to be there first.'

'It's not even a proper wedding, they're only going to say their vows to each other.'

'The vows are the important part.'

'Who told you that? Everyone knows it's only the sex that's important,' she said, leaning in to the mirror to pluck her eyebrows.

'Pity you didn't award it the importance it deserved then, when you conceived a baby.'

They both huffed and sighed, knowing it was a stupid, futile conversation, quickly halted by Jess' mobile ringing. She glanced at the caller ID, then switched it off and began to rub cream into her face.

'Are you not going to answer it?'

'It's Cal, *again*. I don't want to talk to him. I don't want him involved in my life. He's a freakin nutcase!'

'He might calm down if you agree to let him see the baby. Like Dad says, in one of those controlled environments.'

'Like a cell, you mean?'

'Why don't you talk to him and diffuse the situation, like an adult?'

Jess screwed the lid back on one pot, opened another and began to dot cream carefully under her eyes. 'No point. I've told him my plans and he's gone mental.'

'What plans? Have you been deliberately making him jealous over Sam?'

'What if I have? Like my future is anything to do with

him.'

'It's got *something* to do with him, he's Krystal's father!'

A huge shrug and a sigh. 'Whatever.'

'We'll talk about this later.'

Jess inserted earpieces, despite Krystal beginning to grizzle again on top of the bed amongst a huge pile of clothes and bags. Heart racing, Maggie closed the bedroom door and went back down the stairs before she exploded. If she could just get Laura to the church and happily on her way to a golden future with the local horse-whispering hunk, all would be well in at least a small part of the world, but the second she stepped into the kitchen, Armstrong's outline appeared behind the frosted pane on the back door. Maggie's pulse shot through the roof. A barrage of thumping began, and then his distorted face, up close and personal through the dimpled glass. 'Granny Meddle! I know you're in there! Jess? *Jess!* I just want to see our kid.'

Thankfully, she could hear the hairdryer droning upstairs in Laura's room. Maggie shrank back behind the fridge-freezer and considered calling the police. No, not today, she simply couldn't, and Pete would be home soon enough. All she had to do was brazen it out and get Laura to the church. If Armstrong sensed any urgency or fear on her behalf, he'd lap it up. Impatient, he stepped away from the door and looked up at the back bedroom windows. '*Jess!* Get down here and explain yourself! I'll find out what's going on... you sneaky bitch!'

Of course there was no response. He moved towards the door for a last look inside, gave the frame a single solid kick, swore, then retreated down the side of the house just as the hairdryer went quiet. Moments later, her sister materialised in the kitchen, holding an almost empty glass of fizz watered down with orange juice. If she'd heard anything untoward, there was no evidence on her face. She looked completely composed and beautiful. Unlike Maggie, who opened the fridge in order to hide her flushed face, certain her hammering heart could be seen as well as heard.

'A final drink before we sway down the road?'

Laura smoothed the front of her dress with a nervous hand. 'It doesn't look too young on me, does it?'

'Wow, look at you! No, it looks fab, *you* look fab.'

'I don't know why I've gone to any trouble. James will be his usual scruffy self.'

'No, he won't,' Maggie said, sloshing champagne into Laura's glass. 'Come on, drink up. I bet he's already there in his posh suit.'

They clinked glasses and then they had a funny little pre-wedding conversation about the banker's draft Laura's slimy ex had finally coughed-up, and about how Maggie had sent Armstrong away from the hospital with a flea in his ear. It served to remind them that the Brown sisters were no pushover and more than a match for any bloke who might think differently. Further emboldened by the booze, Maggie held out her arm for Laura. They went slowly down the drive, checking their watches with a mischievous air, knowing full-well they were a tiny bit late as the time crept past noon. As they walked along the road, Maggie couldn't help peering closely at any man-sized bushes, and then she worried about Jess being alone in the house with Krystal. Silly, random thoughts that shouldn't be there at all, but thankfully, Laura didn't notice her fidgeting or furtive glances.

The church soon came into sight, an ancient heap of lopsided stones covered in moss. The lych-gate catch was stuck as usual and they struggled with that, then stopped briefly at Mum's grave, admiring the mass of speedwells in the rough grass.

'This is it, then,' Maggie said. 'Are you ready to do this?'

'God, yes.' Laura sighed and turned her brown eyes to meet hers. 'James and I… we've both been through so much to get to this point. Just wish Mum and Dad could be here.'

'I know. Well, Mum is, kind of.'

Laura nodded and managed a tight smile.

A musty smell greeted them through the wedged-open church door, along with some tuneless music. Even the organ sounded out of breath, wheezing and full of dust. Maggie tutted but Laura seemed a tad overwhelmed, as she usually did with anything even mildly sentimental. Maggie patted her hand, and they prepared to enter the gloomy interior – advancing no more than three steps – before they realised that other than Mrs Wynn Evans bent double over the organ and Owen swaying over an open bible on the pulpit, the church was empty. The shock was awful. The absence of the groom was the last thing anyone could have predicted. Of course, once Laura had taken it all in and checked her watch and her phone, she marched right back out again. And she kept going at a fairly brisk pace all the way back to Hafod House.

Maggie trailed behind, cursing her new court shoes. 'Laura, wait!'

It didn't make sense. James was the most reliable, honest man she'd ever known. Oh, he might be moody and depressed from time to time, but if he'd made a promise to Laura there was no way he'd jilt her without a perfectly logical reason. At Hafod House, Laura was pacing on the drive because of course she had no key to get in, and there was no way Jess would answer the door. They moved wordlessly inside and Maggie's eyes fell on the cases and the pile of coats in the hall, and although Krystal was *still* crying upstairs, her sister's quiet distress felt more immediate so she followed her into the kitchen.

'Just call him! There has to be a good reason he's not there. Maybe he's fallen or something.'

Laura filled a glass with water and glugged it down, glanced at her phone again then switched it off and flung it across the table.

'Don't do that, he might be trying to reach you!'

Still, there was no spoken reaction from her, just a pinched face. It was a face which had already endured too much heartbreak. Maggie tugged off her shoes and pulled out a chair. How long did they sit at that table; herself thinking of stupid excuses for him, and Laura trying not to cry? It was probably only minutes, but as every second ticked by and James didn't phone the house or turn up on the doorstep, the worse the prognosis seemed and the more futile their conversation. As if to compound this, Krystal continued to cry the piercing cry of a hungry baby and Maggie was just about to mix a bottle, when the front door opened.

'What the bloody hell's all this?' Pete said, no doubt falling over the luggage in the hall. He materialised in the doorway then, arms full of nappies and greaseproof paper, and lowered everything slowly onto the table. 'What's going on? What you both doing back here?'

'It was a no-show,' Laura said, interrupted by a loud rap on the door. They all exchanged wary glances before Pete said, 'That'll be him now, James.'

Maggie managed a tight nod and a smile at Laura, which wasn't reciprocated. Pete went to answer the door. A male voice, brisk and with a strong Manchester accent floated down the hall and into the kitchen. 'Taxi for Jessica Thomas. Manny Airport, yeah? Are these the bags, mate?'

A long beat of silence from Pete. '*You what?*'

Jess came thundering down the stairs and then pandemonium broke out. Maggie stopped gripping the edge of her chair and rose slowly to her feet. Deep down, she'd known full well what those bags were about, but she'd ignored the significance. She moved to observe the scene of chaos in the hall with as much surprise as she could muster. Jess and the taxi-driver were ferrying cases and bags outside and Pete shot Maggie an almost incredulous look. 'Have you got *nothing* to say about this? Did you know she was

Jan Ruth

planning to take-off today?'

'No, of course not! I have had other things to think about, you know, like my sister's non-wedding.' He seemed partially satisfied with that and turned back to Jess. 'And just where do you think you're going?'

She shoved past her father, 'I'm going to America, duh.'

'You can't drag a newborn all that way to a bloody horse ranch then leave her with strangers all day. We've been through this!'

'I'm *not*. Stella said there's no nursery and not to come over, at the last *minute*. I mean, how unfair is that when we've talked about it for *months*, and I've gone and got a ticket now.' She pulled up the handle on her trolley case with a vicious tug. 'Anyway, Sam's sorted it.'

Pete looked as if he might combust but Maggie was more distracted by Krystal, who was by then screaming with rage. She went quickly up the stairs, glad to be out of the line of fire and lifted the baby from her cot just as Jess slid into the room behind her.

'Don't take her, Jess.'

'Who said I was taking her?'

She spun round, holding the baby's head. 'What do you mean?'

A shadow crossed her daughter's face before she picked up her handbag, ready to flee. 'I'm not taking her, alright?'

Maggie hugged the bundle of squirming baby close to her chest and stroked her downy fine baby hair, a veritable fireball of conflicting emotions dancing in her belly. Oh, Jess would always be a selfish madam but she was hurting and depressed, and that hard exterior was the only way she knew how to function when she was under attack. Armstrong had controlled and bullied her into a pregnancy she didn't want, how awful was that for a teenager? It was Sam who brought out the carefree, passionate side of Jess. It was Sam who made her into a better person and gave her the confidence to be herself.

A holiday, that's what she needed.

Meanwhile, she'd be the best Grandma this poor little mite could wish for. Maggie practically drooled at the prospect of making a safe cozy haven for her grandchild. A routine and a full tummy, that's all she'd need to be content. She carried Krystal downstairs and into the kitchen, just as the taxi prepared to pull away. Pete glared at her, his expression mostly unidentifiable.

'She's… *without* the baby?'

'Looks that way,' Maggie said, jiggling Krystal. 'Pete, listen to me. Let her have some freedom, and she'll come back ready to be a mother.'

'This is Jess we're talking about!'

'She just… needs a break.'

'What *from?*'

'Everything,' she said, cradling Krystal in one hand and trying to heat a bottle in the microwave with the other. She paused to kiss Krystal's head. 'Hardest job in the world, being a mum.'

'Maggie, I've stayed out of your relationship with Jess for years, and then you *begged* me to get tough with her. And at the first major crisis point, I'm overruled! She'll never learn how to grow up and be a decent person when you keep giving her easy options. She's bloody spoilt, Maggie!'

It was a time-worn argument, cut short by the arrival of James and his best-man, Rob. They both looked sheepish, filling the kitchen with testosterone and ripped jeans. If it hadn't been for Pete snarling at her and Krystal yelling to be fed, she'd have done a disappearing act and gone back upstairs. As it happened, Pete shook the bottle without securing the teat and the contents spewed everywhere, all over her hair and her lovely Debenhams outfit.

'For goodness' sake!'

'Well it's not as if you'll be needing it now, is it?'

'Where's Jess off to in that taxi?' Rob said, as if that was the most important item on the agenda while her poor sister sagged against the kitchen units. Pete filled them in, in between mopping-up the spilt milk and wringing out a smelly cloth in the sink. And it sounded awful, what Jess had done. Rob cleared his throat and rubbed the back of his neck. 'So er… she's gone without the baby, then?'

'What's this here, a bloody apparition?' Pete said, pointing unnecessarily towards Krystal. Rob exchanged an odd look with James, then sloped off outside.

Maggie fixed the bottle and dragged Pete out of the kitchen and into the sitting room. The bride and groom needed to talk. At least Krystal fell silent once Granddad had settled in the armchair and cradled Krystal securely in the crook of his arm, milk poised at the correct angle. It seemed only minutes had passed though when they heard the front door open and close, and Rob's car roar back up the road.

'That doesn't bode well,' Pete muttered, 'He's been here for all of five minutes.'

Why did all this drama happen to Laura? All she wanted was marriage and a baby. It seemed life was determined to rub her nose in what she couldn't have, whipping it from under her nose at the last minute. As Krystal was dropping fitfully to sleep and Pete was walking up and down with her over his shoulder, Laura came into the sitting room. Her eyes went straight to Krystal, then she perched on the edge of the sofa. Her hair had come loose and she'd kicked off her shoes.

'It was Armstrong.'

'What do you mean?' Maggie said, aware that her face was sweating and her chest felt tight.

'He burst into the bungalow, convinced James was helping Jess. It just goes on and on, doesn't it?'

'What happened?' Maggie managed to squeak. 'He is alright, though, James?'

'Well, fortunately Rob turned up. Otherwise I dread to think.'

'You've not sent him packing because of this, please tell me you haven't? Laura?'

A huge sigh at this, and her eyes fell to the floor. 'He's waiting down at the church.'

'Well, then! Let me make a drink, and let's see if we can put this right,' she said, grateful for something to do. 'Go and fix your hair, go on.' When Laura didn't move, she squeezed her sister's shoulder with as much solidarity as she could muster. 'Laura, you'll only have yourself to blame if you let this hiccup ruin everything.'

'*Hiccup?* My fiancé was almost beaten-up by your daughter's boyfriend!'

'*Ex.* And James is *fine.*'

Maggie escaped to the kitchen and filled the kettle on autopilot. *Bloody hell!* How was she to know that Armstrong would do such a thing? She had only a few seconds to rearrange her face because Laura came to hover in the doorway, determined to have her say. 'They got a written confession out of him. More than the police managed.'

'That's good.'

A huge sigh at this, arms folded. 'Is it? This is supposed to be my wedding day! Everything James and I plan is somehow destroyed by Jess and Armstrong.'

Maggie concentrated on pouring boiling water over three teabags. 'I don't know why he went round there.'

'I bet Jess does, but we can't ask her now, can we?' she said, then narrowed her eyes. 'Did he come here first and they argued or something, is that it?'

'Well, you've been here the whole time, so you tell me,' Maggie said, going into the fridge for the milk. Thank goodness she could keep her hands busy and her eyes averted, although there was only so many times she could hide behind the fridge door in one day.

'I guess he doesn't need to be here in person though, does he?' Laura went on. 'Jess can send provocative texts whilst hiding in her room. And she's very active on Twitter, according to Ben and Lucy. She's a proper madam when it comes to making men jealous, but it's a dangerous game with someone like Armstrong.'

Maggie endured everything Laura had to say, feeling it was her duty to let her get it all off her chest. It felt horrible, but it's what you did when you were a mother. Eventually, Laura took her tea and announced she was going to her room to fix her hair – which hopefully indicated that the wedding was back on – but Laura took her time about it, and Maggie fretted then that James would give up waiting. Pete began to grumble that he had work to do and he couldn't sit nursing the baby all afternoon. She found some comfy shoes, then carefully laid the sleeping Krystal in her pram. Pete helped her get it over the front step and out onto the drive.

'What a bloody day this has turned out to be!' he said, lowering his voice when Maggie flapped her hand at him but he was still determined to have his say. 'If you speak to Jess you can tell her from me that she can't just swan back in here when she's fed up of the new fella, or fed up of working, or fed up of being on holiday, whichever comes first.'

'Oh, Pete you don't mean that!'

'No, Maggie, I do. She can find somewhere else to live when she comes back. You let her have her own way too often when she was little,' he said, then when she began to make a feeble protest, held up his hand. 'I admit I didn't help at the time, but she needs to learn a hard lesson now for her own good.'

Maggie pulled the hood up on the pram with a dispirited sigh. 'Just… make sure Laura follows me back down to the church.'

'That's up to her, not us. Give your sister some space.'

Maggie set off walking, the sour odour of baby formula clinging to her clothes, but it hardly mattered. She'd forgotten how wonderful it felt to push a pram. It was a big, old-fashioned one too. None of those modern contraptions that fold up without warning and nowhere to put your shopping. The memories it brought back! The day had warmed, releasing the scents of the hedgerows and highlighting the drystone walls across the hills. The church soon came into view and what a relief to see Rob's car. She quickened her pace, peering through the rhododendron bushes bordering the graveyard, glad to spot James sprawled across some ancient family tomb. He'd seen her of course, and once he'd manoeuvred himself upright, looked distinctly crestfallen to see she was alone.

'I've come to check you are actually here,' Maggie said, hoping that was enough to give him some hope without confirming anything one way or the other.

'I'm a man of my word, as you can see.'

'Hmm.' She found her reading glasses, and sent Laura what she imagined was a commanding, no-nonsense text: *HE'S. HERE.*

The pram wouldn't go all the way down the path because the wheel frame was far too wide, but she managed to push it within speaking distance of her sister's fiancé. How did he manage to look so handsome after everything he'd been through and with no obvious attention to his appearance? There was even a splash of blood on his crumpled white shirt. Hanging around the mossed gravestones he looked more like a character in a historical vampire film than someone about to be married in the 21st century. She made sure the brake was on, then lifted Krystal out of her pram.

'My sister's world collapsed again.'

'Circumstances beyond my control. If I ever had any to begin with.'

Krystal immediately began to grizzle in the harsh

sunlight, so Maggie made to move inside the church. It was so gloomy it took her several long seconds to recognise James' sister, Liz, sat next to Rob on the front pew. They were both discussing the altercation at the bungalow, and Maggie was glad she had Krystal to rock and sway, patting her tiny back long after she'd gone to sleep. After a moment, James shuffled back in and sat down.

Rob announced he'd not got the rings.

Liz turned in her seat to snarl at him. 'Oh, *what?* Are you kidding?'

'Is there time to go and get them, where are they?'

'In that souvenir dish from Spain. On the mantel,' James said.

'You're not to go anywhere! Either of you,' Liz hissed, and both men fell silent, arms folded and staring ahead. They waited for what felt like an eternity, listening to Owen snoring, and Rob going through his pockets, but every time Maggie looked at her watch the hands had barely moved. *Come on, Laura!*

She heard Rob whisper to Liz, 'I could make a temporary ring, out of straw. A symbolic one. What do you think?'

And then the door creaked open and Laura stepped inside. Some birds flew in. There was an audible intake of breath from all of them. She looked terribly serious, for a bride. Rob nudged Owen awake and helped James get to his feet. The poor groom looked in bad shape the way he needed to hold on to the opposite pew like that, but his eyes were locked on to Laura's. Her sister continued to move down the aisle purposefully, and came to stand in front of James. She placed her hand in his, and they embraced. No words needed.

The service was short and sweet, with Owen forgetting half the words and mixing it up with the harvest festival. Liz said it was the blessing of the straw ring which confused him, but no one cared, not really. Owen gravely pronounced them '*Man* and… *Woman,*' and then they were all laughing and kissing. They moved outside to throw blossom and take selfies, and then Rob drove James and Laura up to the yard.

Maggie pushed the pram home with a smile on her face, Krystal finally content in her pink nest. Her sister's wedding day had actually happened. It was going to be an amazing summer! Business would pick up at the B & B. Laura would fall pregnant and the focus would move away from Jess. Her daughter would return home happy, with Sam? Who knew! Pete would come round in her absence and they'd sort out Armstrong in a calm, adult manner. Never one to be whimsical or romantic, she surprised herself with her own optimism, although when she discovered Pete already packing-up their daughter's belongings and pulling down the loft ladder, decided it was perhaps more rooted in blind hope, after all.

CHAPTER ONE

Laura

Pregnant. *Not pregnant.* She tore the cellophane from the packet and studied the contents. How many times had she done this? Too many.

Through the open bedroom window, the sounds and smells of summer floated into the room on a westerly breeze. The Welsh hills, rising like a blue shadow in the middle distance, vibrated with new life. Horses, birdsong, the distant hum of farm machinery, and sheep… always sheep. Hundreds of lambs, grown sturdy now and not needing the ewes so much, still bleated for milk and reassurance. Closer to home, the drone of a bee hovering around the top of the wisteria. She moved to the bathroom, peed on the plastic stick and set it down on a slip of tissue.

If she perched on the sleigh bed, she could see her husband's horse browsing along the flowering hawthorn and tearing at the cow parsley. His mouth was so full of foliage he looked to be carrying a bouquet. A lorry bounced down the drive, carrying a load of steel girders and fence posts. O'Malley shied away from the resultant cloud of dust and Laura moved closer to the window. The foundations for the indoor riding arena were already in place, and now they'd begun on the roof. The structure looked angular and ugly, but it would be the most incredible space once fully enclosed and the best possible antidote to the cruel Welsh winters and the wettest of summer days. And she could plant shrubs and hanging baskets in time to soften the lines. Rhian and Lucy were already planning indoor competitions and Laura had dared to suggest non-horse related events too; anything to supplement their income. James had grudgingly agreed. Despite the second chance they'd been given, Laura believed the greatest prop to her husband's recovery – both physically and emotionally – lay in James allowing her to fulfil her role as his partner in every sense of the word.

The jewel in the crown for both of them, would be a child.

Her phone buzzed with a text message from her sister: *Something I need to tell you. Ok to pop round?*

She checked the time and steeled herself to look at the pregnancy test for a full two seconds, before slinging it in the pedal-bin. She responded to Maggie, then took her old shirt from the back of the chair and went down the stairs and out into the yard. Did it show on her face? She could feel disappointment twisting her guts and forcing its way out, but it had no right to be there so she swallowed it down. She and James had had the most amazing second-chance, not only to be together but to be here, in this special place. Alive, and planning a future.

Since the horrific accident the previous November which had put him in a coma and damaged his spine, James had somehow worked himself better around the yard. The current heatwave helped; beautiful lengthening days full of deep, all-encompassing serenity. Sometimes, by mid-afternoon when the grazing horses were stationary beneath the trees and whisking flies, she'd discover him asleep in the hay meadow with a hat over his face, the dogs panting nearby in the shade, ever watchful. He was involved in specialist teaching again, using Ben for muscle power where necessary and walking well enough with a stick, an aid which frequently went missing thanks to his inability to remember where he'd left it or to the mischievous antics of Washboy, the Lurcher.

The quad bike had not been replaced.

She found him directing the lorry-load of roofing with Ben. On sight of her he shuffled over the rough, hard-baked ground and they both stood in the centre of what would eventually be the new schooling area.

'I can't believe how quickly it's all come together,' she said, looking everywhere except at his face.

'There's nothing much to it, is there? I mean, now the foundations are in it's literally four walls and a roof.'

'And the flooring, what did you decide? Rhian said the best one is made from synthetic rubber.'

'Have you seen the cost of that stuff per tonnage?'

'Get the best, whatever it takes.'

'That cash won't last forever you know.'

He meant the money which her sister had finally managed to get out of her ex-partner; another reason to be optimistic about the future. In fact, both of them could put past demons to rest, in every sense of the word. The sun blazed down, illuminating the overflowing dustbin of discarded builder's materials, and the area sectioned off for spectator seating. She made her way to a stack of plastic chairs scattered across the makeshift plinth. 'Should we move the tannoy system into here? Perhaps we need a new one, what do you think?'

When he made no response, she turned to look at him and his eyes travelled over hers. 'What's wrong?'

'Am I that readable, honestly?'

'Mostly.'

She moved into his arms then and it was an embrace which usually made perfect sense of everything. She rested her forehead against his chest. 'I did another test.'

Was it her imagination, or did his intake of breath mean he was already tiring of her butterfly approach to everything?

The pressure to keep everything going on the yard and live in an upturned house as well as accommodate her obsession to become pregnant as soon as possible, was no easy ask. On top of this, the proposed renovations to the house had been fraught with anxiety. A big sum of money fixed most practical problems but while a huge refurbishment project was a job she relished, she was aware of the personal cost to James as she went about ripping out what was left of his life with Carys, although he often went out of his way to assure her that he was fine with it.

'Come here,' he said, drawing her closer, tighter. His lips grazed the top of her head. 'There's no rush, is there?'

'I guess not, but you know what my reproductive system is like.' She pulled away so she could look at him. 'James, I want to look at the options, you know, IVF.'

'Not sure I'm ready for any more hospital stuff.'

'There won't be any of that initially, and anyway, it'll be me. Not you.'

He shrugged.

'Is that a yes, then?'

'It's… a guess so. More of an eventually, not a right away.'

Her spirits dropped. 'You floor me with your enthusiasm.'

'I can't keep up with you as it is,' he said, not unkindly, but then began to count items off on his fingers. 'You're trying to get the house done-up to some impossible standard–'

'A new shower is *not* an impossible standard, it's a bare necessity!'

'Alright, alright! You want to learn to ride, you want to start your own design business again and what's this I hear from the builders about external offices?'

She folded her arms. 'Only when they've finished the school. And it's only a couple of cabins. One for a general yard reception and one for me, well, for Cariad Designs. So we can keep all the office stuff separate and out of the house.'

'And inbetween all of this I find you ordering fifty fancy

trees to line the drive.'

'It's just a few cherry trees. I wanted apple but decided against those for obvious reasons.'

He ran a hand through his hair at this and his face broke into a hesitant grin. They were interrupted by Rhian waving a sheet of paper. 'Them local dog trainers are up for it. Two hours every Thursday night from October.'

Laura smiled. 'That's brilliant.'

'What dog trainers?' James said, looking from Rhian and back to Laura.

'The local fly-ball team. Renting out the indoor school when we're not using it is simply good business practice. James, you *agreed*.'

'Did I?'

'Yes. I showed you the spreadsheets.'

'I remember we had an argument about the size of the thing.'

'And you were overruled,' she said, prodding his chest.

Once she'd started to apply her business brain, it made sense to Laura to go for the largest size school possible, so if needs be, they could divide the space and have dual use at any one time, and then open up the entire area for dressage and show-jumping competitions. Rhian wholeheartedly agreed that the full size arena would attract the key players and therefore a bigger entry fee. But James wanted to keep his round-pen where it was and he'd grown exasperated when she'd suggested he used the indoor school instead.

'No. It needs to be the exact size and shape, and I need isolation. I'm not trying to work a horse next door to the bloody pony club.'

'Fair point. Alright, well, we can keep the round-pen where it is and extend down the other side then.'

'Well, *thank* you.'

He'd shot her a mutinous look but when she'd shown him her reasoning on paper and Rhian had agreed with her, he'd backed down.

Ben came into view and shouted something about drainage. James hobbled gratefully back outside and melted into a huddle of builders peering down a ditch.

Her sister was of the same opinion when it came to forging ahead and expressed genuine surprise at the speed in which she'd got a team of plumbers in to sort out the downstairs shower room.

'I just want to get this, and the kitchen done before winter. I can't understand why everyone thinks I'm going too fast.'

'Everyone? You mean James. Men don't like being steamrollered, you know.'

Laura kept her eyes firmly on the floor as she scrubbed away on her hands and knees. At least it was dry mud and the new non-slip flooring was proving a dream to clean. She'd gone for black, cream, and grey in the end and it looked masculine, clean and fresh. The smell of rotting horse-blankets and whatever else had lurked in there, had gone. The important part of it was the huge walk-in power-shower, complete with grab-handles, which made life easy for James. It made life easy for her in that all the outdoor clothing could be deposited in the same area rather than be trailed into the sitting room or God forbid, upstairs. She'd even bought black and grey towels as further endorsement of keeping it real, although currently they looked especially stylish in an alternating tower on the ottoman. It wouldn't last.

'Looks great in here,' Maggie said, her voice echoing slightly in the mostly empty space.

Laura got to her feet, wrung out the cloth and dropped it into the bucket, then rubbed her back. The room did look great. She'd not add anything decorative, she knew better than that. It was to be a purely functional space. But once the old office had gone from the front parlour opposite, she could make a small guest bedroom and go to town on the decor. If she could persuade her father to come and stay, he'd appreciate not having to climb any stairs to the bathroom.

'How have you got a team of builders to be this motivated, that's what I want to know,' her sister said, and followed her down the hall into the kitchen. Laura filled the kettle and found a couple of clean mugs. 'I still have contacts in that area as you well know. I simply dangled the promise of future work and cash up front. Easy.'

'What's next, then?'

'Kitchen. I expect that will take us up to the end of summer and then we can find easier jobs through the winter.'

Maggie pulled out a chair and sighed. If she'd noticed her terse manner then her sister clearly knew better than to challenge her, and at least she'd not brought the baby. Krystal was impossibly sweet and innocent while her impossibly selfish mother gallivanted around America with Sam. It was an equally impossible situation with no comfortable solution in sight. James hated the fact that his son and Jess were together, but at least they were out of sight. Maggie clearly enjoyed playing the doting grandma despite the steadily increasing awkwardness. The longer Laura took to become pregnant, the more petulant animosity she struggled to hide. Of course, it was shameful that such feelings festered around a three-month-old baby, but the cruelty of nature and the cruelty of random circumstance was a bitter pill to keep forcing down.

'It looks like you've already made a start in here,' Maggie said, nodding towards the brand new boiler sat on the floor, and several shrink-wrapped radiators.

'A new system was cheaper in the end. It needs doing before anything else but I've chosen some units in the meantime. Seasoned oak with granite worktops.'

'Wow.'

'I'm keeping the original slate floor, the dresser and the

table, it all just needs cleaning and resurfacing really.'

They took the tea outside, to a picnic table which had seen better days but was pleasantly sheltered from the sun, and the noise and dust of the building works over by the menage.

There was no garden to speak of, just a raggedy strip that used to be grass and petered out into the general area they called the yard. The only division of privacy was a line of half-dead shrubs, beyond which the staff respected as private territory. Laura eventually intended to erect a smart fence and half a dozen flowering climbers to keep any wandering horses and the nosy public out, and the dogs *in*.

'So, what was it you wanted to tell me?'

'Oh, nothing much, it'll keep. It's nice to have a catch-up.'

Laura took a sip of tea and looked at her sister's strained face over the mug. Was it her imagination or did she look nervous, and sort of furtive? 'It can't be nothing.'

'Holidays,' she said, suddenly. 'You've got the best set-up here, or you will have. I've seen your ad for staff in the local rag.'

'We need a qualified instructor, to replace Liz,' she said quickly, not wanting Maggie to get any wild ideas. She knew how James felt about employing family, and it had always been a disaster in the past.

'I've done the research, and there's a massive gap in the market,' Maggie was saying. 'And I just thought… well, you could do the riding part, *obviously*. And the guests could stay at Hafod House.'

'*Obviously*.'

A girly laugh at this. 'We could, you know, offer one of those all-in deals. Work together, imagine that!'

'According to you and James I'm going too fast as it is with new ideas.'

'I thought, if we did it out of season? Say like, weekdays through October, and see how it goes? We could do each other a favour during the quieter times. I'd be willing to pitch in with the horses–'

'And what about Krystal?'

'Oh, we'll manage.'

'So Jess continues to enjoy the trip of a lifetime and you're left holding the baby? How many months has she been away now, three?'

Maggie looked away, then down at her lap. Laura opened her mouth to apologise but instead of coherent words a flood of tears surged to the surface. She banged the mug down on top of the upturned feed bin masquerading as a table and squeezed the bridge of her nose. She had to get up in the end to go and find a tissue in the shower room. Once in there, Laura splashed her eyes with cold water and looked in the mirror at her flushed complexion. Maggie's matter-of-fact response had unearthed a dark well of discontent. Laura knew her feelings were laced with venom where her niece was concerned. She buried her face in one of the new towels and sounds of activity on the yard filtered through the small open window above the shower. Monday afternoon, but it was school holidays and that meant the constant high-pitched chatter of teenage girls. Rhian and Lucy organised the riding school between them, and the place was busy again, albeit on a smaller scale than it used to function, but she had plans for that. It reminded her that this was what she'd wanted, to be married to James and breathe new, vibrant life back into the bones of the place, and most importantly, into the bones of her gorgeous, recovering husband, who didn't deserve all this stress. Despite the emotional and practical reassurance of her marriage, the desperation to become pregnant almost obliterated everything. What she hadn't wanted, *didn't* want, was this constant yearning for a child. She knew her anger was irrational and unfair on those around her, but every month she failed to conceive she was crushed with an overwhelming sense of failure.

Maggie appeared hesitantly in the doorway, hands on hips. 'Laura… what is it? What's wrong?'

'Nothing.' She sighed and lifted her eyes to the ceiling. 'Everything. I did another test just now and it was negative, again.'

'Oh, I see. You should have said. Tell me to mind my own business but I'm not sure all this frantic activity is conducive to getting preggers, especially when you only have one ovary and some dodgy tubes.'

She dropped her gaze to the mirror. Miserable face, puffy eyes. 'Thanks for reminding me. Look, I know what you're saying, but sometimes I just can't help it.'

Not given to sisterly support of the emotive kind at the best of times, Maggie said, 'Shall I go and find James?'

'What on earth for? Are you going to demand he gets me pregnant, right now?'

Instead of laughing or rolling her eyes, Maggie frowned and pursed her lips, then hitched her handbag over her shoulder and marched outside. Laura followed her as far as the door. Seconds later, she watched her sister's Toyota reverse and roar back down the drive. As the cloud of dust from Maggie's vehicle dispersed, James materialised, and Laura trailed after him into the sitting room.

'What was all that about?' he said, warily.

He was likely expecting news along the lines that Armstrong was causing trouble, or Jess was back on the scene, so she could at least allay his fears in that direction. Predictably, James thought riding holidays were a terrible idea. 'Are you *serious?*' He slung the walking stick across the sitting room floor before sinking into the sofa and rubbing his eyes. 'Sorry, I just don't want to even consider it. Not right now, probably not ever.'

'I think Pete and Maggie are struggling a bit, financially.'

'Remind me why is this our problem to solve?'

'I feel like I owe Maggie, *something*. If it wasn't for her intervention we'd not have all this money in the first place. And I hate this situation with Jess coming between us as a family. Look, I actually think holidays might be a good idea, in principle.'

'Principles don't count when it comes to making money. Neither of you have thought it through. First off, we'd need a team of quality horses that could carry weight up and down hills all day. In other words, an expensive investment. Kids ponies are easier and cheaper in that respect, and better equipped to deal with the terrain.'

'But a few grubby teenage girls are not Pete and Maggie's ideal guests, plus they'd need 24-hour supervision.'

'Exactly. It's a dumb idea.' He pulled off his boots and shot her a sideways glance. 'Look, just give Maggie some cash.'

'She wouldn't take it. She wants to be practically involved in something we could develop together.'

'And she's planning on pushing a pram at the same time, is she?'

'I suspect she's planning on Jess coming home at some point. Her visa will run out by October.'

'Jess? As if she's going to be reliable, or any *help*, or support to anyone,' he went on, echoing her own thoughts. 'Look, I don't want Jess anywhere near this place, you can tell that to your sister as well, just to be sure.'

'She knows that,' she said, quietly. 'Let's not argue over something we agree on. But why have you got such a downer on the riding school?'

'I haven't, not especially. I'd just prefer not to commit to stuff that attracts rules and regulations and sky high fucking insurance.'

'Maggie says there's a massive gap in the equine holiday market in North Wales.'

His shoulders sagged at this. 'And why do you think that is, huh? Trust me on this.'

'But if we were small and *bespoke* it would be easily

manageable and that would hopefully attract only older, experienced riders *and* the right clientele for Hafod House. James, I honestly think it would make money.'

'*I* can do that, if you'll let me.'

He wasn't wrong. But James' way of making money was erratic, and there was always the nagging fear that one day he couldn't or wouldn't want to re-train crazy horses or teach disabled ex-servicemen to ride, and then what would they do with this huge place they'd sunk everything into? Maybe it was all part of her broodiness and nest-building which had her strung-out about future security. Bickering about the details was madness though, and by the time they'd had a late dinner and decided to test the shower-room together, she'd already made a mental note to rein herself in. She told James as much and he actually grinned while he lathered the soap. 'If you were a horse I'd reduce your high-energy cubes as well. Plain old grass for you and maybe a fixed martingale. Or a curb, or a gag. Stop you charging off till I said so.'

'I don't like the sound of any of those.'

'Me neither, as it happens. If you have to use brute force, there's something seriously wrong.'

He shot her a quizzical look. James always managed to illicit a suggestion of parallel living when it came to equine behaviours. Admittedly, she was wound-up about not being able to conceive but James was right, she couldn't force it to happen, and he didn't want to have to force her to stop behaving like a bolting mare. Her husband and her sister were both right about the frantic nature of her days, she needed to slow down in every sense of the word and allow it to happen. The difficult aspect about this was that given her track record in the fertility stakes, it most likely wasn't going to happen at all without some sort of medical intervention.

'Your reasoning is partially flawed if you're trying to apply it to me,' she said, trying to lead him round to her way of thinking. 'For one thing, a horse is so much stronger–'

'With a brain the size of a tennis ball. Combine that with strength and speed and you've already got a dangerous combination.'

'But with the addition of your man-brain it's a beautiful partnership, so long as the mare is compliant?'

'You've worked it out,' he said, smoothly and pleasantly.

She was tempted to laugh. 'I still think the holiday thing is a good idea. How about… two days riding, three nights at Hafod House?'

'You really are a hot-headed, stubborn thoroughbred *type*, aren't you?'

'You make that sound so insulting.'

He laughed for both of them. They stepped out of the shower and James grabbed a hand towel, pausing to hold it across his man-parts. 'Small, and bespoke, huh?'

'Look, just say you'll think about it, then I can tell Maggie something positive,' she said, shoving a bath sheet in his direction. He rubbed his face and hair then tied the towel around his waist with a defeated sigh. 'Alright, if the figures stack up I'll *think* about it. But Laura, I don't want to come home from the suppliers to find you've agreed to run a donkey sanctuary or… I dunno, booked-in a dozen car-boot sales selling second-hand martingales.'

She looked at him for a full two seconds. 'No, that's really tacky. I promise, no car-boots. And,' she went on, kissing his damp face, 'I am sorry. I know I've been bolting in every direction.'

'Like I said, I know a really tacky cure for it.'

He took her hand and they moved wordlessly up the stairs to their bedroom. It looked much the same as it had always done, with a few new additions and a lot less dust. There was an antique vase on the windowsill, full of drooping wild roses. A pair of William Morris curtains pooled stylishly onto the dark oak floor, along with a few errant rose petals. And the hundreds of old sepia photographs she'd rescued from the second bedroom, were sorted into wonky piles for framing. She intended to make a huge collage and hang it in the hallway. Reading about the Morgan-Jones family history, she'd discovered strong connections to clogau gold and copper mining, and Great Grandfather John had been an impressive horseman too.

'I love this room,' she said, luxuriating in their recently acquired ivory bed linen. James propped himself on one elbow and his hand fell onto the curve of her hip.

'Laura, just promise me one thing. Promise me, you won't agree to anything, or sign anything without talking to me first.'

'I thought we were business partners, you have to trust me.'

'I do. Business plans *this* year–' She took a breath and was about to try and explain her worrying obsession in more detail, when he placed a finger over her lips. 'Baby next year.'

'Next year?'

'I promise. Whatever it takes, yeah?'

The conversation wasn't especially conducive to making love, but then she wasn't close to ovulating and the fact that this came into her head at all, had Laura detach from his olive-green gaze. It was only when she was on the point of falling asleep and wondering whether to add a third cabin onto the building list – for selling riding clothes and tack, how could she have overlooked an opportunity like that? The livery owners were forever asking for stuff, it was a no-brainer – that she remembered Maggie had been going to tell her something. Something that had her nervous and giggling. The holiday idea was a smokescreen for something else, she felt sure.

The morning sky, visible through a triangular gap in the curtains where James had roughly drawn them back, promised another scorching day. He'd gone out early, leaving a trail of dirty work clothes across the floor. She rolled into his space and placed her head where his head had lain and inhaled his fragrance. There was a battle in her head. On one side there was logical, practical thought which agreed with everything he had to say about having a child. She pictured the other side of her brain as a mass of building cloud, mushrooming into something she could no longer control. The force of nature won hands down when it came to ripping apart rational thought. It manifested itself in the relentless, desperate yearning that constantly seared her insides. If anyone could help with her anxiety, it was her own husband. James knew all about emotional circuit-breakers, it was how he dealt with his depression. Not only did it feel selfish to burden him with something he couldn't deal with yet, but he would only ever look at it from a male perspective. On top of this he was still recovering from his accident, and why would anyone in their right mind want to heap more stress onto someone who'd gone through the nightmare that James had?

The natural answer was to turn to other women in the same situation as herself. On her laptop she'd bookmarked several blogs and sites that discussed fertility issues, and all of them impressed the fact that it took time, years even, to go through fertility tests and treatments. Some of the stories were heartbreaking, some of them joyous and uplifting. All of them, reflected how protracted the programme could be and how impossibly brave these women were to put themselves through uncomfortable, often painful medical procedures which could fail at any given moment. She tried to look past the personal stories and stay with the facts. The overriding one was age. Obviously, the younger the prospective mother and those without previous children were more eligible for in-vitro-fertilisation. For women up to the age of thirty-nine, the NHS offered three attempts at IVF for couples with unexplained infertility. The other priority cases were women like herself with one ovary and suspect tubes. In a couple of months, she'd be thirty-five…

She swept the duvet off her legs and reached for her phone.

CHAPTER TWO

Laura

Blue sky and a shimmering heat haze across the hills failed to lift her mood completely, but she already felt better in doing something less passive than simply waiting another four weeks to pee on a fresh pregnancy stick. Her doctor's appointment was the result of a cancellation. James looked mildly puzzled as to her early departure, but she explained it as wanting to beat the heat and the holiday traffic for shopping purposes, and then she was meeting Christy for lunch. After that, she planned to call at Maggie's to apologise and give her chance to spit out whatever it was she'd meant to say before she'd flounced off.

'If you're going all that way, get me a sheepskin girth sleeve and a cob-size leather halter from Horse and Farm Supplies, will you?' James said, leaning in through her car window and scribbling down a measurement on her book of road maps. 'And ask them where my order for twenty rubber buckets has got to, will you?'

'Rubber buckets. Right.'

He cupped the back of her neck, drew her towards him and kissed her firmly on the lips. She watched him amble back across the yard towards the construction site and into a sun-filled cloud of dust, and then her eyes were drawn to Song as she spooked at the flapping tarpaulin on the builders' lorry. Lucy had her hands full as she led the feisty mare from stable to field, but once the palomino was safely within the confines of the field, Lucy wandered across to Laura's car swinging a halter.

'You know the village show, can I enter Song in the Clear Round?'

'I've absolutely no idea what that is, but I'm sure you don't need to ask me.'

'Well, she is still your horse. Just hope the crowds and stuff don't freak her out. Jamie said we could put balloons and flags on the gate and ring the old fire bell.'

She grinned. 'Right.'

'Thing is, Rhian says stabling costs are going up this winter, is that true? And I've got books to buy for Uni. I asked Mum for show entry fees and now she's seriously on my case. Is there any chance of some more hours? I don't mind what it is.'

'We'll sort something out,' Laura said, then as the girl turned to go, 'Luce... have you heard from Jess recently?'

Her face coloured slightly at this and she began to fiddle with the lead rope, twisting it into a long neat knot. 'Kind of, but I've been sworn to secrecy. I hate it when she does this.'

'Don't worry, I'm sure it will all come out for public consumption eventually. With flags and bells on, knowing Jess.'

Lucy managed a tight smile then walked back towards the tack room. She stopped and waved at the last moment and Laura was struck by how fiercely she'd become integrated into a world she'd once misunderstood and shied away from. She had everything she could possibly want here. *Almost.* She returned Lucy's wave thoughtfully, reversed her car and headed through the village.

The surgery was packed, mostly sullen-faced children and wailing babies, or at least it seemed that way. She kept her eyes locked onto her phone and scrolled through dozens of images of her white terrier, Lambchop. James and her youngest niece, Ellie. Blurred ones of Song and Lucy leaping coloured poles, often at considerable speed. The mare seemed to adore jumping but Lucy often seemed a helpless passenger without brakes or steering, and every time she watched, Laura felt sick to her stomach. How did parents cope with this stuff? And jumping a pony came fairly low on the worry list. Catching the last bus home, for example. Or dealing with jerks in pubs, bullies at school. The list was endless and that was without global implications, like war and bombs.

James had agreed the mare was getting the upper hand when the jumps came out.

'Do you think she needs a stronger bit?' Lucy had said to him, her face flushed with exertion.

'To be honest I think you need to take that mouthpiece off the bridle altogether.'

'You're *joking?*'

'Face it, Luce. You're gonna die,' Ben had said, but James ignored him. 'She just needs to be reminded who the leader is. So lead her. *Teach* her. She's intelligent. Don't force her by using more metal in her mouth, because you won't win like that. She'll just end up dangerous. Like Ben.'

They'd all laughed and watched Rhian place poles on the ground like a grid, one canter stride apart, both leading into the jump and out of it. Miraculously, over weeks of practise it had forced Song to slow down and think. The results had prompted Lucy to buy a Hackamore – a bit-less bridle. In fact, she still owed the money to Laura. She smiled at the thought and wondered about Lucy's mother – whom she'd never met – giving her teenage daughter a hard time about her expensive hobby, and tried to imagine what sort of parents she and James might make. He had the patience of a saint, a natural teacher. Would he be a disciplinarian?

No, that would likely fall to her, although whenever they'd discussed Jess they'd always agreed that she'd got away with murder once too often. James said his own father had thought nothing of teaching stuff the God-fearing way, with an iron rod as back-up. Did his parental history mean he'd choose the same indoctrination, or would it in fact result in something roughly the opposite of that? When she watched him working the horses it was clear how love and discipline worked together. Discipline wasn't always a raised hand, an angry voice. The iron rod didn't have to be physical, or feared.

She snapped her phone off and stared at the medical notices on the wall opposite rather than the spotty little girl on the floor by her feet. The young, worn-out mother had her attention taken by a baby in a buggy. She kept calling the older child to come away. *Jenna, get over here. Jenna, put that down, now.* Laura's arms ached to pick up the toddler and wipe her grubby face. She hoped she wasn't turning into one of those desperate women who considered stealing babies from outside shops. And although she could understand their immense need – because it surely sprung from the same deep well – it was something of a puzzle that these very same feelings threatened to overwhelm her, too. Up until eighteen months ago, she'd been a hard-nosed businesswoman without a thought for her biological clock. Now, here it was, ticking loudly in every corner of her soul.

Finally, her name was called over the crackling intercom. She slid into room two and took a seat. Of course, her own GP hadn't been available at short notice, so she was faced with elderly Doctor Grimes. He tapped away at his computer for a full minute before he even acknowledged she was sitting there.

'So… Laura Brown,' he said, eyes still on the screen.

'No, I'm married now. Laura Morgan-Jones.'

'Blasted bloody system,' he grumbled, circling the mouse

with considerable force across the desk. 'It's telling me how to do my job. Check blood pressure. I'll check blood pressure *if* and when I see fit. How can I help, Laura Morgan-Jones?'

'Well, the short answer is my husband and I are desperate for a child. And...' Grimes looked at her for all of two seconds before turning back to the screen. 'I presume you're having plenty of unprotected sex? How long have you been trying to conceive?'

'Oh... *years*,' she lied.

A short silence while he absorbed her extensive medical history. 'You've suffered a miscarriage. And more recently, an unexplained bleed,' he said, frowning over the top of his spectacles. 'So we know you *can* conceive.'

Her turn to be silent, preferring not to dwell on either event. Grimes was quick to observe this before turning back to the computer again. 'You had intensive investigations in 1992... due to an adnexal torsion. Removal of an infected ovary... slight damage to the uterine tubes. You've been treated for depression too. And your partner? Has he had any problems?'

'He already has a son. So no, not that we're aware of.' She inched onto the edge of her chair, anxious to cut to the chase. 'I'd really like to go on the waiting list for IVF.'

His hand left the computer mouse then and he turned in his chair to face her. 'The problem with IVF and a lot of fertility treatments is that they rely on the use of hormones to trigger increased ovulation. Looking at your history, it's a procedure that might result in another torsion.'

'There must be something I can try! Look, I just want some *hope*.'

There, she'd said it, managed to get it out over the huge lump in her throat. Grimes drew his eyes from hers and turned to continue tapping on his keyboard, which may have been patronising under different circumstances but at least it allowed her to recover.

'I think we need to start with an up-to-date scan. Then we can think about specialist referral. And I think it may help if you talked to a counsellor.'

'Is there a waiting list for a scan?'

'For non-emergencies? I'm afraid so,' Grimes said, then for the first time, looked her in the eye. 'Mrs Morgan-Jones, it's early days for considering something like IVF. And we'd need a lot more information from both of you, before we could confidently proceed in that direction. As you might imagine, funding is tight for this sort of treatment.'

He passed her a few leaflets and then did actually take her blood pressure. She went from the room as the next patient was called, walked quickly to her car and took a moment to consider the information he'd pushed on her. The flyer about counselling services hit the footwell immediately. The other brochures were equally useless. *Cut down or cut out alcohol, eat well and get enough rest. Take a good vitamin and mineral supplement. And for your partner, make sure he wears loose, cool underwear.* She tore the whole lot into two, stuffed them at the bottom of her bag then spent a couple of hours wandering around the shops until it approached noon.

At least, as Christy pointed out, she'd started the ball rolling.

They sat crushed in the window seat at Nino's Italian, well before the lunchtime rush, but it was still crowded with holidaymakers and they had to talk fairly loudly to make themselves heard. Soft-hearted, sentimental Christy was perhaps the wrong choice for a heart-to-heart over maternity issues, especially since her mummy status had been confirmed three times over with relative ease. And yet, if she wanted to talk it out, Christy would be her only choice of listener amongst her short list of genuine friends. She related the entire story, from the unexplained bleed the previous summer, to her appointment with Grimes and the leaflets about underwear.

'That's true, about the underwear,' Christy said, sipping a glass of chilled white wine. Laura tried not to look at it too longingly.

'I know, but I need serious medical intervention. I'm a mess, physically and–'

'Emotionally,' Christy said, then covered Laura's hand with hers. 'Can't you go private?'

'I still need that referral.'

'Well, then. Wait till you've had the scan and the result, then you can talk to James about it again. In the meantime–'

'I know. Loads of unprotected sex,' she said, loudly. Too loudly, and a couple seated on the next table along, turned to look. She exchanged a wry smile with Christy, then sat back in her chair as the food arrived. Her appetite was tiny but Laura was determined to plough her way through the wholesome bulk of a carbonara and a side of garlic bread. 'It doesn't help that my niece had a perfectly beautiful, perfect baby girl then upped and left her!

'Jess? Uh, if she were my daughter I'd–'

'Disown her? I think Pete and Maggie have, to a large degree. And the other cross we have to bear is that Jess is actually with James' son, Sam. Having a wonderful time in the States.'

'Oh, God, really?'

'I know it shouldn't, but it rankles. Every time I do a negative test, you know? I'm actually worried about all of this affecting my marriage.'

Christy tore the olive bread apart and frowned. 'Talk to him, talk to James. About this entire situation, and about how you *feel.*'

'I have, a bit, but he's got enough on his plate really. I don't want to keep banging on about getting pregnant, Jess, and Sam.'

'At least tell him about the scan. You can say you haven't been feeling well.'

'Lie to him? I couldn't do that, and then he'd worry.'

'Don't tell him anything, then. Takes months to get an appointment anyway.'

Laura lowered her fork, and stared at her white napkin. 'Enough of me. What's happening with you, any gossip?'

'A bit. Pam and Steve have seriously fallen out with Simon and Alice.'

'Oh? Don't tell me their Spanish business plan has gone pear-shaped already.'

'I think it's more to do with your payoff, actually.'

Laura leant in across the table. 'Payoff? I was owed that money! It's mine, every penny of it. Half the business and half the flat, we agreed.'

'I know but I get the impression Simon has fobbed them off with some story about unpaid tax, and Steve keeps asking to see the accounts.'

She sat back in her chair and wished she had a glass of wine to hand. 'Well, that's his problem.'

'Of course it is. Did I tell you about the extension to Pam's kitchen? Steve designed it. It's totally amazing. I think it was his wedding gift to her.'

Laura kept telling herself it was good to see Christy but their conversation felt rooted in the past and it kept coming back round to old friends and ex-partners, or choosing the right school. Then it was what did Laura think about her new boots and should she get another pair in a different colour? Maybe it was just that she'd changed since her marriage to an essentially serious man who had little respect for the fripperies of the modern world. And yet, James could make her laugh like no one else. Her mind drifted away from the noisy restaurant, back to the golden fields at home. *Home.* It still caught her out that she lived happily at an equestrian centre and regularly found straw and dog hair in mostly everything. At least her ghosts from the past were well and truly under control in that department. Even James had moved on from the death of his first wife with the same positivity for their future.

'... and it seems such a shame that you never got a proper wedding, after all that planning you did,' Christy was saying. 'I mean a proper reception with all your friends, and a cake.'

'We made it down the aisle, that's the main thing.'

'You know what you should do?' Christy went on, heaping olive salad onto her plate. 'Throw a big party at your place, in a barn or something. You could have a cowboy theme with all those horses and bales of hay.'

Laura shot her a weak smile and immediately tried to erase an unlikely image of them all line dancing. 'James hates checked shirts.'

Christy laughed, then began flipping through her phone. 'How about... September sometime? The evenings will be drawing in so you can have loads of fairy lights. Just think, loud music wouldn't be a problem where you live. You could even get a live band.'

'I'll think about it,' she said, knowing full well it wasn't even worth mentioning it to James.

They finished lunch and she walked with Christy to her car, where it was abandoned in a mother-and-child parking slot outside the supermarket. The battered people-carrier sported car seats and booster cushions aplenty along the rear seats. The narrow margin of window space free from Winnie-the-Pooh sun-blinds was heavily smeared, and brightly coloured plastic pockets full of games hung from the front seat headrests. She was fine until Christy hugged her goodbye with those huge misty eyes of hers.

'Oh, I hope you get pregnant *really* soon, you'll be such a smashing mum, Laura. And what a wonderful place you live in to raise a child.'

The simplicity of this sentiment caught her slightly unawares, and she had to swallow down an unexpected swell of emotion. Nevertheless, she still headed towards her sister's house with a fair degree of irritation at feeling outmanoeuvred by Christy's silly party ideas, Simon's tax bill lie and then being fobbed off by Doctor Grimes. Maybe it was more that she found it easier to be irritated than dwell on the idea of a child running through the fields at home, or sat on a fat pony. In her mind's eye it was always sunny and the child was always laughing. Even though she'd been exposed to the realities of parenting for most of her adult life, her dreams were always of the fanciful, romantic sort. She even had a running list of names in her head. The current favourite was Eira, the Welsh word for snow, and now Jenna. Jenna Morgan-Jones.

It was pure fluke she remembered to call in at the Farm and Pet place.

At Hafod House, she could hear Krystal wailing through an open bedroom window even as she approached the front door. She took a moment and studied her sandals before pressing the doorbell. Pete answered, wearing a grubby white apron. He announced her arrival by shouting up the stairs to Maggie, then led the way through to the sitting room.

'How's business, Pete? Weather's amazing isn't it? Have you got lots of guests booked in?'

'Some. Could do with a few more. It's not keeping the baby in nappies let alone paying any bills.'

This was dismal news in the height of summer. She flopped onto a chair and fanned her face with a newspaper. The room was messy with Krystal's things. Through the French windows she noticed the normally tidy garden was heavily overgrown. The hens pecked and scratched around dried-out pots of geraniums and the patio stones were dark with moss. A row of baby vests fluttered in the breeze. Her sister appeared, full of false smiles and bluster.

'Little one's just gone down for a nap. Hopefully!'

'I'll get some tea while you two have a *talk*,' Pete said.

Maggie plonked herself down opposite, wincing as she half-sat on some sort of musical spinning top. Her trousers were splattered with stains and her face looked creased with tiredness. 'I'm sorry about, you know,' she said. 'Going off like that, yesterday. Not thinking straight.'

'Oh, Maggie! I was going to apologise for snapping at you.'

A girly laugh. 'What are we like?'

'Sisters. You look exhausted. Here's you, struggling to cope with a newborn and here's me, struggling to cope without.'

'When you put it like that, there should be a simple solution in there, but of course there isn't.'

'No.'

'You er, you look nice, have you been out?'

'I met Christy in Chester, for lunch, and I-'

'Oh, her. She's so gushing.'

'And I...'

'What?'

'I went to the doctor, to ask about IVF. Please don't say anything to anyone.'

'IVF? That's not the one for lesbians, is it?'

Laura shot her a blank stare. 'You mean the one they do at home with a turkey baster and some dodgy sperm off the Internet?'

Her sister's mouth dropped open.

'Maggie, I really worry about your comprehension of modern medicine.'

'Yes, well, you know why. Don't you remember what happened to Marjorie Evans?'

'I'm sure you're going to remind me.'

'She went on one of those insemination programmes. Only she took bull semen to the hospital by mistake. Glan Clwyd didn't know what to make of it.'

Only Maggie could make in-vitro-fertilisation sound and

feel like a weird religious sect, or bring it down to farm-yard status. Making wild assumptions was something she did whenever she was nervous or avoiding serious issues. Laura was about to enlighten her with the correct facts, when Pete barged open the door with a tea tray and Maggie leapt up to fuss with some small tables, and then it was cups and saucers. Laura waited until Pete had left the room before taking the bull by the horns and changing the subject. She sweetened the atmosphere first by telling Maggie that the holiday idea hadn't been completely overturned by James, but they were a long way off confirming anything and they really needed to get the right staff in place first. If they called them mini-breaks instead of holidays and they kept the vision small, then maybe they could build on that. Her sister's face lit up but Laura's immediate problem was that Pete and Maggie looked to be some way off being able to cope with any kind of addition to their workload, but then if Jess was coming home… 'What were you going to tell me, anyway? Why do I have the feeling it's got something to do with Jess?'

'Isn't everything? Pete is *so* angry with her.'

'This is affecting your business, isn't it?'

'I won't lie,' she said, this time with a monumental sigh as she poured the milk. 'Much as I love Krystal, I'd forgotten how tough it was, looking after a small baby.'

'Is Jess coming back, is this what it's all about? I really think she should and you don't have to worry about me, *us*, making anything awkward.'

Maggie frowned, poised to say something at the precise moment Laura's mobile began to ring, and then Krystal started to cry again. Her sister visibly deflated. 'Oh, *Lordy*. She must have trapped wind! I wish she'd take some solids, that's what it is. Why don't you answer that call, and I'll be down again in a minute.'

She waited until Maggie trailed back towards the stairs, before glancing at her phone and accepting the call. 'James?'

'Where are you?'

'At Hafod House… what is it? You sound cross.'

'You need to come home, *now*. I've just had a phone call from Sam. Has Maggie said anything?'

'What about, is it–'

'Just come home, will you?'

He ended the call abruptly, leaving Laura to slowly pace up and down the sitting room, full of indecision. Krystal's wailing increased when the landline phone began ringing. She heard Pete answer it, and a loud conversation ensued about available rooms and dates. Laura slipped into the hall, noticing en route the mess in the kitchen. Everything looked busy, from the spinning washing machine to the semi-loaded dishwasher. The worktops were cluttered and the paused food mixer had dough slowly detaching from its beaters. Clothing was piled high on the ironing board and there were two buckets under the table, full of old-fashioned nappies soaking in water.

'I'll er, speak to Maggie later. Crisis at home,' she mouthed to Pete, waggling her mobile by way of explanation. He stared and nodded, one finger in his ear.

Although Laura closed the front door on it all, Krystal's vocal discomfort followed her back down the drive and into her car, so she closed the window on it too and drove away, then stopped at the end of the lane where she opened the car door, so she could fully inhale. The towering oak trees created a cool green tunnel, and the sweet smell of summer filled her senses. Clumps of cow parsley swayed silently along the verges, and in the adjacent fields sheep lay panting in dusty hollows beneath every inch of hedgerow. On the level land sandwiched between two farms, preparations for the village show were well underway. Standing above the treeline she glimpsed a flag-topped marquee and the commentary stand. Beyond this where the ground rose towards Tal Y Fan, a herd of beef cattle munched the rich pasture, tails flicking. She wondered if they belonged to Marjorie Evans, and if it was her she should be confiding in, and not her sister. It was a cowardly way out, leaving Pete and Maggie like that. Was her crisis any more important that theirs? Somehow, she doubted it. If she'd been any sort of a decent sister she'd have rolled up her sleeves and got stuck in. She started the engine and less than a minute later she was back in her parking spot at home and Lamby was hurtling towards her, her white coat splattered with pale pistachio emulsion. Under normal circumstances she'd also be amused to see happy birthday bunting and silver helium balloons tied to the field gate.

Ben held up a pot of paint and grinned. 'Outside lav. Green, like you told me.'

'Yes, but only on the walls, Ben. Not on the dogs.'

A glance across the yard told her that James wasn't outside. She discovered him in the kitchen, arms partly folded and leaning against the sink unit so that the light from the window gave him an even darker silhouette than usual. He chewed a nail, eyes following her as she dropped her shopping onto the table along with her handbag and keys.

'James?'

A palpable, roaring silence which seemed stretched to eternity before he spoke. 'Sam and Jess got married.'

She thought about those five words carefully before she opened her mouth, but even after considering them, she couldn't think of anything to say. She sank onto a kitchen chair and watched him move towards the wine rack, select a bottle of Shiraz and slosh a good two thirds of it into two glasses before sitting astride a stool. He pushed a glass towards her and rubbed his face.

'Apparently, it's a marriage of *convenience*.'

'For Jess?'

'Who else? So she can work at the ranch. When that's not

on the agenda, she can have fun with Sam. When Sam's busy she can come back here for a while. Whatever she fancies.'

He lifted the glass to his lips and she held his eye contact before letting her gaze fall to the shiny bags on the table, and the halter. It smelt like an expensive handbag and her fingers stretched across the table to touch the soft suppleness of the leather. No wonder Maggie had been hesitant, Pete stony-faced.

James said, 'It's instead of a work visa. Seemed the obvious solution, Sam said.'

'Are they both getting back at their ex-partners, is that it?'

He shrugged and lit a cigarette, throwing the packet towards her, something he hadn't done for a long time. Normally, she'd stop him. Normally, they'd not be drinking red wine and smoking in the middle of the afternoon. One burning question forced its way out, but despite its gravity, her voice was reduced to a whisper. 'Has he given her the rings? James?'

'Course he has! After all, it's just a bit of metal at the end of the day and they were *right* there, in his pocket. Convenient.'

She reached for the wine then. The clogau gold which used to belong to James' deceased first wife, Carys. Those beautiful symbolic rings which Laura had passed on to Sam when she thought James might never recover from his accident. Precious and blessed, the rose-tinted gold from the mountains of Bontddu, mined a century ago and revered in the Morgan-Jones family for generations. It reduced them to a worthless, manipulative device; pushed onto the third finger of a young woman running from an abusive relationship. A way out for her and a kick in the teeth for everyone else.

CHAPTER THREE

Maggie

Pete looked up expectantly when she plodded back down the stairs. 'Well? Did you tell her?'

'Laura? Where's she gone, I heard the car?'

'Some sort of crisis at home. I knew you'd bottle it again, Maggie.'

'I didn't get chance! Anyway, they'll find out soon enough,' she said, and trailed back to her chair in the sitting room, although Ellie would be home soon and no doubt Krystal would be awake again. There was a hundred and one things to do but she stayed sitting. 'To be honest, I'm surprised Sam hasn't phoned his father by now.'

'Putting it off till the last minute. Probably hoping we'd do his dirty work for him.'

'Dirty work? I doubt everyone sees it like that. I'm not sure *I* do,' she dared to add.

'You know something? You and Stella are in a league of your own! At least Sam's mother probably got to attend the wedding as a witness. We didn't even get a bloody phone call till it was all done and dusted!'

'Yes, well, it's not like we'd have rushed over there, is it? It was a spur of the moment thing. Anyway, Sam's a lovely man.'

This had Pete on his feet, rattling his loose change and grinding his teeth. 'Have you heard yourself? This is *nothing* to do with love's young dream. Not only are they making a mockery of those marriage vows, they're breaking the law by using the certificate to dodge work permits.'

'They're not the first couple to do that. Anyway, I honestly think there's more to it than just permits. I don't know why you're so down on Sam and Stella. They have a different view of the world, that's all.'

'One that suits them. It's the bugger-everyone-else view of the world. No wonder Jess fits in so well.'

It was a familiar conversation, the Stella, Jess and Sam triangle. Occasionally, Maggie would receive a photo of Jess riding a horse western-style against some desert-like scenery, and once, a blurred shot of a moose. In another, she and Sam were dressed-up to go out on the town in Maine. Maggie usually reciprocated and sent one of Krystal reclining on her play-mat, but Jess never responded much to those.

Pete sat down again and poured a tepid cup of tea from the pot. 'Did your sister agree to that holiday idea?'

'I think so.'

'In the meantime, we're bumping along the bottom, as bloody usual. We can't go on like this, Maggie.'

Right on cue, a half-hearted grizzle went up from Krystal and they stared at each other across the sitting room, willing her to go back to sleep. She wasn't an easy baby; did she know her mother wasn't there? Maggie had never known tiredness like it. She was ready to admit that weeping was close to the surface some days. Even after she'd given birth to Ellie, faced with a full house again while Pete went back to work, all those times shrank to insignificance. It was like her bones were filled with cement. How did women give birth in their forties and carry on working? They probably had help, that's what happened.

'I don't know what else we can *do.*'

'Well I do. I've been thinking. Even you must agree that responsibilities come with babies and marriage certificates. As soon as it's convenient to call, because we wouldn't want to disturb anyone's sleep, would we? You can phone the newly-weds and tell Jess that she either comes back for the baby, or I'm giving Krystal to her real daddy. Let's see if either of these fellas have got a backbone. If Sam's the pillar of decency you seem to think he is, he'll help Jess out with Krystal, won't he?'

Something caught in her throat, a mix of shock and fear. 'And what if he doesn't?'

'Then at least we'll know the truth about Sunshine Sam and this sham of a marriage, won't we?'

'You can't hand her over to Armstrong on that basis.'

'Maggie, that waste of space hangs about in the village watching us, or leaning on my bloody car smoking weed. And I'm sure it's him putting one-star reviews on Trip Advisor. One of these days, he'll feel the back of my hand.'

'That's what he wants you to do, retaliate.'

'Playing the poor, victimised *daddy*. Pretending to care about Krystal. Staring at me from under his hoody like a thirty-year-old teenager.'

'He's trying to get to Jess.'

'How? Jess isn't witness to any of this, is she? Either Jess and Sam start being a proper family, or I'll call Armstrong's bluff.'

'Pete, no! You *can't!*'

'Then we may as well go bankrupt here, Maggie. Sell up and buy a flat. Is that what you want?'

'Course not. But we can't hand Krystal over, just like that. He's a criminal.'

'Jess knew that when they made a baby together. He didn't physically harm Jess, did he?'

'Pete... we *can't*.'

The irony was she'd wanted Pete to make a stand against

Jess for years and now he was doing just that, but with a nasty vengeance. He'd even sold her rapidly deteriorating second-hand car to make room in the garage for the boxes of beauty products and waxing-kits she'd left behind. Her old bedroom was back as a guest room and all her personal stuff was stored in boxes in the loft. It was as if she'd died. Except that when Maggie looked at recent photos of her, Jess looked happy and radiant, enjoying herself. But of course, it was all at the expense of someone else.

There was a lot of sense in Pete's logic, but it was brutal. And in the midst of it, an innocent baby.

Sunday was another scorching day, too hot for riding gear but it didn't bother Ellie. She scooted off to find Lucy the second Maggie pulled into the parking area next to the permanent builder's truck. A glance in the rearview mirror confirmed that her face was already as red as it felt. The place was busy, but then her sister had the Midas touch when it came to business, any kind of business. It was beginning to look smart too; everywhere weeded and tidy, the loose-box doors varnished a dark oak and sporting brass name-plates. Her eyes were drawn to the old-fashioned iron hayracks on the barn wall, filled with white begonias and trailing fuchsia. The surface in the outdoor menage had been topped-up and raked, with baskets of bright geraniums hooked over the newly painted white fence, and there was a neat wall round the manure heap. They'd even bought a new caravan for Rhian. And then the indoor school, rising majestically where a scrubby bit of pasture used to grow. The building had been done tastefully, using lots of natural materials, and the cluster of oak trees beyond the round-pen at the rear already softened the height.

She spotted her sister by the wheelbarrows and made to walk over, trying to gauge how the land lay. Laura had been on the phone a couple of hours after she'd left Hafod House on Tuesday. The crisis at home had indeed been that phone call from Sam. Talk about timing! Laura said that both she and James were extremely... *disappointed.* However her sister dressed it up, Maggie had felt the animosity towards Jess travelling down the phone line. And despite numerous attempts through the week, she'd not been able to discuss anything further with Jess because her phone seemed to be switched off at all times.

'How bloody convenient,' Pete had snarled. 'When you go over to the yard, get some contact details for Sam, and Stella. Find out exactly where Jess is. I want this sorting out.'

Maggie wondered if this was cheeky, given the strained circumstances. She fixed a benign expression on her face and walked across to where Laura was busy hanging the pitchforks and yard brushes onto a row of new hooks. She seemed perfectly at ease with these tasks and Maggie felt a needle of jealousy, trapped as she was with the baby and not having any real sense of direction, *again*. Horses were, after all, her own particular domain and not her sister's. Laura stabbed a fork into some straw and looked up with an equally benign expression.

'Hi. James might be a bit late. He's asleep, but I'm not waking him. I told him he was overdoing everything yesterday.'

'Oh. Should we come another day?'

'No, if it comes to it, I'm sure Lucy or Rhian will take Ellie.'

'It er... it looks great everywhere.'

'It's getting there, almost back to where it was when Liz was here. Just need another full-time Liz then we can really get cracking.'

'Staff, huh, not easy.'

'No, and James is so picky. Actually, I want to talk to you about staff.'

'Really?' Her pulse quickened and they walked across

to the house. Inside, it was dusty and full of builders with lengths of copper piping and sacks of plaster stacked in the hall, and a lot of noisy banter over the top of a loud radio. 'How on earth does James sleep through all this racket?'

'Oh, he's not asleep in the house, he's in the hayfield.'

Under normal circumstances she might have found this amusing but the underlying tension between them easily suffocated any mirth. The kitchen was virtually a shell, all the old units partially ripped out. Laura made coffee in a jug and Maggie followed her into the sitting room and closed the door to muffle the noise. Anticipation kept thudding in her chest, mentally working out how they'd manage Hafod House if she had a job as well. If anything, it would perhaps help Pete feel less stressed. All too often, they forgot about his heart condition.

'Maggie, I know you're struggling and I… *we*, want to help. It happens that Lucy needs to work more hours but when uni starts again that means she only really has early mornings free, and we won't need her then. So I was thinking… she could come to you?'

'Me? I don't understand.'

'We'll pay her, so you don't need to worry about that, she'll still be on our payroll. I thought, maybe a couple of hours every morning? Whatever needs doing, what do you think? I've spoken to Lucy and she's more than willing to do it.' She paused to take a slurp of coffee. 'Oh, and Ben's happy to give the garden a good tidy-up for you. Just say when.'

Maggie put her mug down, undecided how this made her feel. Grateful and ashamed, but mostly *annoyed*. They were offering her domestic help when for a fleeting moment she'd imagined herself as one of the new riding instructors, striding into the indoor school in a smart jacket, shiny boots and a long schooling whip. Children clamouring for her attention, nervous adults desperate for her reassurance. She forced herself to stay sitting down. 'As it happens, Lucy won't be needed, but thank you for thinking of us.'

'Oh, don't go all huffy on me! What do you mean, she won't be needed?'

Maggie explained the dead phone and outlined Pete's plan to force matters in another direction entirely, and Laura's expression darkened.

'I see.'

'So, if you could let me have whatever contact details you have for Sam, or Stella? That would actually be more helpful.'

The door opened and James came into the room. He nodded at Maggie, then yawned and rubbed the back of his neck. Laura immediately jumped up and went to fetch another mug from the kitchen. When she returned, he slid a protective arm around her waist and kissed her firmly, once on her cheek and then again more thoughtfully, on the lips. Maggie felt a shiver of embarrassment, not only at his sensuality but at the open show of emotion and how her sister lit up like a beacon in response.

They remembered she was there. James shifted his eye contact reluctantly from Laura, to herself, and raised his mug.

'I'll take this outside. See what Ellie's up to.'

Maggie managed a smile in his direction. He must hate that they were doubly related in this weird way; married to her sister with his son married to his wife's niece. And now Pete wanted to force his son to take care of Armstrong's baby. The man who'd almost killed him. She hoped her face didn't reflect any of this, but then Laura was called away by the electrician and became immersed in bulbs and inset light fittings. Maggie slipped outside into the sunshine, grateful to have some time alone on the picnic bench by the menage. Ellie was riding confidently and chatting to James as she made Seren trot first one way, then the other. He perched on a shooting stick these days rather than walk about, but it was obvious from time to time that his back injury was still a problem. When Ellie got the canter aid wrong and almost slipped down Seren's shoulder, his quiet intervention with the schooling whip came at exactly the right second, like a hand reaching out. Seren came to a halt almost in front of him, and Ellie managed to recover herself.

His invisible control of the situation had Maggie feeling enormously humbled on a number of levels.

What on earth made her think she could do anything like this? She wasn't qualified to teach mucking-out, let alone anything else. And her way of teaching involved a lot of shouting and impatience. She plonked her handbag on the table and did her best to avoid crying or looking at Lucy as she went to and fro with bags of shavings, in case awkward questions were raised about the Domestic Goddess job. She found her sunglasses and a tissue, and then Carla gave her a cheery wave as she rode towards the gate on her mare. What she wouldn't give to be out riding on those dry, sun-dappled hills. Some days, she doubted she'd have the strength and energy for such pursuits again, although Carla always had Maggie feeling like she'd drawn every short straw going. Even her supermarket shopping was reduced to a basket of bespoke items, but then Carla only had herself to think about. It wasn't as if there was anyone at home waiting for corn plasters and indigestion remedies. She used to think Carla must be a bit lonely and cold-hearted, but now she wasn't so sure. Did women always want what other women had? Laura had everything except a child. Maggie had three children and not much of anything else. Carla had exactly what she wanted, but unlike Jess, she didn't rely on anyone else to provide it. She looked up just as Ellie managed a full circuit of the school at collected canter in beautiful balance with the pony, and her heart soared with pride, quashing any sense of martyrdom with shame. How could she think even for one second that she had nothing?

James helped Ellie dismount and run-up the stirrups, loosen the girth and pull the reins over Seren's head so she could lead the pony back to her stable. This took an absolute age because Ellie insisted on doing everything herself, then she begged to be allowed to stay; something about helping Lucy move all the saddles and bridles. Laura walked across, holding her squirming dog under one arm and a clipboard in the other. She directed Ben towards the partially emptied tack-room and he staggered inside with a huge tub of white emulsion and a brush in his mouth. Ellie darted after him and Lambchop wriggled to the ground.

'Maggie, look, please don't be offended by my idea,' Laura said, then when Maggie made no reply, assumed the same benign expression she'd worn earlier. 'I was just trying to help. Are you going to the village show, on Saturday?'

'Oh, we don't know yet. Any chance of those phone numbers?'

A huge sigh at this. 'James thinks it best he asks Sam to call you. He rarely speaks to Stella, but you can always email her from the ranch website, if you like.'

'Oh. Rightio.'

'Jess is always on Twitter, if you get desperate.'

Maggie knew Laura meant it in jest but the throwaway remark rankled. There might be a part of Maggie that wanted to whoop and clap that Jess was with Sam, but she had to face the fact that she might not actually be *with* him. And clearly, and perhaps understandably, James and Laura didn't like the idea of their union one bit, nor did they wish to sanction Pete's intended plan concerning Krystal. Why would they?

All this examination of other people's lives and relationships brought her own into sharp focus. If nothing else, an hour of navel gazing had gone to prove one vital fact: that they'd reached the end of the line with Jess, and Maggie could no longer realistically cover for her. Oh, she might have had a hard time with Armstrong and giving birth, but she had help right *here* at home and she'd snubbed it. Snubbed them. Snubbed Krystal. Pete might not ooze sensuality but he was right to be angry about the mess Jess had left behind, and part of that anger was for all the times they'd had to get up in the night, rocking and walking and cradling. Part of his anger was on her own behalf that she could no longer be proud of her grandchild in the way other grandparents were, like the happy way they billed and cooed when they were left with some arranged babysitting for a couple of hours. Part of his anger was about Linda, their next door neighbour, constantly asking where Jess was with that smirk on her face. And a lot of his anger was on behalf of James and Laura, whatever they might think. His idea might be harsh, but what if Jess planned to never come home? It wasn't just their livelihood falling into a black hole, it was their lives too.

Her spirits sank further when she pulled onto the drive at home. She could hear Krystal crying. Linda twitched her curtains.

Inside, Pete was slowly pacing up and down the sitting room with the baby against his shoulder, like he used to do with Jess. She waited till he placed Krystal carefully into the Moses basket, and then they both tiptoed into the kitchen.

'Well?' he hissed, 'did you get a phone number?'

She did her best to present the information in a calm manner, then spoilt it by mentioning Twitter.

'Twitter? So your sister suggests I try and sum this up in 140 characters, does she? Let's see… Fetch baby now or heads up real baby daddy. Hashtag call home.'

'I don't know what you're talking about.'

He was all set to carry on spouting until she stopped him in his tracks with Laura's domestic help idea.

A long beat. 'And what did you say to that?'

'I said, no thank you.'

They looked at the website for Stella's ranch. Riding, fishing. On-site accommodation. The photography was stunning, and there was an online booking form. Head-shots of the horses travelled down the left side of the screen on a revolving loop. She even found herself automatically picking one out.

Elvis, 16 hands. Big-hearted schoolmaster. Home raised and loving those trails!

Surely they could do something like this in collaboration with the yard? Admittedly something a bit less cheesy, but then Stella's market was different to theirs. Laura easily had the skills to set something up and sell the idea. Snowdonia easily sold itself. Hafod House could look special too, especially the dining room which Laura had designed. If anything, it at least gave Maggie some resolve to pursue the idea.

Pete typed out an email. It was polite and upbeat, enquiring after Stella's health and business and finally, a friendly remark about the marriage of their daughter, to her son.

'I'm not asking directly about Jess. I want to get a conversation going first,' Pete said.

Maggie went along with his British restraint, although she could well imagine Stella casting a wry smile at some of his wording. There again, it wouldn't do to go in all guns blazing. Conversation was after all key to resolving most problems. But when another weekend loomed and they'd still had no response from Stella, and no phone call from either Jess or Sam, Pete was back on the ranch website looking for phone numbers. Of course, the advertised number for the Lazy River wasn't Stella's personal landline, it was something attached to an answer machine in an office.

'Are you sure that's the only number you can find?' Maggie said, finding her reading glasses and peering over his shoulder at the screen. She frowned at the complicated table of departures and destinations and realised then that he was actually looking at flights. For a magical moment she imagined them going over there and enjoying a family bonding session round a campfire. Maybe she'd even get chance to ride Elvis!

'Are you thinking of going over? Stella did say she'd put us up… when they were here at Christmas, do you remember? Been ages since we had a holiday. We could have a proper heart-to-heart with Jess.'

'We don't even know where Jess is, not properly. This ranch, it's in New Hampshire. Nowhere near an airport from the looks of things. And a whole state away from where this Sam lives, in Maine. Look at these bloody prices! We couldn't afford flights for one of us let alone both of us. And temperatures in the nineties every day… not sure I'd like that, and anyway, I'm not sure what it would solve, either. Jess needs an ultimatum, not a cosy visit.'

'But it would be better to speak to her face to face.'

'Maggie, there's nothing I'd like more than to present the happy couple with their ready-made baby,' he said, closing everything down and pushing the computer mouse aside. 'Fact is, going over there looks like another huge problem to me, at our expense.'

Reality sunk in, and Maggie had to agree. It would more likely be Pete trailing exhausted across half of America looking for Jess, bags stuffed with baby paraphernalia with holes in his shoes, and his wallet.

Another dose of reality kicked-in when it took forty minutes to get out of the door on Saturday morning. Then they had to go back inside for a last-minute nappy change. It was a spur of the moment decision to go to the village show but Maggie was determined to get out of the house on such a beautiful day. Ellie had already gone ahead with her strange school friend, Willow. It was a comfort that despite her low-spectrum autism Ellie seemed perfectly settled in secondary school. And Nathan seemed to be equally settled in a long-term relationship with Christopher, the rugby-playing hairdresser. It was just Jess, the middle one. The one who'd probably had the most advantageous start in life, the one who still had the ability to get them running in circles, both metaphorically and otherwise.

'I'm not sure it's a good idea, Maggie,' Pete said, fanning his face with a canvas hat. 'Walking all the way up to Bryn Derwen. I don't like this heat one bit.'

'It'll be nice to forget all about Jess and the Americans. Put that hat on.'

'They'll probably ring while we're out.'

She fiddled with the parasol, trying to secure it at the right angle. 'Then they'll have to call back. Anyway, isn't it the middle of the night over there?'

'A week to respond to an email or a text, it's bloody rude. Insulting, that's what it is,' he grumbled, helping her to lift the pram over the step. 'You know something? I'm *fed up* of waiting for other people. It's time to get tough.'

'I know how you feel, but let's just take one day off.'

'I'd actually like a day off babysitting, Maggie.'

She set off walking and he fell into step.

The best thing about the pram was that Krystal always seemed content with the rocking movement and everything she could possibly need was stored underneath. It was oppressively humid, and the smell of burgers, fried onions and donuts seemed to permeate the entire village but at least the long spell of good weather meant the ground was bone dry, and the lack of ruts ensured a smooth passage for the pram. They paused at the trade stands around the entrance to inhale the leather of a new saddle and gasp at the price of a handmade rug. Or at least, Maggie did. Then it was vintage tractors and a loud fairground organ. Krystal kicked off her cotton cover and sucked her fingers.

'Look, Pete, she's smiling!'

'Nah, be teething. Or wind.'

'No, I know her wind face. I think she likes the music.'

'She's the only one then.'

He marched ahead, pushing the pram past the sheep and cattle pens. Maggie followed wishing he'd slow down, and lighten-up. They stood ringside for a while and watched the final line-up of heavy horses vying for a rosette. Few people failed to be moved at the sight of Shires and Clydesdales in their full regalia, despite few people actually having a use for them these days. Although a couple of places around the country had set up riding centres using heavy horses and she'd watched a television programme once where they'd all galloped down a beach in South Wales, kicking up spray like a tidal wave. It had been quite stirring, watching that slow power transformed into something modern and exciting.

The horses moved round the judge for one last time, the gentle giants of a past world, all gleaming coats and brasses, white feathers like snow. The handlers had to run to keep pace with their flamboyant trot. A lot of people clapped, including Maggie. Pete wasn't even watching. If things had been different with Jess and Krystal, she would perhaps have gone over to Ireland and brought her father over for a visit. He'd always loved a country show, everything produced by honest sweat and toil off the land, although not all the participants were traditional die-hards these days. She'd spotted a lot of old, rare breeds making a comeback amongst the hobby owners, the smallholders and the less commercial sorts. No doubt her father would have strong opinions about the decline of traditional farming but like the heavy horse riding centre, it was at least a way of keeping the best part of it alive. Even he couldn't argue with that.

She nudged Pete. 'I've had a brilliant idea. I'm going to suggest to James and Laura they have a heavy horse on the riding holiday team. Be a great advertisement and it might encourage more men to come along. Be one in the eye for Stella, that would.'

'There's not a cat in hell's chance of any holidays happening. And you know why.'

She tutted at his glum face.

The red rosette went to the black Shire. Annoyingly, the running commentary was out of sync with what was happening, so she had no idea who it belonged to. First of all, the information was delivered in Welsh, mostly loud and stumbling with frequent mistakes and there was a lot of throat clearing and rustling paper. By the time Jones had translated it, the situation was already fifteen minutes ahead. It could be amusing though, especially when a random announcement for a lost dog was confused with the winner of the dog agility show.

'They need to retire him. How many years has Jones-Rag-and-Bones done this job?' Maggie said.

'He's out of date. Gone past his sell-by. Like all this has. Like we have.'

She let him walk ahead.

At the far side of the ground the horse-boxes were lined up in the shade. It was easy to spot the palomino mare, despite the cluster of teenage girls around her. She was tied to the side of the small trailer and Lucy was fixing up a hay net. Ben sat on the ramp, a plastic pint of something in one hand and a hog roast sandwich in the other. Maggie was torn with wanting to interrogate Lucy, but not wanting to get drawn into a conversation about anything else. As it happened, she looked up and read the situation anyway. The same old questions were probably etched into Maggie's face, along with the tiredness and the slightly despairing joviality.

Lucy continued to rub away at the sweat marks caused by the girth, keeping her head close to the mare's flanks. There was a red rosette fluttering on her halter.

'Oh, is that a first place I see?' Maggie said.

'Yep. She was totally brilliant.'

'Well done! No James or Laura today?'

'James is busy on the yard and Laura's in the floral art tent, with Mum.'

'Oh, typical. Sounds dead boring,' she went on, then smoothed a hand down Song's shoulder. 'Lucy, I don't suppose–'

'Look, Jess lost her phone when she was on the Congo River ride in Busch Gardens. And that's *all* I know.'

'How do you know that?'

'Sam's Twitter.'

'Busch Gardens? That's in Florida.'

'Yep. She's on *honeymoon*. With Sam, and about twenty of his friends.'

She watched Lucy sort through the travel bandages spread out over the grass. Of course, she and Pete hadn't thought about a honeymoon, even if it was a pretend honeymoon for the sake of the authorities. At least the lost phone went a tiny way to absolving Jess and her tardy behaviour. She wasn't sure if it absolved Sam from ignoring them as well, but then it was highly likely that James hadn't even sent a message in the first place. And an email to Stella that didn't actually demand an answer was hardly going to motivate an immediate response, at least not one from a busy person. And if Jess was away Stella might well be very busy indeed.

This combined information might at least buy some time into the following week and stop Pete doing anything stupid. She looked around for several anxious seconds through the milling crowds until finally, she spotted the parasol on the pram. Pete was standing braced, both hands on the pram handle. And standing equally braced in front of the pram with his hands on the hood, was Armstrong.

CHAPTER FOUR

Laura

The long, humid nights were compromising sleep but the extended heatwave was so rare, no one dared grumble. All too soon they'd be moaning about the wind and the ice, but for now it was full summer and early mornings were the only time they could bear to be physically close enough to make love. The faintest movement of cool air found its way through the open window, disturbing the curtains and flushing the room with dawn light. She turned to face James, to taste the sweet saltiness of his lips once more. A loud clatter outside and the scrape of a wheelbarrow reminded them that they weren't the only ones awake, and the moment was lost.

'Rhian's up and about early,' James said.

'It's show day. I bet Lucy's already here.'

Once he'd padded down the stairs to the shower room, Laura shuffled round in the bed and propped her legs up against the wall. These days more often than not, she had a scientific vision of her reproduction system. This was down to the screwed-up leaflet she'd rescued from the bottom of her bag. Point three suggested that this particular post-coital position may allow better bathing of sperm to the cervix. Hopefully, it might also allow a microsecond of magic to occur.

James returned sooner than expected, with wet hair and

wearing a towel, both dogs in tow from where they'd spent the night downstairs on the tiled floor. On sight of her, he smothered a huge grin. Lambchop leapt onto the bed.

'I'm willing to try anything,' she said, trying to dodge the terrier's hot kisses. 'Dignity is not an option.'

'I'm not laughing. You're just… I dunno, beautifully committed.'

He went about his daily routine of hunting for clothes through the discarded items on the floor, which she no longer picked-up since it had the power to create a silly argument. His pockets were the equivalent of a busy office desk. Important scraps of paper, a special screw which had fallen out of the security camera, something he'd customised for the horsebox engine, nearly always covered in oil and crushed dog biscuit. Much as it bugged her, she consoled herself with the fact that he was pretty much perfect in a lot of other ways; ways that mattered.

Beautifully committed.

He opened several drawers, noisily and randomly.

'If you're looking for clean underwear you'll find there isn't any since it's all still on the bedroom floor, or behind the laundry basket where it's clearly been lobbed from a distance.'

'That's disgusting. How do you put up with me?'

'If you're desperate, there's a bag on the chair. It's the present I bought for you in Chester. You've not even looked at it.'

'That reminds me, what happened to those rubber buckets?' She heard the bag rustle and then a disparaging grunt. 'Fancy pants.'

'Silk *boxers*. Nice and cool for the heat.'

'I suspect this might have some allegiance with your morning yoga,' he said, but ripped off the packaging anyway and held a pair in front of the towel. 'Not sure about the pattern. Bit jazzy, aren't they?'

'Who's going to see?'

'Me. They might affect me psychologically, as I go about my business.'

'I just want you to be beautifully committed too.'

'I am. But I don't need pink paisley to confirm it.'

'It's the silk that's key, not the design,' she said, finally righting herself, bemused at his idea of pink and paisley. She reached for her wrap and her eye caught the photo of his son, propped on the dressing table. 'I want to give you what you missed with Sam. Those first precious ten years, when you never knew him. And beyond that, obviously. That's got to be worth putting up with a bit of magenta-mix.'

'*Pink.*'

She sighed. 'I'll do everything else. You know… grow the baby, give birth to the baby, breastfeed the baby.'

He crossed the room then and kissed her, a lingering kiss full of hope and understanding. A kiss which somehow delved into deeper territory than any words could possibly explain. His eyes left hers, reluctantly, as a pair of filthy torn denims went on over the delicate silk.

'Did you text Sam?' she said.

'What about?'

'Getting Jess to call home.'

'Nope.'

'Oh, *James!* I've told Maggie now.'

'And I've told you, I'm not getting involved.'

Relationship complications, especially anything to do with Jess, tended to have James switch off at the best of times. She knew this, but theirs was a unique situation. Jess and Sam's latest escapade prompted awkward questions and raised plenty of speculation. Maybe James was right to blank it for the moment, but it was difficult to see Pete and Maggie struggle and in her heart of hearts she had to agree that Jess should be at home by now looking after Krystal, although that looked less likely as time went on. Much as it was easier not bumping into Jess at every turn, her sister couldn't go on forever like they were. Pete's threat of a solution was unnerving, but she couldn't actually think of anything they could do as a viable alternative. It was irksome that her sister had refused Lucy's help as it would have solved more than one problem, at least in the short to medium term.

She slipped on a practical summer dress and a pair of flat sandals. Not the best choice of footwear around horses, but temperatures were again forecast into the eighties. Although this was an ideal prospect for the village show, the downside was the unrelenting ground and the possible fight for shade and water. Lucy had already asked Laura if she'd be there to watch her jump and although it had been a casual invitation, it had her feel enormously secure in the knowledge that she was firmly accepted as part of the scene. And then Lucy showed her the programme.

Number 32, Morning Song, owned by Mrs Morgan-Jones and ridden by Miss Lucy Ford.

'*Morning* Song?' she said to Lucy.

'It sounded better.'

It sounded wonderful. Furthermore, it was an endorsement in print, and no one could argue with that.

When she arrived down on the yard it was still early but Song was already in the trailer, fully plaited and preened. Ben was loading water containers, a hay net and tack into the empty side.

'Problem. Me. Driving with that trailer,' she said to James. 'Can Lucy not ride down there?'

'I'd rather she didn't, roads are full of idiots on show days. Take Ben. He's due an easy morning before we start baling.' She caught hold of his hand. 'So are you, due for an easy morning. I'm worried you're doing too much. Come with me.'

'Problem. You. You're taking two thirds of the staff, so I'm needed here. Haven't you given the builders till the end of play today to get the boiler in? I'm waiting for the electricians to fix the lighting in the school, if they turn up with the right fittings this time. Then Rhian's teaching all morning, and I've got a private client.'

'Oh. Should I stay? There's so much going on.'

'Well, it is you who's cracking the whip.'

'Sorry, it must be some sort of nesting syndrome.'

'Seriously big nest. How many kids you planning on us having?'

She ignored his jibe. 'I have advertised for staff. Another part-time Ben, a part-time stable girl, and a full-time instructor from September.'

'Have you?' he said, warily. 'Look, I'll come over at lunchtime for a hog-roast, and a beer. Be too hot for anything else by then.'

She climbed into the Land Rover with a nervous Lucy and James stuck his head through the rolled-down window. 'Have fun. No falling off and disgracing our exceptional reputation.'

'As if!'

Ben pushed the ramp home and Song whinnied her concern as they sashayed slowly down the drive and onto the village road. The fields looked especially parched and brown and the hedges bordering the narrow lanes had grown impossibly high and wide. Along with a line of impatient cars trying to get onto the A55 to join the morning rush hour, it was obvious why James had insisted on them taking transport. Two children and a pony joined the line of horse boxes and animal trailers waiting to get into the ground and Laura found herself constantly checking the wing mirror for sight of them as they inched along. How did parents deal with this sort of constant anxiety, more to the point, where *were* the parents? She stole a glance at Lucy and tried to imagine what it must feel like to have a daughter about to jump in a competition. She hoped she wouldn't be one of those overzealous mothers who suffocated their children with worry, but then she thought about James and how steady he was. She was most certainly the Yin to his Yang.

Their pitch was in a good spot; on the perimeter of the hustle and bustle and close to the shade provided by a bank of trees. Song was a handful the second she clattered off the ramp, whinnying and spinning round to look at every passing horse, and spook at every unfamiliar noise.

'Oh, crikey, she's already sweated-up,' Lucy said, tying her to the side of the trailer.

'Like a tin can in the back of that trailer,' Ben said, getting in Lucy's way at every turn. 'Or it might be the smell of them bulls making her nervous. I knew a girl once with a ring through her nose like that.'

'Ben. Listen to the PA. They want people for the boot throwing competition,' Lucy said. 'You'd be good at that.'

'What do you have to do?'

'Just chuck a boot as far as you can. You know, like you do in the tack room.'

'Is that it?'

'That's it.'

While Ben went to stand in line at the admin tent and Lucy careered over the practice jumps, Laura wandered through the throngs of people already eating burgers, candy floss and bacon sandwiches. There was little hope of finding Pete and Maggie, that's if they'd decided to attend given her sister's frostiness the previous week. Unsure of how the land lay with regard to Sam and Jess, she hadn't tried phoning or texting. She watched the *Barren Veteran Welsh Mountain Pony Mares* lining up in their class and wondered at the odd name, preferring to move on to cast a sly glance around the cattle pens in case she spotted Marjorie Williams. A sign on one of the pens bearing their name and the breed of cattle, alerted her to the right place. Maybe she expected, *hoped*, to see her with a brood of children and it felt like an anti-climax then to see her wearing a grubby white overall and struggling to adjust a halter on a Welsh Black – alone. Was she really a barren veteran too, or was she hiding six strapping farmer's sons somewhere, or a set of triplets? Fertility treatment tended to do that. She tried to imagine the look on James' face if she ever announced they were expecting twins.

A strong hand grabbed her arm and she spun round.

'Sorry, sorry, didn't mean to make you jump,' Rob said, kissing her firmly on both cheeks. 'Advance apologies for the smell, it will hit you any second now... Jamie here, is he? Need to ask a favour.'

She suddenly pinched her nose. 'Not till lunchtime. Are you on call?'

'What makes you ask that, huh? I always stink and walk about covered in guts and shit.'

She laughed. 'Rob, you do, often! Not too busy though?'

'Mostly heatstroke so far, a Gloucester Old Spot with a swollen nearside hind and a couple of cases of mocking-up grey hair with black boot polish. And that's just the old folk.'

'Cheating?'

'You bet. The stakes are crazy high. A first place can earn... oh, at least a tenner in prize money.'

'Ah, yes, but it's about the resultant sale price on the ram's head if he wins the red. Everyone knows that.'

'Well, well, I'm impressed. Not just a pretty face, but I knew that.'

'My father was a farmer. Although it was Maggie who took to it all, riding, shooting.'

'So it's in your genes whether you like it or not, and you're married into the community now. You do know you have to grow a moustache and have arms like a couple of marrows to look like a proper farmer's wife?'

'Idiot.' She smiled and linked the cleaner of his arms as they negotiated the crowds heading towards the main ring. 'What was the favour, anyway?'

'Oh, if I tell you, you'll be bound to say yes, I know you will. And then we both might get into trouble.'

'I'm intrigued.'

They approached the cordoned-off veterinary area and she watched his broad back duck beneath a rope. 'Back at the surgery I've got this really weak Carneddau foal,' he said. 'Days old. His mammy was killed on the mountain road last night–'

'Killed, how?'

'Car. You don't want to know the details. Ideally we need a foster mare and I've tried all the usual leads, but nothing so far. The only alternative is bottle feeding artificial mare's milk but then we'd need a constant chain of teenage girls, and I thought… now where can I find that sort of loving devotion around the clock?'

'You don't need to ask.'

'I knew that. Catch you later.'

Announcements for the open novice show jumping had her head over to the main ring to find a good position. She knew she'd have to wait a while for number 32 but it was almost too warm to walk about and she perched on a vacant straw bale by the collecting ring. The bright start had given way to an altogether more oppressive, darkening sky. She rooted out a bottle of water from her bag and watched 31 competitors. When she heard her name over the PA system it sounded surreal. Lucy Ford and *Morning Song* entered at a smart pace. They looked so breathtakingly bright; Song's summer coat like clogau gold and Lucy impossibly smart in white jodhpurs and a dark jacket. They performed a square halt in front of the judges, Lucy bowing her head. The starting bell rang, loudly and suddenly. Song didn't flinch, thanks to the old hand-operated fire bell Laura had discovered in the barn and they'd 'tested' it within hearing distance of Song at regular, random intervals. Ben had bitten his own tongue and dropped the same pot of paint at least twice.

The mare galloped rather than cantered towards the first fence, clearing it with at least a metre to spare, her legs tucked up and her little golden ears flicking to and fro at the hundreds of distractions in the jostling crowd. A loose dog ran across the ring carrying a leek, then crawled beneath a caravan. A roar of laughter went up but the mare was used to the antics of Washboy and Lambchop and she was unperturbed as they went into the second; an uncompromising upright brush fence with small flags drooping at either end. Laura had never known tension like it. She had to remind herself that it was just a country show and not the Olympics. And *not her daughter.* Stupid thoughts, and totally out of context, but she couldn't stop her heart thudding. They soared over everything, Lucy struggling with the mare's steadily increasing speed as they approached the last, but they jumped clear. Laura rose to her feet and then everyone was clapping. Song wasn't ready for the sudden applause and her ears flattened as she made a sudden swerve towards the exit.

Lucy recovered quickly and they slowed to a trot, a beaming grin on her face.

Laura hurried across the field, cursing the way her sandals collected the long grass. Lucy had already dismounted, her face flushed with heat and excitement. She pulled off her hat and shook out her hair, and a woman quickly moved in for a hug. Clearly, Lucy's mother, but then it was a mother's job to *be there.* Her privilege. Laura slowed to a more respectable pace, forcing away the immature, overblown emotion which must be plastered over her face, until Lucy eventually spotted her.

'Laura! Did you watch?'

'Yes, of course. Well done, you were both fabulous.'

'If there's a jump-off against the clock how can I ask her to go any faster? She'll just bolt everywhere.'

'Then *don't,*' Lucy's mother said, pointedly. 'Why aren't

you wearing that body-protector you pestered me to buy? *Eighty* pounds, Lucy! It's meant to protect you in a fall not reside on your bedroom floor.'

'In this heat? It's really uncomfortable, as well. Don't nag.'

She led the mare out of earshot, back to her spot at the side of the trailer. A few teenagers from the yard came to pat Song's sweaty shoulder and they were both soon lost in a huddle of admiration. Her mother turned to Laura and offered a hand. 'I'm Pauline. You must be Laura?'

'Yes, hi. You must be so proud of Lucy.'

Pauline gave her a barely-there smile, then folded her arms. 'Hmm. She's a tad obsessed. Honestly, that horse is all she talks about.'

'It's good to be… beautifully committed to something though,' Laura said. 'Better than hanging about pubs, like I did at her age.'

'For now, until uni starts. To be honest, I'm not keen on these competitions. Sooner or later she'll want a bigger horse to do the nationals. We'll have the cost of fuel and transport on top of the farrier, the special rugs, the livery fees… I mean, some of these girls have sponsors, don't they? And now her brother is hitting on me for his car insurance. The cost of these kids is endless! Sometimes I think I work full-time just to pay for their hobbies.'

'Lucy works really hard on the yard.'

'I'm not being funny, Laura, but her wages only cover running her moped to get her there and back. It needs more than a… a *beautiful commitment,* as you so elegantly put it.'

Ouch. James had warned her about this. It was one of the reasons he generally disliked anything of a competitive nature – he simply didn't like the conflict it could create – and exactly why he shied away from talking to parents, unless it was specifically about an equine behavioural problem. She didn't have an answer for Pauline, at least not a constructive one. Growing a business and making money had always come easily, but this was different. This wasn't about coordinated curtains and lampshades; she was dealing with real lives, hopes and dreams. Including her own? It was still something of a revelation to swallow the answer to this because not only did the driving factor come from the man she'd married, but now it was also connected to the horses she was coming to know, and understand. Stupid to think it had been safer to deny all that emotion and immerse herself in facts and figures for most of her life. She'd probably got locked into this mindset since the death of her mother, because it was easier, like being with a man who couldn't, *wouldn't* commit. Thank God he hadn't. Climbing out of her chrysalis to be the person she was meant to be might be invisible on paper, but it was infinitely more powerful than any profit margin.

Perhaps her real challenge was to pull these two forces together and make them work. Profit with empathy sounded about right.

She stood with Pauline Ford to watch the timed jump-off. When Lucy gave the mare her head to gallop around the shortened course they certainly lacked the style and composure of the other two more polished competitors, but the crowd got behind them. A lot of this was down to the sheer exuberance of the mare, and she did look very striking with her flaxen mane and tail against that puce sky. A couple standing to the left of Laura said it was refreshing to see a new face on the circuit, especially someone from the Morgan-Jones yard after years of bad luck for James. Further along the row of spectators, there was talk about the new indoor school. This was definitely profit with empathy, and she had to stifle her desire to shout and clap too loudly when they were presented with a red rosette. Pauline's reaction was a split between parental pride and the unwelcome resignation that they now likely qualified for a bigger competition elsewhere. Laura couldn't decide if she felt guilty enough for encouraging Lucy, or sad that Pauline found it such a stress.

'You must think I'm really rude, I'm sorry,' Pauline said, as they wandered slowly back towards the trailer. 'I haven't thanked you, for being so supportive of her. Lucy thinks a lot of you.'

'She's a credit to you. Honest, hard-working. I've enjoyed the learning process with the horse too.'

'It's just that, well, I suddenly find myself a single parent and…' She paused to exhale, and looked skyward, 'and it's… *tough*.'

'Lucy never said.'

'Like I say, she's obsessed with the horse. Like *you* say, maybe that's a good thing.'

Perhaps she'd misjudged Pauline Ford.

A small crowd of teenagers, including Ellie and Willow were clustered around Lucy and Song, taking mobile phone selfies. Pauline announced she was off to do her own networking. 'I'm going to head over to the floral art, fancy a look?'

'Sure. What is it you do, for a living I mean?'

'Florist. Don't you have a design background?'

'Yes, although I've no idea when I'll get back to it on a full-time basis. I'd like to get everything up and running on the yard first and then maybe think part-time for Cariad Designs. I'd like to get to the stage where I can cherry-pick jobs around whatever else is happening.'

'I'm sure you'll succeed. You strike me as being especially motivated.'

She chose to ignore Pauline's slightly sarcastic edge. After all, she'd got her wrong before. It was airless in the marquee, combined with a mix of hot bodies and both types of hot dog. It was just about saved by the considerable perfume of wilting foliage. They stopped at the winning table decoration, a towering contemporary structure of bamboo and calla lilies.

'You mentioned sponsors,' Laura said. 'How does that work, exactly?'

'Oh, well, it's all about branding and advertising. Some of the clothing manufacturers for example, might sponsor a horse and rider they see as an asset. You know, wear our boots when you compete and talk about them, and we'll sponsor you.'

'I'm guessing it would be inappropriate for Cariad Designs to do such a thing?'

Pauline pushed her spectacles up onto the top of her head and studied Laura's face. 'Thing is, I'm not sure I'd want that for Lucy. As I said earlier, she has uni starting in September and I'd rather she didn't get distracted.'

'Right.'

They moved down the line of wedding bouquets but she wasn't really paying attention by then. When Pauline stopped to talk to the judges, Laura motioned she was heading outside for some air, not that there was much to be had. And then she saw him, Armstrong. Any remaining stale air was sucked from her lungs with a single gasp. She'd recognise that stance anywhere, but it was Krystal's cry that facilitated the quick connection. Everything happened in seconds, the way he shoved the pram back against Pete, the angry retaliation of both men and then Pete clutched his chest and collapsed to the ground. The crowd surged, dispersed, regrouped, and she lost sight of what was happening. Several shouts went up for medical assistance. Someone took charge, moving people back and shouting into a walkie-talkie. Laura's first instinct was to grab the pram handle, but several people had taken it upon themselves to interfere and there was a complicated, anxious few minutes where no one fully understood what was happening. Until Maggie came charging in.

'Pete! Oh, my God has he had another heart attack? He has, hasn't he? Has anyone called an ambulance?'

'It's probably just the heat,' someone said, still licking

an ice cream, while Pete lay white-faced and motionless on the grass, flat on his back. A stray balloon landed gently on his chest. One of the stewards fanned Pete's face with a programme, and Maggie sank to her knees. Laura moved into the fray and kept a firm hand on the pram handle, scanning the crowds for sight of Armstrong, but he was long gone, of course he was.

Maggie looked round to check the pram. 'Oh, Laura! It's Pete, he just dropped to the ground! He's not moving.'

The milling crowds began to part quickly at sight and sound of the resident ambulance as it trundled over the grass towards them. Laura squeezed her sister's shoulder. 'He'll be alright, Maggie, doctor's here now.'

'He's still breathing, love, don't panic,' the steward said, still on one knee and flapping at the sultry air.

The doctor quickly produced an oxygen mask, then they all had to step back as Pete was carefully manoeuvred onto a stretcher and a phone call was made to Bangor A & E. The entire scene had the look of a field hospital but on the other hand, it was infinitely more hospitable than the wild place on the Carneddau where James had lain after his accident. She'd never forget the way her sister had knelt on the rocks, holding his head for hours, covered in blood. The scene couldn't be more different but it held exactly the same shaky expectation of life or death.

Maggie struggled to her feet, sweaty and beaten, two round spots on her knees where the trampled soil had stained her cream pants. She clasped hold of Laura's hand and moved in close enough to whisper.

'Did you see, Armstrong?'

'Yes, I saw.'

They spoke with their eyes, understanding the significance but unable to quantify it into words.

'I'm worried *sick*. And I'm sick to death of all this,' Maggie said, her eyes following the slow progress of the stretcher.

'I know, I know you are. You just look after Pete,' she said, but Maggie began to look round wildly, torn between wanting to go in the ambulance and then obviously wondering what to do about Krystal, and Ellie.

'Go with him. I'm here,' Laura said. 'I'll look after Ellie and the baby.'

'But I don't even know where Ellie is! She's here somewhere, with Willow.'

'I know where she is. Maggie, just *go.*'

Finally, her sister climbed into the ambulance. She waited till the vehicle pulled away slowly across the field and then someone must have opened an emergency exit, because it roared up the lane, siren full-on, orange light flashing through the hedge.

It didn't take long to pack up.

She lifted Krystal from her sticky slumber, then took Ellie to one side and explained what had happened while Lucy set about loading Song. The pram was pushed unceremoniously into the spare side and strapped to the fixings with a length of baler twine. Song eyed it suspiciously.

'I bet she thinks it's a horse with round legs,' Ben said.

Lucy rolled her eyes, 'By that reckoning she'll have you down as a donkey with two legs.'

His face lit up. 'That's the sort of thing Jess used to say. I miss Jess, she was a right laugh.'

'Well, there's nothing funny about this,' Laura murmured, 'she needs to come back.'

They squashed into the Land Rover and Ellie had to sit on Lucy's knee with the seatbelt round both of them. Thankfully they had less than a mile to get home but it took an age given the unlikely cargo. Lucy looked at Krystal with a fair degree of trepidation, then flicked her eyes onto Laura's. 'She dropped her phone in a water park, Jess did.'

Laura looked firmly out of the passenger window, a vision of the wedding ring sliding off as well, sinking to the bottom of a concrete pit and floating amongst the weeds. At home, she slid out of the Land Rover carefully, cradling Krystal close to her chest. Ellie followed close behind carrying the parasol off the pram and a grooming kit. She hadn't said a word to anyone. Ben let down the ramp and wheeled out the manure-splattered pram with a jaunty whistle. James did a double-take, then frowned and ambled across the yard, his eyes immediately drawn to the baby. 'What's happened?'

'We was robbed,' Ben said. 'That boot-throwing was a fix. Pretty sure mine was a left foot. Either that or it had cement in it.'

James continued to stare at her. Krystal felt like a lead weight under his scrutiny. 'Pete's been rushed to hospital,' she said.

Behind her, Song backed obediently down the ramp, the red rosette still pinned to her halter but no one mentioned it. Laura felt sorry for Lucy, that her glory had been so short-lived, overtaken by Jess' trail of never-ending misery. O'Malley whinnied a greeting but other than that, their reception was cool.

After several seconds of digesting the information, James drew his eyes from hers. 'I'll call Sam.'

CHAPTER FIVE

Maggie

Jess came home on the Wednesday of the following week. Maggie heard the taxi first and then the slam of a door. She'd just got Krystal back down for a mid-morning nap but either she was getting more settled or she was zonked out from being awake half the night, because she didn't stir. Nevertheless Maggie opened the front door before Jess hit the bell, meeting her eyes for a fleeting second as she walked up the drive carrying an array of matching leather luggage. Her clothes seemed smarter too and her long dark hair had been cut into a super-sharp jaw-length bob with chestnut highlights. Her appearance wasn't the only marked difference. She moved in to give Maggie a perfunctory hug and a waft of expensive perfume filled the space between them. There was a long awkward moment, perhaps because there was no mention of Krystal. No enquiry of general health, no race up the stairs to see her. A throb of something behind her eyes had Maggie root out the tissues she had permanently jammed up her sleeves. It was tiredness, that's all.

Nathan looked over her shoulder, drying his hands on the pot towel.

'You took your time getting here,' he said, to his sister.

'I got the first available, *affordable* flights I could, alright?

81

New Hampshire's not exactly round the corner.' She shoved past and marched into the kitchen. 'Anyway, it's not as if anyone's died, is it?'

Oh, yes, she still had the backchat but there was something different in her demeanour, a sort of detached coolness. Maggie wasn't sure what to make of it, but preferred to think it was a combination of jetlag and a desire not to fall to pieces in front of her older brother. She exchanged a weary glance with Nathan then followed Jess into the kitchen, where she was brandishing a Disney bag. 'Where's Ellie? I got her something.'

'At Willow's house,' Maggie said, filling the kettle. Her reflection in the kitchen window above the sink looked wild and dried-out, much the same as the back garden. 'Seems to prefer to live there these days. Either that, or she's helping out at the yard with the foal.'

'Foal?'

'Oh, one of the Carneddau mares was killed on the road. Little thing needs feeding round the clock. Good job it's in the school holidays, Ellie's there morning, noon and night.'

'A bit like what's going on here,' Nathan said, but Jess ignored that. 'So… how's Dad, then?'

Maggie lined up three mugs on the counter and threw in teabags. 'Poorly. He has to rest.'

'So it's not an emergency, as such?'

Nathan rounded on her. 'Yes, it *is* an emergency! It's been an emergency since you decided not to come home from America and went and got yourself hitched instead.'

'I'm not talking to you about it. It's none of your business, Nate.'

'Damn right it's my business! Mum and Dad have put up with your crap for too long. Sort it out!'

'Sort out, *what?*'

'Well, let's see. I've taken four days' holiday to come and help out here and support Mum. I've got to go back to work tomorrow. So you can sort that out for a start.'

'I'm not actually *back* back. And I'm on leave as well–'

'Oh, *leave*, is it?'

'Whatever. Anyway, all my stuff's gone, even my car. It's not like I live here anymore, is it?'

'You'll find your *stuff*, upstairs in her cot waiting for you.'

Maggie spun round from the sink. 'Stop it, both of you!' She cast her eyes towards the stairs in what she hoped was a warning and they both stared back with frowns like deep ruts. 'All your things are safely packed away, Jess. We simply needed the space.'

'That's not what Dad said a couple of months ago.'

'It was a spur of the moment reaction, he was cross.'

'With good reason,' Nathan added, before quietly leaving the room, the pot towel still stuffed in his back pocket.

Rather than dive upstairs and slam a door, Jess remained curiously passive and went to pick up the tray bearing the tea and some cake, into the sitting room. Throughout the silent sipping, the landline phone rang several times as it usually did on Wednesdays and Thursdays. Nathan dealt with it all. Sometimes it was Pete's mum, and with more good weather promised for the weekend they'd had plenty of enquiries for rooms. Pete kept saying they shouldn't put anyone off because they couldn't really afford to and anyway, Nathan seemed hell bent on playing host.

'Let him do it, why not?' Pete said.

'It doesn't seem right, not with you being all wired-up in here.'

'Better than being over-wired at home. And tell your sister you want that girl to help as well.'

'Lucy?'

'I don't know why you refused in the first place.'

Her shoulders had sagged at this.

'We can't afford pride, Maggie.'

At least having guests, albeit sporadic, gave them some focus. Nathan's energy and enthusiasm made everything seem so much easier. Maggie cooked the breakfasts and looked after the baby during the day. Nathan did everything else, including the night feeds. But then first thing Thursday morning he brought her a cup of tea in bed and announced he was setting off for the long drive back to London.

'That lad from the yard's here, to sort out the back garden.'

'Already?'

'Make sure Jess pulls her weight, Mum.'

'I'll be having a talk with her, don't you worry.'

'She needs more than that.'

'I *know*,' she said, and pressed a placatory hand on Nathan's arm in what she hoped was a gesture of kindly authority. Once he'd left the room she dressed hurriedly and waved him off into another beautiful, sun-filled dawn. She heaved a huge sigh at the *talk* to come, picked up the milk from the step and looked up at the bedroom windows. Jess was still zonked out with jetlag, Krystal would be awake soon and there were two couples waiting in the dining room for an early cooked breakfast before traversing the Snowdon Horseshoe. Their enormous boots and rucksacks were already lined up in the porch. Jess would have to wait. Although Maggie was itching to know what her plans might be, she didn't want to wade in too heavy in case she was feeling her way to coming home. There was no point both of them suffering with pride and missing a chance to fix things. Now that Nathan had gone, Jess might open up. Later, they'd get the baby to sleep, pour a glass of wine and have a proper talk.

Back inside, she switched on the coffee machine and pulled down an apron from the back of the door, then began to whisk the eggs for one scrambled on brown, plus three full Welsh, one without tomato. They only called it a Welsh breakfast because it included sausage and bacon made from Marjorie Williams' rare breed pigs, local mushrooms, and their own eggs. Well, most of the time. At the thought of

Marjorie, an uncomfortable vision of Laura holding Krystal came into her mind as she tossed the mushrooms in butter. Why had Maggie even mentioned her? Poor woman never did get pregnant. And then on Sunday morning Laura had turned up on the doorstep with the pram. She'd been fully expecting it but at least the whole episode had prompted action of some sort, and now Jess was here, *finally.*

Just after seven, Lucy's moped turned in and Maggie had to admit the relief was enormous, and the support appreciated. And it looked so much better to have someone young and pretty serve the breakfasts in a white pinny. Lucy was a morning person too, full of chatter and knew what needed doing without Maggie having to point things out. As Maggie cooked, Lucy washed-up then began sorting through the washing.

'Oh, the foal is *so* cute,' she said, folding and separating everything into piles. 'Doesn't seem right it's a colt. Not when he looks so pink, especially in the evening light.'

'First a palomino, now a strawberry roan. I think my sister must be collecting one in every colour, like handbags. What have they called him?'

'There's a competition to choose his name. Ben wanted Pimple.'

They both laughed, just as Jess craned her head round the door, still in her pyjamas. She yawned and reached her hands up through her hair, exposing a bellybutton piercing and a Celtic cross tattoo. That was new.

'Luce… What you doing here? How did you know I was back?'

'I didn't,' Lucy said, slightly startled at her appearance.

'So… what *are* you doing here?'

'Helping,' she said, then went to depress the plunger on the cafetiere. She pushed past Jess with the coffee pot and the morning papers.

'And very good she is, too,' Maggie said, dropping bread

into the toaster. 'You'll find a bottle for Krystal, already made up in the fridge. And she's started taking some of that baby cereal as well, just a spoonful.'

All of this was met with an expression more associated with imminent dental treatment. Jess removed the bottle from the fridge, shook it, then cast a disinterested look at the label on the jar of porridge. If her father had been here he'd have already exploded, but if she'd learnt anything about Jess it was never to respond to provocation. Pete's ultimatum churned relentlessly through her mind, as did the unspoken incident at the show. The incident where Armstrong had grasped the pram and Pete had collapsed to the ground. She and Pete had discussed neither, choosing to keep to safe, bland conversation. She concentrated on the special slate platters from Llanberis, measuring out Heather Honey and Welsh Hedgerow jam into pots, then adding delicate scrolls of butter. All presented exactly as Pete liked it with a sprig of fresh heather on the side.

Jess warmed the milk through in the microwave and measured out the porridge into a plastic bowl and Maggie felt a pathetic wave of gratitude flood her insides. And as if to compound the good start to the day, the hikers were extremely pleased with their breakfasts and paid in cash, leaving much praise and a generous tip for Lucy.

'That's very kind of you,' Maggie said, hovering in the hall as they brought their cases down. 'When you get home, would you consider putting a review on Trip Advisor? It's just that I think we've been trolled.'

She could hear Jess snorting with disdain in the kitchen, but one of the guests did promise to write something nice. Maggie handed over the folded note to Lucy with a small flourish. 'From Mr-scrambled-eggs-on-brown.'

'A twenty quid tip!' Lucy said, wiping round the sink.

'Well deserved. What a good team we make. And it's almost nine, so off you go.'

Maggie cast a satisfied look at the clean and tidy kitchen and helped herself to the left-over coffee. Jess made to carry Krystal into the sitting room. 'You coming through, Luce? Not had a catch-up in ages.'

'Well… just five minutes. I'm on the yard at ten and I still need to get changed.'

Maggie stayed at the kitchen table and flicked through the paper. She could hear their loud conversation but it was severely muffled, partly due to Ben's radio but mostly down to the whine of the strimmer. It was only when it stuttered to a mangled halt that she caught any of the words.

'Are those her rings?' Lucy said. 'They are, aren't they? They used to belong to Carys. It's *sick*, Jess. That's what it is.'

'Sick? In what way?'

'You've still got a thing about him, haven't you? *Uncle* Jamie.'

Maggie didn't dare turn the page for fear of it rustling.

'Change the record,' Jess said, and her short sigh bled into an uncomfortable silence until she said, 'Is that Ben thrashing about in the jungle out there? It is, isn't it?' Cue hysterical laughter and then Maggie heard the French doors being forced open, followed by Krystal's protest as she was disturbed and carried outside. Soon after, Lucy marched down the hall and out through the front door. Maggie stayed frozen in time until the sound of Lucy's moped faded into the distance, and the agony aunt page keeled over.

In the afternoon, they went to visit Pete.

Ellie wouldn't come. She'd barely acknowledged Jess and her Disney present. She was obsessed with the foal, and seemed to prefer being farmed out between Laura and Willow. It was, after all, the early teenage years so she tried not to worry about it. Maggie strapped Krystal into her rear baby seat and Jess sat alongside with the bag of baby wipes and nappies. Every time her left hand moved, Maggie's eyes were drawn to the flash of dark gold nestled next to a traditional glittery diamond. Why had she not noticed this before? Somehow, she'd imagined a cheap, contemporary wedding ring but the ones Jess wore were old-fashioned in style and setting, possibly Victorian. There was a wide wedding band and a truly stunning solitaire. They didn't seem suited to Jess and her hard, modern exterior. But then she thought about the Celtic cross ingrained into her hip bone and wondered how superficial the American shell actually was.

They joined the dual-carriageway towards Bangor, and the intimacy of the car prompted her to speak.

'So, where did you get those rings? Or rather, where did Sam get them?'

'Walmart.'

'Very funny. James gave them to Sam, did he?'

'It was Laura, actually. When Jamie was in hospital.'

'With his blessing?'

'Well, she didn't hand them over without asking, if that's what you mean.'

'They look–'

'Serious? Yeah, that's the whole point.'

'Yes, but you and Sam are *not* serious?'

'Not in the way you mean, no.'

What *did* she mean? The opposite of serious was frivolous and amusing, but then love and laughter wasn't a bad foundation for marriage. But one without the other never worked. Maggie risked a glance in the rearview mirror and Jess stared right back.

'Look… Sam was engaged, and then he called it off.'

'Those rings were passed on to Sam in good faith, in respect for a genuine family marriage.'

'So?' Jess shrugged and looked out of the side window. 'Me and Sam are on the same wavelength where love is concerned.'

'He should have given those rings back to James, not you!'

'Charming. Since when did you get all sentimental over two bits of metal?'

'I'm not especially. But what you have to understand is that other people are. And those rings used to belong to Carys, didn't they? They likely have significant meaning for James.'

'Then he should have kept them. Or given them to Laura.'

Maggie gritted her teeth and rammed the gears into second as they turned into the car park. She shouldn't have broached anything until they'd seen Pete. It wouldn't do for them to turn up at his bedside with faces like thunder.

They negotiated the lifts, the stairs and the long corridors, to discover he'd been moved to an open ward. It was busy with visitors and noisy with other children, but this was enormously reassuring. And he looked so much better wearing a simple oxygen mask rather than wired up to all sorts of bleeping machinery. They exchanged the usual remarks and Maggie put his Cook Now magazine on the side, along with his phone charger and a bag of mint imperials, which he opened immediately. He pulled the mask down and managed a wan smile at Jess.

'Oh, you're here, are you?'

'Wow, Pops, hold the enthusiasm,' Jess said, but she did stoop down to kiss him, then plonked Krystal into his arms.

He cradled her appreciatively. 'She's grown again, hasn't she? I bet you see a difference in her, eh, Jess?'

The merest acknowledgment at this. She settled herself in the only available chair, then began to scroll through her new mobile.

Maggie perched on the bed. 'How are you, really? Can you come home yet?'

He shook his head and sucked furiously on a mint. 'I've got to have coronary angioplasty. They're keeping me in till they can do it.'

'Oh, no.'

'It's only putting a stent in, to fix a blocked artery. I'll be home a couple of days after, I don't even get fully knocked-out, it's just a local anaesthetic. They go in through the groin though, not looking forward to that.'

'I'll cancel the bookings after this week, you'll need peace and quiet when you come home.'

'No, I've *told* you. That girl can help out and you've got Jess home now, it'll be fine.'

Maggie wondered if anything would be fine, ever again. They managed to keep the conversation light and bland, Jess readily going along with general, albeit guarded chat about the ranch.

'So you enjoyed it over there, did you?' Pete said. 'Hot, was it?'

'Yeah.'

'Your Auntie Laura's thinking of doing something similar. Horse holidays. And we'll put them up, you know, all in.'

'You're going to copy Stella?'

'Not copy,' Maggie said. 'But we're thinking of joining forces with the yard.'

'Stella doesn't cook for them, they get a self-catering lodge on site.'

'Yes, well, we haven't got that at our disposal, we'll be offering the British version. And we'll be more tailored, exclusive. Experienced riders only,' she said, pinching a mint from the bag. 'Hack with Hafod House!'

'Your sister won't go for that, Maggie,' Pete said, unnecessarily.

A dark look from Jess, before she went back to her phone.

Pete gave the mobile a scathing look and tried mouthing various questions to Maggie, avoiding Jess' eye, but it was hopeless really. She knew what he wanted to know, but there was no way she was getting into a heated discussion at his bedside. The issues were too big, even for a two-hour visiting slot. And anyway, she had none of the answers yet. It was all very well Pete thinking and talking in the past tense when it came to the ranch but it was clear Jess was going to scuttle back over there the minute Maggie's back was turned.

For the sake of Pete's arteries and the other patients, she pretended that everything was fine. The funny fake marriage with the genuine jewellery – all gone in a puff of smoke along with the job. Armstrong, her daughter's thinly disguised reluctance to be a mother, and her possible continuing obsession with Uncle Jamie, was swept away along with the incident at the show and placed in the same shady corner.

Later, Laura called to see if it was alright for Ellie to stay over again.

'She's practically living there as it is! Are you sure?'

'I thought it might give you and Jess some, er… space.'

'Right, yes. If you're sure,' she said, hugging the phone under her chin and removing a chilled bottle of wine from the fridge.

'She's been helping with the haymaking, and now she's back on feeding duty.'

'Oh… sounds idyllic. I have to say, from a mother's point of view it's far preferable she's there than wandering the streets or hanging about at Willow's place,' she said, painfully aware of every mothering reference but it was unavoidable. 'How's the… how's the foal?'

'Gorgeous, like Bambi. We've called him Magenta. He does get Mags for short, though. I hope you don't mind.'

She laughed, and poured some of the wine into two glasses. 'I don't mind at all. Better than Pimple.'

It was good to be back on better terms with her sister, just a shame that it had taken Pete's accident to pull them together. Still, it's what families did when the going got tough. 'Sophisticated name choice. Magenta, I mean, not Mags.'

'Ah. Down to James. It was either that, or Paisley, but no one could spell Paisley correctly.'

'Goodness.'

A muffled giggle. 'How's Pete doing?'

Maggie filled her in on the latest and apologised again for being stubborn over Lucy and Ben.

'Oh, Lucy's happy to oblige,' Laura said. 'Her mother a lot less so.'

'Pauline Ford? Used to see her at the school gates. Problem?'

'Hmm. Lucy saw my ad for staff. So now she wants to pack in uni and work for us permanently. I mean, from our point of view we'd have Lucy in a heartbeat. She's personable, reliable. Can *talk* to people.'

'I know. She's a gem. But if her mother has other ideas… Pauline isn't easy.'

'Maybe one day we'll have a nice, calm discussion about it.'

Maggie ended the call and pondered on those words as she carried the wine through to the sitting room. A nice, calm discussion sounded like a grown-up, mature way to handle most disagreements. A warm glow filled Maggie at the thought of a proper mother-daughter heart-to-heart without Ellie eavesdropping, or Pete putting his two-pennyworth in and telling them to keep their voices down. She heard Jess come down the stairs, fully expecting to see her in pyjamas and a dressing gown. After all, she'd been in the bathroom for over an hour. When, after a few minutes she still hadn't materialised Maggie went through to the hall to discover a model-like apparition in a strappy summer dress and killer heels. Three months on the ranch had given Jess her pre-baby body back and she was tanned and toned, pouting into the hall mirror and poised to apply a bright pink lipstick.

'Where do you think you're going?' Maggie said, aware that her voice was already strident.

'Clubbing. Liverpool. Have you got Krystal's birth certificate? I need it.'

'Now? What on earth for? And what about Krystal, while you're out enjoying yourself?'

'What about her?' Jess said, replacing the cap on her lipstick. 'You're here, aren't you?'

Maggie moved across the hall, slid the bolt across the front door and pressed her back against it. 'Oh, no, you're not going *anywhere!*'

'Don't be ridiculous. You can't keep me prisoner. Like Cal did.'

'I think you'll find I'm the prisoner here. Jess, we need to *talk.*'

A big theatrical sigh as her handbag and a small holdall slipped from her shoulder and slumped to the floor. Then it was eyes to the ceiling and a heated session on her phone, rearranging a taxi and muttering to whoever she'd arranged to meet. She finished her calls, moved into the sitting room and perched on the sofa arm with a bored face. 'Alright, so... I have a forty-minute window. The certificate?'

Her own father would have slapped Jess many moons ago. There'd be no opportunities to talk things through, let alone the constant emotional games and the mental manoeuvring they went through to force any sort of compliance, let alone the opening and closing of windows. So far, they'd barely said anything important to each other and Maggie was already sitting on her hands. So much for a calm, grown-up conversation. What she wouldn't give to swap problems with Pauline Ford. A full-time job or a university degree... what sort of problem was that in the grand scheme of things?

'I'll close the window when we're done, *not* you,' Maggie said, braced for a childish retort, but none came. 'Why Liverpool, all that way just to go dancing?'

'Well, I'm hardly going to pick Chester for a night out, am I? Where *he* lives. Look, I'm staying over with a mate.

Then in the morning I need to go to the passport office to get something sorted for Krystal. You have got her birth certificate here, haven't you?'

This was typical of Jess, throwing out curveballs at every opportunity.

'Er, yes, somewhere,' Maggie faltered. She went to the sideboard where they kept paperwork. The action of flicking through inoculation records and leaflets about teething gave herself some breathing space. She'd not expected this. She threw the folder down on the table.

'All in there. So, what are your plans, exactly? Other than going clubbing tonight and the passport office tomorrow?'

'You're asking me like I have a choice.'

'Of course you do!'

'Look, if you want me to talk, then you need to *listen*.'

Maggie sat back down and twiddled with the stem of her glass.

'I'll be taking Krystal back with me, on Sunday.'

'Oh… so, you're settling over there with Sam, are you?'

'Mum, I'm not *with* Sam. We hang out in Maine sometimes, at the weekends. Sam married me so I could build a life over there, *away from Armstrong*. I can't stay around here with Cal stalking us and everyone else hating me for what happened to Jamie.'

'Oh, *Jess!* No one hates you.'

'No?'

A long pause, which Maggie failed to fill with the right platitude. Her eyes were drawn instead to the wedding rings, catching the soft evening light as the sun vanished over the Carneddau. Closer to home, the garden looked bald and exposed. 'They helped me, Sam and Stella did,' Jess went on, quietly. 'They got me some counselling.'

Maggie's mouth must have dropped open a little at this but she managed to remain quiet while the idea was digested. She couldn't imagine her hard-nosed daughter ever agreeing to such a process, but then the time she'd spent with Armstrong was still a mystery to Maggie. She had to concede that there was much she didn't understand about the control he'd had over her. 'You talked to a stranger rather than your own family?'

'Yes! I talked about his control and the way he made me give birth to a baby I didn't want. How that made me *feel*.'

This was awful, not how she'd imagined their chat at all. Pete's unspoken ultimatum had her shift uncomfortably in her chair. The thought of handing Krystal over to such a man because they were both tired, was suddenly abhorrent. She swallowed down some of her wine.

'Jess, look, surely we can work something out… you've got all the support you need right here. James and Rob have got a signed confession, did you know? If Armstrong puts a foot wrong they'll go to the police–'

She threw her head back in a gesture of disbelief. 'I'm sure he's quaking over the thought of that. And do you really think I want to play happy, separated families with *him?*'

'No, alright. But let's recap on the alternative,' Maggie, said warming to her subject. 'Your life will be about a false marriage and a baby you never really wanted, in America. How is that better than being here, with your family and working it through? And what about Krystal in all of this?'

'What *about* Krystal? I'm doing all of this for *her*. And I'm actually doing it for the good of everyone else. Why can't you see that?'

'But you'll be burying your head in the sand! Krystal won't stay a baby forever and you can't keep her on that ranch in the middle of nowhere. Sooner or later she'll ask questions about her father. And her… her *pretend* stepfather, the one you meet up with when the fancy takes you! What sort of example are you setting to a young girl?'

'I know what I'm doing. I've had three months to heal, and time to think it all through.'

Maggie's first thought was that the mention of healing time meant the shock of labour, but of course Jess was talking about the emotional and mental scars she'd discussed with the counsellors. Maggie fought every fibre in her body not to yell and instead, forced herself to concentrate on the folder, hands gripping the edge of the chair for a long moment. When she felt composed, she continued in a gentle, modulated tone like a counsellor might do. 'Alright. So, this American future you've got all planned out, none of it is about you? Because permanent self-sacrifice isn't going to work, Jess.'

The rumble of a taxi and the pip of a horn.

Jess gathered herself together, smoothed down her dress and her hair. 'I'm done talking. It's best this way.' She picked up the birth certificate and slid it into her handbag, then her hand reached out for the spare glass of wine. She downed it in one. Maggie stayed sitting on her hands and transferred her attention to the terracotta carpet. She listened to the sound of heels clacking down the hall. Then the front door opened and closed, like the window of opportunity which had come and gone.

There was a huge chunk of something vital missing from her daughter's story. Love, most certainly.

And not only in her account of the American dream but of herself, healed or not.

CHAPTER SIX

Laura

At her sister's request, Ellie was sent home on Friday. Maggie said she wanted both of her daughters to spend the weekend together before Jess flew back to America on Sunday afternoon. *With Krystal.* Rather than be tempted to ask any pertinent questions about this over the phone, Laura invited her sister to the staff barbecue they had planned for Sunday evening.'We're celebrating getting the roof done on the indoor school, and all the building work finished in the house.'

'Oh, fab. Yes, count me in. Take my mind off things. We're seeing Pete first, he's got his op on Monday, did I tell you? And then I'm driving Jess and Krystal to Manchester Airport. She was going to get a taxi, but really, all that way! She has to check-in three hours before the flight, and all the stuff she has to carry... Ellie won't come because she doesn't want to miss her lesson with James. Is it alright to drop her off?'

'Yes, of course. That's a lot of driving, Maggie. But you will join us, later?'

'Yes, look forward to it. I'll er... fill you in about Jess, when I see you.'

She passed on this information to James as they shunted the farmhouse table back into a more central position.

James pushed the chairs under and Laura placed a heavy antique jug full of white roses in the centre. It was difficult to quantify how she felt about this latest development for Maggie. On the one hand it was good that Jess and the baby were seemingly reconciled and from her own point of view, easier all round that they would be out of sight. She knew James would second that, but then she fully understood how difficult it must be for her sister, despite the fact it would allow them to get back on their feet, not only with the B & B but to aid Pete's recovery too.

'I never expected that, did you?' she said to James. 'Taking Krystal to America.'

'I never know what to expect with Jess. I just hope Sam knows what he's getting into.'

'Have you spoken, recently?'

'Nope.'

He pulled a beer out of the fridge, flipped the ring pull and took a long draft before shooting her a studious look. 'Do you need me for anything else in here?'

Laura shook her head and he went from the room. The subject was not only closed but it seemed he'd pulled the bulletproof shutters down too for good measure. She stood back from the table and decided the single, rustic vase was perfect. In fact the whole space was pretty perfect; practical and authentic without being over-styled or pretentious. Getting both bathrooms and the kitchen functional and finished meant they could sign-off the builders until next spring. Although as a last-minute thought, she'd asked them to fence around the garden area and to use some sort of power drill to get the cherry trees planted up along the drive. The verges were, after all, like concrete.

She found James outside, watering the cherry tree saplings and rinsing a thick layer of dust from their wilting leaves.

'If there are any trees left, they can go in the garden,' she said, to the builders. 'If you can get them into the ground.'

James shot the men a look. 'You do realise you're not getting out of here alive, don't you?'

They grinned and a smile creased Laura's face. She shielded her eyes and looked towards the hazy skyline. The dry weather had turned the paddocks into hard-baked areas of compacted mud, even the menage needed to be watered down before they could use it. Although the drought had enabled them to finish lots of jobs, the grass had virtually stopped growing and the fields were brown and tinder dry. Fires had flared up across the mountains and James was concerned about having to start feeding hay in August. Laura was concerned about her hanging baskets. Not only did everyone forget to water them but O'Malley had managed to scoff every single marigold. Anything else fresh, green and trailing had been tugged out, leaving most of the compost on the ground and any surviving plants hanging on by a thread.

'Told you,' James said, catching her expression as she surveyed some of the remains.

'No, you didn't. You told me which plants weren't poisonous.'

'Same thing. Our herbivores see them as smorgasbord.'

'I'm afraid O'Malley is the sole culprit.'

'That's a bit unfair.'

'None of the other horses can reach! Anyway, he's been caught red-hoofed. I've seen orange petals on his nose.'

'Busted.'

She folded her arms. 'James, you haven't forgotten about the interviews tomorrow, have you?'

Judging from his expression, he'd forgotten. Or more likely, chosen to put it out of his head. He paused as he rewound the hose. 'If anyone turns up, just remember I need to see them work the horses before you go promising jobs to anyone.'

'I know, it's all in hand. The short-listed will come over to you, for final choosing. I'll be looking at their experience, qualifications and social skills and then you can–'

He laughed.

'*What?*'

'You're treating it like they'll be working in a fucking office. And anyway, I'm not interested in paper qualifications and I don't give a fuck about social skills.'

She blanched at his hostility but made sure to lower her voice. 'If we're doing holidays, the staff need to be able to talk to the clients. We can't rely on Ben and Rhian for that, as good as they are in other ways.'

He drained the can of beer, crushed it, stuffed it into one of the overflowing builder's bins and walked into the tack room without a backward glance. She raked a hand through her hair and worried not only about their difference of opinion over staff and the holiday idea, but at the lack of interest in any of the roles she'd advertised. So far, she'd had one phone call from a fully qualified BHS instructor, who not only sounded extremely personable but ticked every single one of her boxes. Until he'd started to ask his own questions.

'Is accommodation provided, with the job?'

'Accommodation? No… sorry.'

'Oh. It's just that I don't live in North Wales and given the salary and the hours you want, I can't really see how I'd be able to–'

'If I could find something in the local village, you'd still be interested?'

A beat. 'I… guess so.'

'My sister may be happy to take a permanent lodger.'

'I'd have to see the place first. Some of these boarding houses are grim–'

'Hafod is my sister's guest house, there's nothing grim about it.'

'...and with having no transport, I'd really need a room on site.'

He rang off with a vague promise to turn up first thing on Saturday morning, but Laura had already drawn a line through his name.

On Saturday, James dutifully made himself available at nine o' clock – the time Laura had stipulated via the job-centre, two local papers and several equestrian websites. She tried not to keep watching the entrance or looking across to where James sat waiting on the picnic bench with a newspaper and a mug of coffee. O'Malley stood in the outdoor menage displaying almost the exact same body language; resting a hind leg and nodding-off in the rising heat. When it crept towards ten-forty-five, James closed the paper, turned O'Malley back out into the field and led his latest recalcitrant project into the round-pen. Laura admitted temporary defeat. She considered calling the job centre, just to check there was no mistake with the day and the time, but who was she kidding?

She contemplated Lucy as she marched past with a handful of halters, and Laura shot her a wry smile. 'Have you sabotaged my recruitment drive?'

'You know I'm the best candidate,' she said, skipping backwards. 'Maybe the only candidate?'

Laura's resolve faltered, surging first one way, then the other. James had warned her about this, about getting personally involved with staff. Pauline Ford had warned her as well. If Lucy were her own child she'd likely feel as aggrieved as Pauline that her clever daughter was considering giving up long-term prospects for a well-paid career, to be a full-time stable girl. And chasing the dreams in her head? The dreams that she and Song had put there? Children began to arrive for the ten o' clock lesson, although another reality was that any profit from this would be swallowed-up

– literally – by the cost of Magenta's milk formula and a sack of milk-replacer pellets, which Rob had thoughtfully dropped off with his monthly invoice. A foal which, when fully grown would be worth in the region of five quid, or so James had informed her as he'd cooked dinner a couple of evenings ago.

'Well, what was I supposed to *do*? You saw Rob carry the foal from his car. It was *heart*-breaking!'

'If you took a walk across the Carneddau in January, no… scrap that. If you walked into Rob's nice warm recovery room at the surgery, you'd find any number of stories to break your heart.'

'I *know* that. But Mags is here now. Can't we use him in the school, eventually?'

'In a few months, he'll need castrating,' he'd said, chopping the top off a large carrot. 'That's another few hundred quid. Then three years of growing his bones before you start sitting kids on him, and that's only after you've spent enough hours breaking and training him to be safe.'

Despite his pragmatism, James had been first on the scene when Magenta had tried to scramble to his feet for the first time, his own spinal injuries forgotten as he lifted the swaying foal onto its splayed legs. Magenta's tiny hoof could fit into Laura's hand, and it didn't seem possible that an animal designed in such a gangly way with such huge hocks and a neck so short it couldn't reach the grass, could ever be practical by its own volition. But survival was by far the strongest instinct. James often berated her for bestowing human feelings onto the horses, but when the foal took his first unaided step, James had quickly turned to look at her. Laura had responded, but it was something of a crooked smile because her mind was busy controlling a wall of emotion. The same wall of emotion which had almost crushed her when he'd lifted a fractious Krystal from her pram, and cradled the baby close to his chest.

That time, Laura had slipped away unseen, but both images moved and haunted her with equal passion.

Only a few days on from that momentous moment, and Magenta already had the power to stop everyone and everything in their tracks. Every twitch of an ear, every breath which dilated his tiny, delicate nostrils and the occasional squeal when he saw Rhian with the feeding bottle, was commented on and marvelled at. Now, it was decided Mags needed a non-human companion to remind him that he was an animal, and allow an exhausted Rhian to move back into her caravan. Ever resourceful, and no doubt solving a problem for someone else, Rob had found them what he described as a motherly old ewe, called Dorothy. Laura looked over the loose box door and they were both busily eating the milk pellets out of a raised bucket, well, mostly Dorothy was. Magenta's pink nose appeared at the top of the stable door, already trying to ascertain what lay beyond the confines of his square box. A stable which, as James was apt to point out, was meant to be filled by a no-hassle, *paying* livery owner.

Laura wandered out of earshot down the yard and called Liz in Spain, ready to admit that she was feeling slightly out of water. She was used to dealing with commodities, not these powerful emotive subjects which were worthless in any commercial sense. At first, Liz was mostly incredulous that the weather across North Wales was hotter than they were currently enjoying in Tenerife.

'Why the hell did we retire here, that's what I want to know? I certainly didn't sign up for grey and cool.'

'I love the heat, although I think James would actually prefer heavy torrential rain right now.'

Liz laughed, understanding her reasoning. 'My bro the stubborn humanist and his savvy, empathetic wife. On paper, you're the perfect business combo.'

'Whereas in reality?'

'Look, how many arguments did James and I have over running the business? And it's tough employing people, and expensive. Horses are expensive! That's the real rub, isn't it? We could never afford to pay a decent salary. I guess we were always fortunate enough to be able to keep it in the family.'

And wasn't that the truth? Carys and Liz had kept the home fires burning between them, but Laura couldn't step into their shoes if her life depended on it. She turned her face towards the sun and closed her eyes. The gaps in her knowledge about this business were beginning to tear and join as one, making one huge black hole. She slid her phone into her jeans pocket and turning, almost fell over a girl standing right behind her. 'Oh! I'm sorry, I didn't see you!'

The girl muttered something in Welsh first, then flicked her eyes towards Rhian. 'Told me to speak to you. Looking for work. Horses.'

She was slight, with startling violet eyes and a nose stud which didn't look too hygienic. Dark, beautifully smooth sallow skin and tight, knotted black dreadlocks.

'You saw the advert?' Laura said, 'You're a bit on the late side.'

'I walked.'

'Ah. Are you local?'

'Enid Evans. Penrhiw Uchaf.'

She spoke quickly and softly and combined with her Welsh accent, Laura found the exact words difficult to decipher. 'Alright, well, I'm Laura. Let's go over to the house, shall we?'

Several eyes were upon them as they walked through the yard and entered the cool hallway. Enid's eyes were everywhere, taking in the freshly painted walls and then pausing at the framed set of collages Laura had made of the old photos. When they reached the kitchen, the girl sank onto a chair and sat on her hands, seemingly spellbound by the floor-standing wine rack and several items on the dresser, including the open cash-tin. Laura made a mental note to have a word with James about leaving it open and in full sight.

'How old are you, Enid?'

A slight jut of the chin at this. 'Eighteen.'

She looked no more than fifteen, at a push. 'And, what experience can you bring to a yard like this?'

'I know how to handle horses. Can drive a tractor and stuff.'

'That's a good start,' Laura said, smiling. 'Where did you learn about horses?'

Another long, awkward silence. 'Taid had a farm horse. And I used to gentle the Carneddau ponies.'

'Gentle them?'

'I took them straight off the hill to train to halter, and my brother sold them on, sometimes. Only he got done for it.'

'He went to prison?'

She wrinkled her nose. 'Nah. Got beaten-up by the Griffiths boys.'

Laura looked down at her list of questions and found them to be inadequate. When she looked up again, Enid was staring right back at her. There was an unspoken hesitance between them, a complicated need which seemed to magnify time and space. And it was something Laura couldn't quite quantify but it was unnerving, not being able to recognise who or what Enid was about. Aware of how desperate it felt, and of how painfully unprofessional it would probably look to anyone else other than this girl, she texted James for help. Minutes later, he shuffled into the kitchen complaining of an aching back. Almost immediately he began to converse with Enid in Welsh. Laura was left to make drinks, but before she could even get the teapot, three cups and a plate of fruitcake onto the table, the girl had disappeared.

'So… you didn't trust her either?'

He studied a black thumbnail, then flicked his eyes onto hers. 'Starts on Monday.'

'But we don't know anything about her! And why haven't we discussed this first?'

'I can't see anyone else standing here. Anyway, she's only after stable work.'

Laura reached down the packet of painkillers from the top of the dresser and passed them thoughtfully across the table. 'We still need an instructor.'

'Yeah, agreed.'

She shot him an incredulous look. 'Wow, really?'

'Just had an earful from Rhian, pissed-off teaching kids all the time,' he said, popping out two tablets into his hand.

This was news to Laura but then she wasn't entirely surprised. 'That settles it, then. I'm going to offer Lucy permanent full-time on the proviso she gets qualified to teach. That way, I'm hoping Pauline Ford will be more forgiving.'

James sighed, leant back in his chair and studied her with his head on one side. This was probably as much enthusiasm she could hope for.

'I mean, at the end of the day we have to do what's right for us, don't we?' she went on, encouraged by his compliant expression. She poured the tea. 'So, Rhian, Yard Manager. Lucy, hopefully working towards Assistant Instructor. Rhian tells me she's already done a stage two, whatever that is. Is that the right title, by the way, BHS AI?'

'Why do we need fancy titles?'

'So everyone knows what they're responsible for,' she said, anxious to get everything agreed before he switched off, or backtracked entirely. Any major changes now would spoil everything, including the fabulous new website she'd drafted. Before they went live, she needed some professional photos of the staff, the indoor school and the magnificent scenery. And then some of the horses, especially Magenta, Song, and O'Malley. She'd need one of the dining room at Hafod House with a blazing fire in the grate, and then maybe an arty shot of Pete's signature breakfast, the one with the local honey and the heather on the side.

James folded his arms. 'Go on. I'm still waiting for my bespoke title. I know, how about… *The Boss?*'

'Specialist Instructor and Trainer. Then Ben, as… just Ben, I guess. And Enid–'

'As Just Enid.'

'I was *going* to say, as assistant to Lucy. If she stays,' Laura said, pushing a cup towards James. 'Such an old-fashioned name for a young girl, although it sounds positively lyrical when *you* say it. The name comes alive.'

'Enid is Welsh, or at least I'm pretty sure it has Welsh origin. Means soul, or *life.*'

A long beat before she could draw her eyes from his, then he glanced at the details she'd managed to scribble down. 'Penrhiw Uchaf? You must have got that wrong. Been derelict for years.'

After an uncomfortable moment, she said, 'Did you invite her to the barbecue?'

'What barbecue?'

'For the staff, tomorrow! And did you get a phone number?'

He drained his tea, eyes on hers. 'I'll go after her.'

On Sunday, Maggie arrived in a fluster. Laura could hear Krystal wailing before Ellie even got the passenger door open.

'Mum, come and see the foal.'

'I'll look at him later, I promise. Say goodbye to your sister, and your niece.'

'Bye.'

Ellie, monosyllabic at the best of times, darted across the yard and was soon swallowed up by a posse of teenagers swinging on the paddock railings and being scowled at by Rhian. The scowl magnified when Rhian caught sight of Jess clambering out of Maggie's car, brushing her outfit clear of crumbs and rubbing at a stain with a tissue. Her niece looked different, more mature certainly, although she treated Ben to the usual glare when he paused theatrically to drop the wheelbarrow handles in order to shout a greeting from the top of the muck-heap. Laura cast a glance over to the menage where James was working, and his disapproval felt complete when he made no move to even look in their direction. Laura found herself constantly drawn to Jess' left hand, if only to cement the truth with some visual proof. If anything, recognition of the rings drew her closer to Carys, which was curious. She also felt cut to the bone on her behalf.

Maggie stuck her head out of the car window. 'Can't stop. I need to get some fuel from somewhere.'

'Right, well, drive safely. See you later. I'll have a glass of wine ready for you.'

'Make it a large one. I'm going to need it.'

'Is everything alright? It's not Pete, is it?'

She was about to respond when Ben killed the conversation by jogging over to the car and peering in at Krystal. Her chubby hand held a rusk, her cheeks were red and her face was smeared with tears. This didn't change, despite Ben's funny faces routine and a lot of tapping on the window.

'Has she got quidditch?' he said. 'One of the horses has got that. It like, chews stuff then it falls out of its mouth.'

'That's called *quidding*,' Maggie said. 'Quidditch is Harry Potter. Even Ellie can tell you that. Krystal's teething.'

'Can we go?' Jess snapped. 'I *really* need to get on this flight. You should have let me order a taxi like I wanted to.'

'It's too late for that now. Just get back in!'

Maggie waited till she'd secured her seatbelt again then reversed awkwardly, offering a token wave as she roared back up the drive in a cloud of dust. Jess turned to look through the rear window. It was only when the car had gone from sight that Laura recognised what she'd seen. Wistfulness wasn't something she'd ever associated with Jess, but it was the only way she could describe that curious expression. When she mentioned it to James, he remained mostly impassive but she knew he was inwardly seething about the whole business. And it wasn't just the fake marriage to Sam, it was the way Jess managed to get Maggie running all over the country in a frenzy. No doubt the minute Jess landed in New Hampshire, Sam would be caught up in the same bubble. So far as James was concerned, Jess was an attention seeking user. Laura knew he took a hard line with behaviours, because that was the way he'd been brought up. In his eyes, Jess was being allowed to take the soft option and Maggie's actions constantly sanctioned her daughter's approach to life; that someone, somewhere, would pick up the pieces. Emotionally, there was every chance that Jess would stay a wayward teenager, and maybe Sam would learn a hard lesson. Armstrong would simply remain a dangerous prat on the loose.

Laura wasn't sure exactly what to believe, especially when the parental elastic was constantly stretched to such an amazing length. Whether it came back to hit you in the face when the child let go, was something she had no knowledge of, yet. She did know that she loved her husband's logic and values, and his quiet discipline was something he integrated into his life on a daily basis, not only with people but with the horses, too. He looked up from the menage when Maggie's car had gone, and for a long while, the atmosphere on the yard felt as oppressive as the heat. But as the sun relinquished its fierce hold and slipped away over the Carneddau, the mood gradually improved as preparations got underway for the barbecue. By late afternoon, the horses were all turned out, the dogs were safely shut into one of the looseboxes with marrow bones, and everywhere looked tidy and watered. Ben had fixed Laura's homemade banner across the school doors by way of a private declaration of being open for business. She planned on getting the local press interested at a later date, but for now, this was all about their personal aims to forge new beginnings with the staff and celebrate what they'd achieved so far.

Lucy was bursting with enthusiasm. 'Right, so I've downloaded the syllabus, and booked the exam. It's in Cheshire somewhere. This is the preliminary exam to the AI but it means I'll be qualified to teach straight away.'

'Have you told your mum?'

A shrug at this, and no eye contact. 'Yeah, yeah, it's all good.'

Clearly, she hadn't mentioned it to Pauline yet, but as Laura wandered through the house, bathed as it was in the mellow evening light, everything felt purposeful and *right*.

James was oiling steaks in the kitchen. He paused to hand over a glass of something cold and fizzy. 'To my wife.'

'Hmm, thank you, husband.'

She touched her lips to the side of his face and he turned to envelop her in a bear hug. 'So, this is it, kind of.'

'The beginning.'

'You've worked hard. On the house, everything. And I've been a grump and got in the way.'

'Uh huh.'

He grinned at this. She met his eyes over the rim of her glass and they moved in to kiss just as Rob announced his noisy arrival in the hall.

'Hey! Would you look at this place,' he said, wiping his feet vigorously on the new mat before walking through to dump a carrier bag full of clinking bottles onto the kitchen table, along with a box of horse worming syringes. 'Looks bloody brilliant.'

'Yeah, all down to my wife,' James said, handing him a beer.

He flipped the cap off the bottle and winked at Laura. 'I know that.'

They laughed and moved outside, Rob and Laura carrying platters of food to where Ben was keeping a strict eye on the barbecue coals. His face looked as scorched as the lawn but at least there was nothing flammable within several metres. She looked round at the sea of happy faces – noting with dismay that the dogs had already made a sizeable hole beneath the new fence, at least big enough for Lamby to slip under – and wondered why Maggie was so late. She was about to check her phone when Enid appeared, waiflike in a floaty white shirt, flip-flops and grubby denims. Ashamed that she'd partly forgotten about her, or perhaps she hadn't really expected the girl to turn up, Laura went to slip an arm across her shoulders in what she hoped was a friendly, non-threatening gesture. Half the time she expected Enid to simply vanish or dissolve into the ether, like a wood-nymph. She certainly had an aura which was more folklore than modern teenager.

'It's nice to see you. Would you like a drink?'

'Water. Please.'

She followed Laura to the kitchen sink, then back outside again where Ben couldn't take his eyes off her, and was soon deemed unfit to be in charge of the grill. Carla arrived with a bottle of sloe gin, then a couple of their long-serving loyal livery owners who'd kept their horses on the yard since Carys had been alive. Once upon a time, not so long ago, their presence might have left Laura feeling awkward, but the camaraderie between everyone was growing and the Morgan-Jones yard was developing into a good place to be. Dismayed that there was still no sign of Maggie, she was about to check her phone when Rob clinked something against a glass.

'Listen up everyone, Laura's got some stuff to say before she cuts the ribbon, so charge your glasses.'

An expectant silence fell as Rob handed over a pair of surgical scissors. 'Do I?' she hissed.

'Yeah, then we can all get to the food and drink.'

A smatter of laughter as they walked the short distance from the end of the garden to stand in front of the indoor school, drinks in hand. Laura cleared her throat, looking over to the car park one last time for sign of her sister's car. *Where the hell was she?*

'I'd just like to say thanks to you all for your continuing support, and I hope we can really take the business forward and make some happy memories here. We've got all sorts of exciting plans. First, I'd like to welcome a new member of staff…' Laura began, looking through the small crowd for Enid, but the girl hovered at the back staring into her glass of water. 'Enid Evans. I'm sure you'll all meet her soon. And I'm really pleased that Lucy has agreed to stay on as a full-time trainee instructor.'

Everyone clapped at this, and Lucy beamed back.

'I guess all that's left now is to declare the school open,' Laura said, turning to snip the ribbon and it fell away to another smatter of applause. Ben pushed the huge doors back so they could all stand inside and admire the perfectly raked surface. The evening sun filtered through the slatted sections of the walls, throwing beams across the old show jumps, all of which had been repaired and painted. The chatter stepped up a gear, and it began to feel like a real party as they wandered back to the garden. Soon after, James declared the food was ready, and everyone grabbed a plate. Enid ate like a horse, then seemed to slip away unseen as dusk fell, and Laura wondered how she'd got home. The pink clouds clinging to Tal Y Fan were poor illumination, especially subdued by a faint sea mist which had rolled in across the fields like smoke, and the mountain tracks beyond the village would be pitch black.

When the temperature dipped, she went back inside for another layer of clothing, and to try calling Maggie. There was no reply from her mobile or the landline phone at Hafod House.

James came to find her, swinging a bottle by the neck. 'There you are, come and eat. You're missing all the fun. Ben thinks sloe gin is all about the speed of alcohol poisoning.'

'Something's wrong,' she said. 'Maggie. I'm going to the house.'

His shoulders slumped. 'What's the point of that, if she's not answering the phone, she's not there.'

'But where the hell is she?'

'I don't know, but it's not *that* late. Could be a delayed flight, stuck in traffic… anything! Anyway, we've all had too much to drink to go driving anywhere.'

'But not even a text?'

'Phone out of signal, or out of juice? More than likely it'll be something to do with Jess.'

Laura shivered, pulled on her sweater and followed him back outside.

CHAPTER SEVEN

Maggie

She'd been hoping that Saturday might be a cosy family day. Not that Maggie had planned anything specific, but it would have been nice to at least spend a day where all four girls were together. As it happened, it turned out more or less the opposite of that. Jess didn't even get out of bed after her extended two-night clubbing and drinking expedition, and Ellie had a face long enough to curdle milk. Krystal cried as if her milk *was* actually curdled and for the sake of her sanity, Maggie gave in and slammed the frying pan down harder than she meant to.

'Alright, off you go to Willow's house. Go on! You may as well move in there.'

'Can I?' Ellie said.

Her autism sometimes meant she took everything literally, and Maggie had to find the patience to say no, of course she couldn't move in, she was making a joke. All the years she'd worried about Ellie not mixing with people, and now she was never in the house.

'Come home for five, though. I mean it, Ellie, I'm making a nice meal.'

'The old man who lived upstairs in bed, died. We're making Rabbit Kingdom in there now, it looks awesome,' she said, checking the contents of her rucksack. There was a roll of chicken wire poking out and the outer leaves of a cauliflower stuffed into the side pockets.

'Make sure you wash your hands, *frequently.*'

Ellie nodded and ran to get her trainers. Maggie stared at the ceiling, then closed her eyes. She waited till the front door banged shut then wandered through to the sitting room, where Jess had kicked off her shoes and flung her handbag. Krystal's passport was just visible, peeping out from the inside pocket and Maggie fought a terrible temptation to remove it and secrete it somewhere. The comforting thought that Jess was actually doing something proactive about her child was tempered by the knowledge that as a result of the American counselling plus Sam and Stella's *help*, she felt increasingly helpless and shut out of her grandchild's future. A conversation with Pete about the latest developments was seriously overdue but it looked like she'd have to do it after his operation, and after Jess and Krystal had gone. Would he be mad that she'd kept him in the dark, creating even more stress? Better to come clean about Jess and her plans, or not? The indecision was further compounded by not having anyone to talk to about it, other than Pete himself. Laura was obviously off-limits, and no one else understood the complexities.

Maybe it was already predetermined because in the end, there were no opportunities to have a private talk to Pete about any of it. Jess clearly had no intention of explaining anything to her father, either. The remainder of her Saturday was spent sunbathing and recovering from her hangover until it was heading towards the final hour of visiting time when she reluctantly accompanied Maggie to the hospital for another superficial three-way conversation, only encapsulated into a smaller window because of all the secret ferrying about which was lined up for the following day and required no end of packing and planning, mostly down to Krystal. And then on the Sunday, everything fell apart. The airline cancelled the direct flight from Manchester, meaning Jess had to first catch a domestic connection to Heathrow.

'For *God's* sake, twice the bloody security now and both times humping bags, *and* a kid,' Jess said, '*Sucks*.'

'And timings?'

'Got to be there earlier.'

The sensible answer was to cancel the afternoon trek over to Bangor hospital, and in truth Maggie was more than happy to dodge small talk under such clandestine circumstances. Neither could she trust Ellie not to say anything. She texted Pete with an excuse about running late, and having to take Ellie to the yard, which wasn't a lie. His response came back: *Come over later instead. Bring that skin rash cream.* Oh, for goodness' sake! It was hard enough having to chivvy Jess and Ellie along and keep smiling without pretending everything was fine and dandy for Pete's benefit. The idea that deception would be kinder, was already wearing thin.

Late morning, and they finally managed to pack the car with whatever Ellie needed for riding, and then all the luggage for Jess and Krystal. During the toing and froing on the drive, Linda stuck her head over the fence to complain that Ben had ruthlessly hard pruned her wisteria – presumably where it tumbled over Maggie's back fence – and ruined two years of planned twining.

'I'm very sorry, Linda, but I can't stop now.'

'Cars coming and going at all hours.'

'That's not true. And we're trying to run a business, so extra cars can't be helped,' Maggie said, closing the car window and preparing to reverse off the drive. That's all she needed, a fall out with next door.

Ten minutes later, they were turning into the yard and Ellie remarked how clever Auntie Laura was and how funny Ben was. Then it was all about how Lucy had got a full-time job as an AI but she was scared of telling her mum. This information had come via text to Ellie, and it warmed

Maggie's heart that Ellie was included in the news and part of the 'gang.' It had the opposite effect on Jess, who simply stared at everything, especially the new school and the smartened-up loose-boxes and… *James*. He was his usual rugged self in ripped denim but much fitter than when Jess would have last seen him. Her eyes followed his every move as he instructed a disabled serviceman from the end of a lunge line. He didn't look over, even when Ellie slid out of the car and ran towards Lucy, shouting. Her sister ambled across, the white terrier leaping at her feet and a halter over one shoulder. She looked like part of the fixtures and fittings these days, although she still looked magazine-shoot standard. Even the straw sticking to her top and dangling in her hair looked fetching.

They made arrangements for later, Laura avoiding eye contact with Jess. Her daughter's sad belief that everyone hated her, played on Maggie's mind as she pulled into the service station on the A55. At least Krystal had fallen asleep. Jess got into the front of the car while Maggie went to pay for fuel and bought a big bag of mixed sweets. Finally, they joined the dual-carriageway again and she was about to say something along the lines of being early, when they hit a long line of slow traffic. She tutted, changed into second gear and crawled along on the inside lane. It was so slow she could unwrap a humbug and shake the bag at Jess. Her daughter waved them away and turned in her seat, peering through the side mirror, then checking her phone.

'Stop fidgeting, what is it?' Maggie said, pausing to chew and scrutinise the queue ahead. 'It's always busy here, they'll all turn off for Chester soon.'

'It's *him*. He's fucking following us!'

'Stop swearing! Who?'

A glance in the rearview mirror confirmed that CAL 10 was indeed right behind them!

'*Oh!*'

When she could spare a second to look again, she almost swerved into the car alongside, and someone leant on their horn. Every time she looked, Armstrong gesticulated in no uncertain terms to either turn off, or pull over.

'Mum, come on, step on it, lose him! Come off at the next exit, then lose him on the back lanes. Go on!'

'No, Jess, I'm not doing that. That's dangerous. And who knows how long that would take, or where we'd end up. He'll guess where we're headed anyway.'

The bejewelled hands came up and the eyes rolled over. 'I just want to get away from him!'

Another sly glance in the mirror saw Armstrong give Maggie the V sign, and she frowned back with pursed lips, hoping it looked formidable enough to let him know she wasn't shaken, although as Ellie was apt to point out these days, her Miss Piggy face held little threat. The traffic began to disperse and as everything speeded up, it took all of Maggie's resolve not to be intimidated. Every time she changed lane he was right behind her, not caring about the risks he took or how close he came up behind her, car horns pipping and blaring in his wake. The bag of sweets slid off the dash and hit the floor, along with her phone and a bottle of water. He even came up alongside the passenger door, yelling at Jess out of his rolled-down window at sixty-two miles an hour. Of course, they couldn't hear a word he shouted above the roar of the traffic, and he took his eyes off the road for longer than was comfortable. They endured some thirty minutes of Armstrong's insanity, sometimes getting a couple of cars ahead, but then he'd manoeuvre behind them again or suddenly swerve in front, and brake. He was cunning with it, aware of any police cameras or of making too much of a show of himself to attract attention.

Jess seemed to shrink in her seat, while Krystal slept on.

A mixture of relief and trepidation then, as the airport signs began to appear. Maggie moved into the left lane and dropped her speed as they peeled away from the dual carriageway, then they were being urged to *Get in Lane,* followed by the considerable spaghetti of roundabouts, traffic lights and parking options. Miraculously, they lost Armstrong on the final leg. Of course, there was every chance he'd be heading for Terminal Two where the majority of the big American airlines operated from and not Terminal One. Maggie congratulated herself on keeping calm, at least outwardly. In truth, there were rivulets of sweat running between her breasts. He could easily have killed them all, or at least caused a serious pile-up. What sort of father did that with his child in the car? He was certainly a cowardly man, and a very stupid man, and that made him the worst possible type of enemy.

'See? Gone. He's a bag of wind.'

'You don't know him. Go to the drop-off point, and I'll run in,' Jess said, eyes front.

'Don't be silly. You can't run anywhere with all the stuff you've got to carry. I'll park up and we'll do it properly.'

The crowded nature of the airport was reassuring, despite the protracted business of finding a parking spot in the right multi-storey, then travelling down to the main building with Krystal in the buggy. Jess gripped the handle with white knuckles and Maggie searched the faces in the crowd as they stepped out of the lift. Once inside the glossy interior of the main building she found excuses to look backwards, scrutinising every man who came within a few feet of them or rushed-up behind. And it came to her that Jess was perhaps right to say she had little choice, she couldn't live like this, being harried by Armstrong at every turn.

'Is Sam meeting you at the other end?' Maggie said, as they inched along at the check-in queue.

'Probably.'

Naturally, once her bags were checked-in, Jess wanted to go straight through to Domestic Departures.

'It's better this way.'

She was right, of course, but it didn't stop Maggie wanting to cling onto them both, knowing she could never say what was really in her heart in the thirty seconds they had left. At least they'd both be safe on the other side of the wall which separated the public from those waiting to board a flight. She cast an appreciative look at the burly security guards as Jess headed towards another queue to present boarding passes and passports. It was all a bit dismal, an anti-climax of a good-bye when Maggie had imagined they could sit and chat with a coffee or browse the posh shops first. Instead it was rushed, and emotions were once again buried beneath the false bonhomie they'd managed to create and maintain ever since Jess had landed a few days ago. Somehow, she managed to keep a smile on her face and wave energetically until Jess and Krystal had passed through the door, the door with a stern notice about boarding passes only... *What if he had a ticket?*

What if Armstrong had been fooling them all along, double-guessing Jess would leave with the baby and managed to get himself a ticket for the same flight? No, he wouldn't have gone through all that James Bond style driving if that had been the case. *Get a grip.* She went into the Ladies and splashed cold water wherever she could splash it without stripping off. The certain relief that Jess and Krystal were out of harm's way allowed her to relax a little before contemplating the long drive home. She headed towards the food and drink area to grab some lunch, a large coffee and a small glass of wine. Poor little Krystal, she'd not even managed a last cuddle. She couldn't send a text either, since her blasted mobile was still somewhere under the car seat along with a dozen humbugs. Was it daft to wait and watch the plane taxi across the runway and soar into the sky? Probably, but then the longer she hung about the less likely it would be that Armstrong would be waiting for her in the car park. *God forbid.*

She unwrapped her egg and cress sandwich and sat with the plane spotters and no doubt many other relatives, watching the action on the runway. The heat still shimmered from a heavy sky, but it was a lot less attractive melting the tarmac than blazing across the dusty hills. Down below, trolleys were loaded and off-loaded, some piled high with cases, others stuffed full of meals or cleaning equipment. The details of life's necessities carried on regardless, despite the bomb scares and the endless security checks. Even holidays to Spain continued as if there was nothing else happening in the world. She watched a child get priority boarding because they were in a wheelchair. Someone walked behind carrying a drip, a parent? You didn't need to look far to get help with perspective. And she had to conclude there were far worse things going on in the world than their daughter and granddaughter choosing to live in a different country.

The fact that it wasn't choice, it was more circumstantial necessity was something she'd have to deal with one day at a time.

A smaller aircraft moved out, taxied down the strip of bleached runway and slowly pounded towards the horizon. Was that it? She followed its soaring trail until she was blinded by the sun, and could see it no more. Lifting her glass to the sky, she drained the wine in one go. It was only cheap, low-alcohol stuff but at least it took away the taste of week-old egg.

He must have given up and gone home by now, surely… She made her way out of the concourse and back over to the car parks.

Her hands felt huge and clammy as she blipped open the Toyota and slid into the driver's seat. Then she got out again and looked through the rear window to check no one was hiding in the back. She even opened the boot. That was a mistake because a pink sock, some teething gel and the notebook she'd given Jess containing Krystal's feeding and sleeping routines, had been left behind and sat on top of the toolkit, redundant. Thoroughly dispirited, she slammed the boot shut, climbed back in, and began the journey home.

As the miles slipped by, she justified everything she'd done by genuinely not being able to come up with any alternatives. Jess was an adult, she had every right to make her own decisions, and if that involved an American life coach and a false marriage, then at least with Sam she had the freedom and security to be a mother, away from Armstrong. In a lot of ways, Jess was being incredibly brave. This was how she'd present it to Pete, when the time was right. And wasn't this scenario on his original short list of ultimatums, anyway?

She tried not to drive with her eyes constantly flicking onto the rearview mirror, scanning the lines of traffic behind her, although it was difficult not to become fixated, but then a mere thirty miles from home she spotted what looked like Armstrong's Mercedes, some three cars behind! She could see half the plate as well, CA... *something.* A crazy impulse, or something that made her feel better because it was less passive, had her take the next exit. Sure enough, the same car turned off and followed her along the winding single-track road. She drove up to the speed limit then quickly pulled in to a concealed farm entrance. She misjudged the manoeuvre by several inches and bumped against a sturdy fence post. The Toyota stalled and the Mercedes zipped past, but she was steeled to spot the plate before it vanished from sight. CA... N2LB.

She exhaled and flopped back into her seat, taking a moment to locate her bottle of water and fan her face.

What a stupid, stupid thing she'd just done. This man had them all hopping about like idiots! Well, no more.

Fortunately, the Toyota started first time but then it was a five-point turn and a lot of dodging traffic to get out of the driveway, head up the road to find a turning space and get back onto the dual carriageway. Another waste of time and fuel, plus a likely dent in the bumper. Pete would need another op at this rate! In an attempt to conserve some time and fuel, she drove directly to the hospital, stopping only once at the garden centre to use the Ladies and purchase a wisteria.

Rather than feel calmer in a modulated environment populated with shuffling patients, a knot of anger still had to be reconciled. No wonder Jess behaved the way she did, sucked in by a charming bully like Armstrong. He was cunning, ruthless, and got others to do his real dirty work. Well, he wasn't dealing with a teenager now, he was dealing with Maggie Thomas. She took a deep breath before she pushed open the doors to the men's ward, and relaxed her face before she approached Pete's bed.

'Did you bring the ointment? Where're the girls?' he said, folding his newspaper.

Maggie sank onto the chair alongside and she must have looked at him for a full two seconds before her mouth worked. 'I'm sorry we didn't come earlier, we just… we just ran out of time. And Ellie wanted to go over to the yard, and…'

He plucked a grape, bit into it and spat the pips into his hand. 'Jess at home with the baby, is she?'

A long beat. 'Jess is with Krystal,' she said, avoiding his eyes.

He frowned. 'I've been thinking. If I'd not had a funny turn at that show, none of this would have turned out so well.'

'What do you mean?'

'That there's always a silver lining. Jess would still be in America for a start, and I'd be a walking time-bomb,' he said, prodding his chest, then leant towards her and lowered his voice. 'Popped up in front of me he did, all swagger.' He fiddled with the bunch of grapes again and Maggie resisted the temptation to move them out of his reach. 'So I told him to stop stalking us. I *promised* he could see the baby if he went through the proper authorities and paid his way.'

'Well, you've changed your tune!'

'Maggie, I couldn't have handed Krystal over to that man-child if my life depended on it, and you *know* it. And with Nathan batting for the other side, and Ellie... you know. Krystal's the only grandkid we'll ever have. At least, this way, now Jess is home we can sort this mess out once and for all. And it's only right he sees the kid, in a way. I mean, it won't last, will it? He'll get fed up, knowing his sort. And then he'll leave us all alone.' He studied another grape. 'These are going brown, Maggie.'

'What did he say, about paying his way and towing the line?'

'He said we could eff off, he would only deal with Jess and considering the rumours he'd heard about her, he had every *right* to take the baby – right there and then.'

'What rumours, what's he talking about?' She was aware that her heightened breathing was quite possibly visible, but Pete was more interested in getting his story out. 'That's when he tugged the pram towards himself and I said something like, *over my dead body.* And *he* said, *it might well be, Granddad.* All menacing like.'

Maggie reached for a beaker of water.

'I said he could go eff off himself if he thought idle threats were going to make any difference.'

Pete looked pleased with himself, tossed another grape into his mouth and waited for her to say something, but nothing would form in her mind. She had to get away from his close proximity before her sweaty face gave anything away. She forced herself to talk about the cherry trees, Rabbit Kingdom, and Linda's hysteria, then wished him good luck for the next day. He reminded her to bring the ointment, more grapes and another cookery magazine. Pete might be rested and de-stressed in his hospital isolation but the real world, her world, was like living in a shaken Christmas snow globe, or at least the midsummer version of one.

Once outside in the car park, she located the Toyota and purposefully ignored the dent in the bumper. She rested her forehead on the steering wheel and the trapped heat inside the car seared into her skin. She had to confide in someone or she'd combust. If she pulled herself together she could nip home for a freshen-up and a change of clothes and still make the barbecue. If she felt she couldn't burden James and Laura with any of it, at least Rob would probably be there and he might lend a better ear, since he was less emotionally involved. Motivated by the thought of a beefy ally in the vet and a large glass of decent wine, she fuelled up again at the next petrol station, cast a worried glance at the time and headed back onto the dual carriageway towards Rowen.

The village looked picture-postcard peaceful, everyone enjoying their Sunday evening outside the pub. Reverend Owen's peacocks were strutting atop the church walls, and Hafod House looked especially serene in the evening light. She stuffed her phone back in her bag, drained the bottle of water, collected up the explosion of sweets from the footwell and jammed the wilting wisteria under one arm. Never had she felt so glad to be home and she slid her key into the front door with enormous relief. Inside the house though, it was unnaturally quiet. When she put her keys down on the hall table it sounded far too loud. Maybe she was spooked because for such a long time, the house had always been busy and noisy. It certainly *looked* busy and noisy, dirty washing trailed up the stairs and the usual big clutter of shoes in the hall. As she glanced into the kitchen, a wisp of steam floated heavenwards, confirmation that the kettle had just boiled. But it was silent, and it was a noisy silence, the sort of silence that had her skin crawl for no good reason.

'Ellie, is that you?'

As she moved a couple of steps down the hall she could

see the French doors were ever so slightly ajar and a deep triangular shadow reached into the twilit garden. The doors were rarely used as they were partly glued-up with old paint, but then just a few days ago, Jess had forced them open and gone out into the garden. They didn't come together to lock unless you used considerable force. She knew then, knew she wasn't alone. Her eyes fell onto the wing-backed chair in front of her, to see the outline of a man.

He spoke, his tone low and resigned. 'Granny Meddle.'

'*Get* out. Get out of my house!' she said, rounding on the chair, all fatigue forgotten. 'How *dare* you come in here!'

'I figured we had stuff to discuss,' he said, squinting up at her. 'Your old man made me a promise, for a start.'

She balked at this. Face to face, he looked less of a teenager than Pete always made out. Her phone buzzed and then began ringing at the bottom of her bag in the hall. She knew he'd stop her answering it so she didn't give him the satisfaction of making a move towards it. Her heart might be banging in her chest and her limbs felt all wobbly and useless, but she was determined not to show it. 'How *dare* you try and run me off the road and then walk in here and make yourself comfortable! Make a habit of trying everyone's back doors, do you?'

'Mags… Mags, hey, I'm family,' he said, and threw his arms wide. 'Why don't you get a brew and sit down?'

'I'll do no such thing. I've nothing to say to you.'

'Ah, but I've got something to say to you.'

He took a moment to stir his tea, tapping the spoon on the side of the cup before placing it on the side table, stringing everything out until he had her attention. Then he looked up at her. 'I heard a rumour on the grapevine. And I saw some stuff on Twitter, and it kind of got me thinking. I reckon your only grandchild is going up for adoption.'

Maggie made a dismissive huff, rolled her eyes and swallowed over her dry throat. He was all bluff, trying to wrong-foot her with lies and presumptions, all to cover his own dirty tracks. That's all it was.

His eyes bored into hers. 'You hadn't thought of that, had you?'

'You're being ridiculous.'

'All adds up though, don't it? When you think about it, eh? Jess always was ten fucking steps ahead.'

Her phone rang out again, then the landline phone started ringing. Eventually, it clicked over to the answer machine and a loud, elderly voice sounded down the hall. 'Is it on? Hello, Mrs Thomas? It's Nora Blake. Can you hear me? We want to book a room for…' A cacophony of white noise and then the tone sounded and the whole thing switched off. Armstrong sniggered.

'I want you to go, or I'm calling the police,' Maggie said.

'You do that. I might want a chat with them myself. Let's see… fake marriage in order to stay in the country. That's a jail sentence for a start. Then there's the abduction of my kid so she can give her away without my permission. Not looking good, Granny Meddle.'

He drained his tea and placed the empty mug down, got swiftly to his feet and pushed his face close to hers. 'I don't know what sort of games you're all playing here, but your darling fucking daughter is getting a lot of help. There again, it's always about what *she* fucking wants. And Morgan-bastard-Jones junior is a proper little interfering twat. I don't think he understands that Krystal is *my* kid. But he will do. He fucking will do.'

'I want you to go.'

'I'm relying on you, Granny Meddle. I'm relying on you to do the right thing. Then no one will get hurt.'

His phone made a discreet beep. He checked the screen then sidled out through the French doors and disappeared down the side of the house. Maggie rushed to close them, using superhuman strength from somewhere, to lock them.

She paused to breathe, looking round at the familiarity of the room. Nothing was disturbed, nothing taken, but then he wasn't interested in anything she'd got. Her mind couldn't process what had happened, let alone process his words, his threats. Instead she picked up her handbag, went back outside to the car and twisted the key in the ignition. Barely cooled, the engine sprang to life again. Her foot slipped as she turned to reverse and accidentally revved the engine to screaming point. Linda's curtain twitched but Maggie kept her head down. Back past the church and the busy pub, up along the twisting lane bursting with cow parsley and elderflower. The sun was sinking rapidly now behind Tal Y Fan, flushing the sky for one last time.

Her sister's place was another world, a world she and James had built from the ashes of Armstrong's evil misadventures. Maggie parked up, clambered out and smoothed herself down, pleased to see Rob's vehicle was still there. She stood for a moment and inhaled the evening perfume of summer, listened to the distant whinnies and bleating sheep, and closer to home, the tinkle of glasses and loud laughter coming from the garden. The dogs bounded over wearing funny hats and ties and this almost had her break into a sob. What was wrong with her? Two dogs wearing dickie-bows didn't warrant anything like a show of tears, but then Ellie waved from one of the loose boxes and she knew what it was that had her throat tighten and her insides turn into a wobble of fear. It was the thought that Armstrong could still spoil everything and blow all this apart. That, and the seed he'd planted about Krystal's adoption. The idea swam in her head, trying to find purchase amongst all the other things she had to think about. How she'd manage to keep a lid on it all and make small talk, was anyone's guess.

Maybe she should go home, bolt the doors and *stay* there.

CHAPTER EIGHT

Laura

About to try calling Maggie yet again, Laura heard a car rumble to a stop. At last! She walked briskly round to the front of the house to discover her sister standing in the car park, handbag over one shoulder. Lamby failed to command any serious attention, and so began to dance on her hind legs. As Laura drew closer, she also made out a sizeable dent in the Toyota's front bumper.

'Maggie! I've been calling and texting for over an hour, where have you *been?* Are you alright?'

She turned then, and seemed to spring to life. 'Oh, yes! I'm so sorry. Had a hell of a busy day. Awful traffic, awful everything! Travel plans changed at the last minute, and then my mobile packed in.'

It all came out in a loud gush with funny rolling eyes and she laughed, but it all sounded hollow, somehow.

'Come into the kitchen and I'll get you some food. It's a bit too cool to sit outside now.'

'Sounds good.'

As they walked through the house, her sister exclaimed how wonderful everything looked. She said all the right things but her demeanour was strange, and she clearly hadn't been home to get changed because her clothes were dishevelled with a variety of stains on them. James, Rob and

Carla were still at the kitchen table with coffee and brandies, and for a while the conversation was light and centred around the riding school and future plans. Laura poured her sister a large glass of wine because she looked as though she could do with one. Maggie drank a good half of it without coming up for air.

James offered to fry a steak.

'That's really kind of you,' Maggie said, finally slumping into a chair. 'I'm famished. And I'm really sorry I missed the grand unveiling.'

'No matter,' Laura said. 'So long as everything's alright?'

'Fine! Where's everyone else?'

'Still outside, can't you hear them?' Laura found a plate and began heaping it with herby potatoes, and what was left of the watercress and tomato salad. 'Although it's only Ben and Lucy, and a couple of the livery owners. Rhian's already sneaked off, as is her style. I think she's making up hay-nets with Ellie, and I've no idea what's happened to Enid.'

'Enid's the new member of staff,' Carla explained, for Maggie's benefit. 'Curious little thing, isn't she, Laura?'

'That's one way of describing her.'

James plonked a fillet steak and some mushrooms onto the plate she'd prepared, and Laura slid the whole thing across the table to Maggie with a set of cutlery, then went to switch on the lamp by the dresser. The cash tin was in a slightly different place and for some reason, she opened it and counted the large notes. Forty pounds missing.

'Have you been in the cash tin?' she said to James, who shot her a blank look.

'I didn't think I was allowed without written permission.' Rob laughed.

'Well, someone has,' she murmured, and dropped the whole thing into a drawer and locked it.

The party outside began to break up, everyone blaming work the following day. Ben scuttled off over the fields to

Morwydden cottage, disturbing the horses. Laura stood and watched as Peaches, Mal, and Song cantered through the shadows, enjoying the cool air. Lucy was a bit giddy, but she helped Laura collect all the used plates and glasses from the garden and stacked them by the dishwasher, although she did drop a couple as well.

'Do you want a lift home?' Carla said to her. 'You can't drive that moped of yours if you're over the limit, darling.'

'Oh, I guess not! Thanks, that would be good.'

Once Laura had waved them off into the night, she discovered Maggie was already onto her second large glass of wine and talking ten-to-the-dozen, something about using a couple of heavy horses for the holiday idea. She wasn't the only one who'd need a lift home at this rate. Rob scraped his chair back and finished his coffee.

'Right, that's me. I've got surgery first thing.'

Her sister seemed to become agitated at the thought of Rob's departure and flapped a hand at him. 'Oh, no. Don't go yet. I could do with a chat.'

Rob pulled his jacket on, turned the collar up and began hunting through his pockets for keys. 'What about?'

'The hens! But not here, *outside*. I'll walk to your car with you.' She laughed at his puzzled face. 'Oh, it's probably just me, but I don't like to talk about cocks at the dinner table.'

Rob thought she was being funny, but Laura immediately felt uneasy. Something hadn't sat right with Maggie from the moment she'd arrived. Maybe James picked up on the same vibe too, because he began to load the dishwasher – an unusual event.

Rob sat back down and a frown crossed his face. 'Ask away. Although I'm not much of a poultry man to be fair.'

Maggie exhaled. She looked trapped, her eyes darting everywhere until eventually, Rob leant across the table.

'This isn't about the hens, is it?'

'No.' She glugged down the rest of her wine, then looked

round at their expectant faces. 'Truth is, I ran into some bother today. Oh, *blast.* I wasn't going to heap all this on everyone.'

Still, no one said anything. James stopped clattering the dishes and leant against the kitchen units. Maggie started to speak, beginning with Pete's exact conversation at the show with Armstrong. Some *promise.* The second Armstrong's name was mentioned, Rob thumped his fist on the table and everyone's glass vibrated. Then it was all about some crazy car chase to the airport, ending with Armstrong drinking tea at Hafod House. She spoke about it all in a remarkably clear and concise fashion, all things considered. Of course, they all knew Armstrong had been hanging around watching Pete and Maggie since Jess had left, but this was something else. Another interesting bombshell was Armstrong's belief that Krystal was going to be adopted. Maggie began to babble at this point. 'I mean, why has he said that? Jess would have *told* me, wouldn't she? I mean, there's nothing on this earth that would stop me and Pete having Krystal if we thought the only alternative for her future lay with a stranger in America!'

Laura didn't dare look at James or Rob. She put her arm round her sister's shoulders and that's when Maggie really fell to pieces and the strain started to show. Rob grew agitated and looked at James. 'You know where this *scumbag* lives, don't you?'

'No, sorry. Not going there. This is between Jess and Armstrong.'

'It's not though!' Maggie said. 'My granddaughter is in the middle of this, and she can't speak for herself. Look, if Jess and Sam hadn't gone ahead with this fake wedding, then I might be tempted to call the police. But we don't want them digging around in all that, do we?'

Laura cast a weary glance at her husband, knowing Maggie was right but feeling equally helpless for James.

'Sam was just trying to help,' Laura said.

'Yes, I *know*, but now Armstrong sees Sam as an accomplice.'

James' face darkened at this.

'He's expecting me to *do the right thing*,' Maggie went on. 'How am I meant to stop any adoption plans – real or not – and get Jess to come home? She *won't*. And how can anyone blame her? But everyone *does*, and that's partly why we have a problem.'

There was a short, tense silence.

'Thing is, it's not just Armstrong we're dealing with here, is it?' James said. 'The Griffiths boys are implicated as well.'

'The Griffiths boys?' Laura said. 'Enid mentioned them.'

'Yeah, well, there's a fair few Griffiths round here, but they're probably one and the same. Those are the names on the confession we've got, anyway. Hew and Gareth. If they knew Armstrong had named them, I can't imagine they'd be very happy about it.'

'What are you saying… we blackmail him?' Maggie said, suddenly fired-up by the idea and refilling her glass.

'Yeah, that's a *really* smart move. Look, the Griffiths are hardcore. They own the majority of the grazing rights across the Carneddau. Enid tells me they've been trying to evict what's left of her family for years. Or, at least make life difficult. And they have the same Neanderthal mentality as Armstrong. They also think they own each and every one of the ponies up there even though they're classed as wild. It's as dumb as trying to lay claim to all the birds of prey that fly over Foel Fras, but they don't see it like that. And yet there's only Rob and Pony Jones who actually look out for any welfare issues.'

Maggie frowned. 'So, what are you saying?'

'He's saying not to poke the local hornet nest,' Rob said, leaning back and folding his arms. 'Too close to home, too messy, too complicated.'

'And too fucking dangerous,' James added, then looked specifically at Maggie. 'And your current problem is down to Jess, continuing to poke the nest from a safe distance.'

'What do you mean?' Maggie said, a tad indignant.

'Flirting, taunting. Men like Armstrong don't walk away.'

Laura felt her spirits sinking into a complicated cesspit of family grievances and bullheaded arrogance. Survival of the human race was an ugly thing. Rob was angry and frustrated, Maggie despairing. James was understandably resentful and weary of it all, but Laura felt torn. Probably sensing rising antagonism, Rob offered to take Maggie and Ellie home and to double-check the house, something both women felt grateful for. Ellie ran in, rosy-cheeked and breathless to say thank you, and goodbye. Laura helped her get her riding things together and promised she could come again the following week. She waited until they'd all climbed into Rob's car, then proffered a limp wave as it roared down the drive. Only Ellie responded. The powerful security lights dimmed the yard to an eerie shadowland, leaving only the courtesy lamp outside Rhian's caravan. Dorothy had both front feet on the steps, butting the door and bleating.

Laura locked and bolted the front door and returned to the kitchen. James passed a hand over his face, then met her eyes. 'I thought we were done with this, but no, Jess pulls *another* long straw, then does a runner.'

'What are we going to do?'

'Do? It's nothing to do with us!'

'It is a bit, because of Sam, and Maggie.'

'Laura, Armstrong and his charming subordinates left me for *dead*.'

'I know. I haven't forgotten.'

He slung the remains of his drink down the sink and banged his glass down. '*Stay out of it.*'

The weather broke in the early hours of the morning. As if they needed any further evidence of rumbling discontent.

James slept through it all, the heavy rain battering the windows, a stray bucket skittering across the yard, and then the monotonous sounds of dripping water as the gutters began to overflow. She heard the bedroom door creak open and Lamby leapt onto the bed, no doubt anticipating thunder. Laura lay still for another hour, then decided it was pointless lying there going over and over the previous evening's conversation, and quietly got dressed in the gloomy dawn. Downstairs, she opened all the curtains to see a good few inches of mud in the paddocks and most of the flower baskets saturated beyond all hope. The cherry trees had fared a lot better, although one or two of them were keeling over.

She pulled on wellingtons and a billowing waterproof cape in order to inspect outside. It was still warm, with a strange undercurrent of cooler air against her face. Hesitant sunlight tried to break through a mass of multi-coloured cloud and everywhere, the sound of running water rushing down drains and cascading off the brown hills. The horses stood grouped together, no doubt relishing the damping down of dust and the lack of flies. Occasionally they'd shake out a wet mane or rub a nose on an outstretched foreleg, ears pricked towards Laura as she walked past the field gate towards the indoor school. She walked the entire interior and felt satisfied that the roof was doing a good job and left the sliding doors open so the fresh air could circulate, then went to unlock the tack room. The smell of worn leather, oil and soap, never failed to inspire. And it was a clean bright space now that the bin and the smelly old kitchenette had gone. Since the staff hangout had been moved into the old caravan there was room for a filing cabinet, plus a sturdy chair and table, but because no one wanted a computerised version, the current booking-in system consisted of a large grubby diary. She flicked through the curling pages to see the day was mostly filled with children's activities. Private lessons for adults were beginning to filter in for the evenings thanks to the indoor school, including a half-hour slot reserved for herself and Peaches. She'd almost mastered the rising trot, something which had taken many months and nerves of steel to accomplish, but still, even looking at the pencilled-in entry in the diary had her stomach churn. And then ideas for integrating Enid into their daily routine had been scribbled in the margins. Laura doubted the girl would even turn up. In a way, it might be better if she didn't, then they could draw a line under the missing cash. What a pity they couldn't draw a line under a few other issues too. Rather than focus on the Jess-Armstrong-Krystal triangle, she decided to concentrate on matters closer to home. It was Pete's operation today, and James could hardly be cross if she offered support on that basis.

She texted Maggie, something about collecting her and going for a coffee. A response came back almost immediately: *If you time it right you'll miss Pauline dropping off Lucy - I cancelled her coming over this morning. Neither of us can face the domestic chaos.*

What about Ellie?

Huh. Out.

She was about to head into the kitchen to start breakfast when she heard a yawning sound. Most of the looseboxes were empty because the horses were still turned out at night, although she felt sure the yawn had been a human one. She poked her head over the half-door of each stable, just to be sure. Next door to Mags, and Dorothy – who'd clearly been returned to duty – she discovered Enid, rising from a bed of straw with a horse blanket round her shoulders. The girl jumped, then stared.

'Enid! What on earth are you doing there?'

'Rhian said I could, last night.'

'You *slept* here?'

A beat. 'Yeah.'

A longer beat. 'Won't your parents wonder where you are?'

'No.'

A closed answer. Laura wondered if it was an honest one. 'Alright, well, come over to the house. I think we need to talk.'

Back in the kitchen, she set about making tea and toast. Enid stood like a spare part, with the blanket still round her shoulders and her long matted hair framing her undeniably beautiful face. She also looked grubby and unequipped to work since she was still wearing the clothes she'd arrived in for the barbecue. At Laura's suggestion, she sat at the table, eyes down. When the tea was done, Laura pushed a cup towards her. 'So, tell me about your family. You farm?'

She nodded at this, heaped a lot of sugar into her drink and stirred it for a long time. 'Just… me and my brother.'

'Mum and dad?'

A head shake. 'No.'

Flip, she was hard work! Laura was about to insist she write down her full name and address and produce a P45, when James materialised. Enid came to life and they both began to converse in Welsh. James even offered to cook her some breakfast and set about cracking eggs, and throwing an enormous amount of bacon and sausages into a pan. 'Enid is taking Mags on as her personal project,' he said, after a while. 'That's after she's swept up that ton of sheep shit off the yard.'

Amazingly, the girl shot James a genuine smile. He turned back to the hob. 'Want some of this?' he said, to Laura.

'No, thanks.'

Neither of them responded further, so Laura left them both to it. By the time she'd showered and changed, James was lacing up his work boots by the front door.

'Where's Enid?' she whispered.

'Working.'

'She slept in one of the stables last night.'

He squinted up at her. 'Yeah?'

'Yes! Can you find out what's going on with her, because she won't speak to me. And if we're feeding her as well maybe you can ask her if she's got forty pounds stashed away by way of contribution?'

He sighed, then stood upright, taking in her clean denims, lacy white sweater and smart showerproof. 'Where are you going?'

'Shopping.'

He kissed her firmly on the lips. 'See you later.'

At five to nine, she walked to her car and slicked on some lip gloss using the rearview mirror. Enid was pushing a wheelbarrow across the yard, wearing a pair of overalls that were two sizes too big, rolled-up over a pair of boots. Perfectly timed, Pauline Ford's enormous 4x4 swept in. Laura quickly started her own car and pulled the seatbelt across, managing a quick wave. Pauline shot her an unfriendly look. Lucy was white-faced and only managed a sickly grin as Laura sped past.

At Hafod House, Maggie looked equally pasty.

'Oh, Lordy. I'm too old to have a hangover. What's the latest cure?' she said, sinking into the passenger seat.

'It's still a big greasy breakfast, so far as I know.'

Her sister groaned and they travelled in silence to Llandudno. Despite it being middle of the season the heavy rain had delayed the day-trippers and they parked easily on the seafront. Maggie wanted to walk. The tide was in and the wind produced some spectacular waves, the combined noise of which halted any intimate conversation but then it was difficult to know where to start, how to find a way of helping her sister through the family minefield without betraying James. They staggered against the wind as far as the pier and into one of the Victorian seafront hotels, where they settled at a table with a sea-sprayed view of the Punch and Judy tent, and the restless ocean beyond. The sky was dark and low, a mushroom of cloud building behind a line of silver wind turbines on the horizon. They looked to be spinning vigorously.

A bored waitress brought them coffee and teacakes.

'Not as good as *my* waitress,' Maggie whispered. 'No wonder Lucy gets tips.'

Laura turned the cups the right way up onto the saucers and peered into the cafetiere. 'Really?'

'Yes, and she'll need all the cash she can get when Pauline finds out she's working for you on a permanent basis, she'll stop her big allowance like that,' Maggie said, and clicked her fingers. A warning light went off the size of the old beacon on the Great Orme, but Laura pushed this information to the back of her mind.

Maggie began to butter the teacakes. 'First off, I apologise for spoiling your evening.'

'Oh, it was all bound to come out.'

'You know what upsets me the most? This adoption theory. Sadly, it has a ring of truth. How *can* she, Laura? When here's you–'

'I *know*, here's me. You don't have to spell it out,' she said, pausing mid-pour with the coffee pot. 'But Armstrong might be stringing a line. You need to know the truth, for your own sanity as much as anything else.'

'I know, but I'm not asking Jess. Even though it tears me apart and I'm desperate to know, I don't trust myself to disown her!'

Laura fished her phone out of her bag and scrolled through her contacts.

'What are you doing?'

'Texting Sam. I'm going to ask him to call me as soon as he's awake. If there's something going off, he'll know.'

Maggie put the butter knife down. 'If you think that's a good idea.'

'It's the only one I've got. You do *want* to know, don't you?'

'Yes, but what if it's true?'

Laura had no resource to answer that. There was nothing inside her that could comprehend giving away a child. Before she'd developed such full-on maternal urgency, Laura could argue a perfectly well-balanced debate about abortion or adoption till the cows came home. Her empathy lay in the freedom of personal choice. She'd almost gone through with an abortion herself. But now her own desperate need to be a mother sometimes felt as if her opinions on everything had been turned upside down. Where once upon a time she could understand that women with unwanted pregnancies should be supported in their decisions, the injustice of her own position rendered her unable to deal with Jess rationally.

A small gap in the clouds opened up when Maggie told her that Jess had been to see some counsellors. This at least told her that she was getting the right sort of help. Of course, her sister dismissed it all as a personal affront. There again, Maggie likely placed counselling in the same ballpark as yoga, crystals, and horoscopes. This attitude came from their father, and Laura wondered if Jess instinctively understood this.

Maggie seemed lost in her own thoughts, and continued to gaze out of the window.

'I know it's small consolation, but the adoption process is painfully slow.'

'You think it's true, then?'

'I don't know,' Laura said, tapping her sister's hand. 'Let's not jump to conclusions.'

'How am I going to tell Pete about all this, where do I even start?'

'Leave it till he's home. We might know more by then.'

They walked back along the prom, grateful that the wind was behind them and emptied all their loose change into the lifeboat collection by the bandstand. 'Never know when we might need a life rescuing, huh?' Maggie said.

The yard was busy. Her sister drove the Toyota straight home, claiming there was a sink full of washing-up and an overflowing wash-basket waiting for her, due to the considerable upheaval of getting everyone out of the house the previous day. Laura didn't doubt the truth of that but she couldn't imagine Maggie was especially keen on bumping into James, either. She slipped into the house and checked her mobile to discover two missed calls from Sam while she'd been driving, but before she could turn her attention to this saw that James had opened all the post and left it scattered across the kitchen table. Amongst the feed bills and the usual junk mail was a hospital letter addressed to herself, confirming a date for her investigative fertility scan.
Damnit!

She changed into her scruffs, scooped up Lamby and headed outside to see how the land lay. Ben was busy fixing the paddock gate, and Enid was with Mags in the round pen, persuading him to wear a soft halter. She was deft and quiet, as Laura somehow knew she would be. Magenta had fully recovered from his ordeal, and strutted his stuff round the enclosure with erratic bursts of energy, while Dorothy looked on like a benevolent grandma. A glance into the indoor school revealed Rhian and Lucy trying to control a half-a-dozen children and ponies playing gymkhana games, while their parents looked on. She made a mental note to get a vending machine installed.

James was with a client in the outdoor menage, so she couldn't talk to him. He'd even locked the gate and put a no-entry sign over the post so everyone got the message. He glanced across when Laura settled on the picnic table, then looked away, his expression unfathomable. Laura was prepared to watch and wait. She knew the ex-serviceman he called Big Mick was a tough case, since he was terrified of horses, but anyone with a high level of anxiety always interested Laura. She'd watched these sessions before, how horses could reduce damaged men to tears. Equine therapy was a last resort in an effort to control Mick's PTSD, the most pertinent symptom being a crippling loss of self-worth. He couldn't look a less likely candidate for working in the menage; combat trousers, Mohican haircut and huge tattooed arms. Cutie Pie, the deranged thoroughbred, had perhaps suffered the equine equivalent of post-traumatic stress disorder himself, but even so, Laura was surprised to see this particular horse in the same space.

'*Shit* man, he looks mean,' Mick said. Cutie Pie was unsaddled and standing four-square, head up, ears locked-on and scraping the ground. Mick was sweating, puffing out his cheeks and shifting from one foot to the other. Physically, he almost mirrored the horse.

'No, he's just suspicious,' James said. 'He's trying to decide if you're going to hurt him, or eat him.'

'Fuck. Why does he think that?'

'He's learnt that some men are evil bastards, that's why.'

'Yeah? He's smart.'

'So smart he's going to tell you the truth, about yourself.'

'I know what the truth is. I'm a waste of fucking space. Flashbacks, guilt. *Anger*. Marriage fucked.'

'That's not who you are. And I know it's not who you *want* to be, otherwise you wouldn't be standing here, facing it,' James said, smoothing a hand down the thoroughbred's neck. 'Pie can see right through you, so don't give him any bullshit.'

Mick ran a big hand through his ginger hair. 'That's the honest fucking truth, I'm telling you.'

James went through his routine of having the horse follow him calmly round the menage, then explained the hooking-up principle to Mick, who remained nervous and skeptical. Eventually, he approached the horse and touched his shoulder.

'Feels warm, soft.'

'Now walk away, turn your back on him.'

Ten minutes later, Cutie Pie was following Mick, albeit from a safe distance. Mick kept turning round to check, then yelled from the other side of the menage. 'So, he wants to be my buddy, does he?'

'He's sussing you out as a leader. His survival relies on good men. You should understand that part of the deal, being in the forces. So, let him make up his mind about you. But no arm-waving or shouting, he doesn't get that. This bit's all about your self-control.'

'Self-control, right.'

Mick looked anything but in control. He was twitchy and anxious, as if he might break into a run and skim over the gate.

'Basically, horses are scared of everything,' James went on. 'He's looking to you to be calm and consistent. Give out mixed signals and there's no real communication. You told me communication was an issue.'

'Yeah, but with the missus and the kids, not with a fucking horse!'

'Let's start with simple before we get onto women.'

Mick suddenly laughed, stroked his beard, rubbed his jaw. He touched Cutie Pie's shoulder again, then turned away and started walking.

'You're speaking Pie's language already. You're telling him loud and clear that you're no threat.'

The children piled out of the indoor school, leading ponies. For a while, Laura was distracted by their noisy babble of excitement and a couple of disappointed faces smeared with tears. Enid appeared and began to help untack, and Ben made an excuse to leave the gate and find something urgent to do in the tack room. Presently, Lucy came over to the picnic bench with her packed lunch, although she still looked too green to consider eating it. Lamby jumped onto the table and tried to help by nosing off the lid of the box, and taking a look inside, then feigning abject starvation.

'Laura, can I talk to you? Mum's on the warpath. I told her, last night when I was drunk, and I know, I *know* not a great move, but I told her that I was giving up uni–'

'You've only just told her?'

Lucy nodded and threw a slice of ham towards Lamby. 'Thing is, she's not prepared to pay for Song on loan anymore.' Her face crumpled and she made a heroic effort not to cry. 'So I can't afford her, I'm totally, *totally* gutted.'

Laura took a deep breath. 'Oh. So, I'm in for an ear-bashing, am I?'

'She's been *completely* unreasonable!'

'Are you absolutely certain you still want to do this full-time? If you went back to uni, you'd still have Song at the weekends, the evenings and all the holidays.'

'But I want to teach, and I *want* to work here. I totally love it,' she said, then hunted through her pockets for a tissue.

There was a powerful part of Laura that wanted to hug Lucy and tell her it didn't matter, that she'd happily sponsor her under the banner of Cariad Designs, but the missing cash reared its ugly head again. Somehow she'd have to find the wherewithal to behave as an employer and not as a soft-touch surrogate parent with suppressed mothering tendencies. She'd just have to bite the bullet.

'Lucy, I have to ask you something. I'm asking everyone, so don't feel I'm singling you out, but have you borrowed any money from the petty cash tin in the house?'

Her mouth fell open then her face seemed to freeze into one huge, offended frown.

A bleep had Laura look down at her phone. A text, from Sam: *Hey. At work now so can't call again. No worries though I spoke to Dad.*

The next time she looked up, Lucy had marched off. Could the day get any worse?

Laura exhaled. When she looked across to Mick he was sitting on the ground and Cutie Pie had lowered his head, not quite into his lap but well within stroking distance.

'He reckons you're ok,' James said, grasping Mick's shoulder. 'One of the good blokes.'

If she ever needed a powerful perspective about injustice, it was right in front of her eyes. That, and survival of the equine race was a beautiful thing.

CHAPTER NINE

Laura

They argued. About the secret doctor's appointment and the resultant hospital scan. The letter should have been about his due physiotherapy appointment, so she couldn't feel especially aggrieved that James had opened it by mistake. They argued about her intentions behind contacting Sam, and finally, they argued about her accusations concerning the missing cash. Lucy had worked until five, then gone home without another word. Then Pauline Ford had turned up and stuck her two-pennyworth in.

'First of all, you go directly against my wishes without saying anything, and then you accuse my daughter of being a thief!'

'I did no such thing, on both counts.'

'I don't want to fight with you, Laura, my life is hard enough as it is.'

'Why don't you come inside?'

Pauline followed her into the kitchen. The table was full of their disturbed dinner – hers untouched. James had taken his plate elsewhere the minute Lucy's mother had started hammering on the door. Laura went to the fridge and pulled out a chilled bottle of white wine and poured some into a glass for Pauline.

'I'm not accusing anyone specific of stealing,' Laura said. 'But what do you expect me to do, ignore it?'

A huge sigh. 'Alright. I'll admit, I'm mostly cross about the degree my daughter seems intent on giving up in order to muck out and wait on tables.'

'Look, Pauline. We had a vacancy, Lucy applied for it. It's a qualified position and at the end of her training, she'll be a teacher–'

'Paying the same salary as the local education authority, are you?'

'You know we're not. We're running a business, same as you. I can't be held responsible for Lucy's choice. Besides, she's really happy here.'

'Until today.' A derisory sigh, then Pauline pulled out her cheque book, snapped the cap off a pen and began writing. 'This should cover livery fees to the end of the month for the horse. She's left full-time education, so her allowance and associated perks have to stop. She knew that was always the deal. Welcome to the real world, and all that.'

'As you wish. Your choice.'

'As it's my money, yes, it is.'

Laura couldn't wait for Pauline to go. Her head was bursting with a hundred mother-daughter problems which were not directly of her making. She couldn't help but compare the vast differences between her sister's hit and miss parenting and Pauline's tough love – if that's what it was – the jury was still out on that one. While she was scraping her plate of uneaten food into the bin, Maggie sent a text to say that Pete was groggy, but otherwise fine.

Did you find out anything?

No, not yet. Give Pete our love.

Beaten by the day but not entirely out, Laura fired up her laptop. Jessica Thomas was super private on Facebook, even Laura had been unfriended and party only to a black and white profile picture. She logged-on to Twitter, something she'd not bothered with since her early Dragon Design days with Simon, when they'd tried to drum up restoration business via social media. She couldn't find Jessica Thomas there either, but she did find Krystal Chandelier @ JessThom. She had 130k followers. Her stream amounted to a continuous diary of conscious thought. Some of the tweets were disturbing and provocative, but overall, they represented a fairly active personal hate campaign against controlling men and mental abuse.

Hi5 to my baby girl on her way to freedom! #stopmentalabuse #Abusivedads #Adopt is the safe option #freedomfromabuse just because you can't see my scars doesn't mean they're not there RT

James had been right about Jess poking the hornet nest from a safe distance, it was a significant red rag to a bull. Although this was typical of Jess, it was perhaps her own form of therapy. She wasn't sure Pete and Maggie would see it like that and she didn't dare ask her husband's opinion, nor did she dare fill him in on the latest loss of income, thanks to Pauline Ford, although he'd find out soon enough.

They slept apart. She hoped James was simply being his usual capricious self, rather than any desire to prolong a feud. Although he was disappointed in her and heading towards one of his depressive interludes, a tricky combination. She knew his back was hurting a lot as well, and sometimes he did sleep in the sitting room rather than constantly disturb her by getting up and down. This time though it felt more hostile and although she made drinks and fetched his painkillers, they didn't really communicate.

In the morning, she braced herself to call a staff meeting. She couldn't challenge Lucy about the missing cash and then not talk to the others, but when she arrived at the old caravan and saw them all sitting there, her resolve dropped through the floor. These weren't her employees, they were her friends. Rhian carried on eating a pork pie smothered in mustard, and drinking tea the colour and consistency of crude oil. Ben slurped a can of cola. Lucy stared at the floor with her hands in her pockets and Enid stared right through her with a mildly startled expression.

'I'll come to the point. There's some cash missing from the house. No one's in trouble, I'm not accusing anyone. If you've forgotten to fill out the little book or leave a receipt, then now's the time to say. Thing is, if no one comes forward, we'll have to change the petty cash system. I need to account for it, you see. So, if you need anything, just come and ask. Is that alright?'

Complete and utter silence. Rhian screwed up a paper bag and wiped her mouth on her sleeve. Enid kept her voltage death stare fixated on Laura's face, and the other two couldn't meet her eyes. It was soul-destroying, and she scuttled back inside the house as soon as she could, to discover James had partially surfaced. Against her better judgement but feeling compelled to be completely honest, she filled him in on the meeting and promised that was the end of it, while she helped him to pull on a shirt. Sometimes, his shoulder joint ceased rotating and behaved as though it was frozen. He shoved his good arm through the other sleeve with considerable force.

'Right. Good. Now *stop* hassling the staff. Leave Lucy and her mother alone, and stop racing ahead with things I thought we'd agreed to leave until next year, and that goes for those horse holidays, any more building works and *definitely* includes scans and plans for babies. And don't get me started on your sister's mess! I *specifically* asked you to stay out of that.'

It hurt, the way he'd included their child in the general scheme of things, as if her trying to get pregnant was as irritating as losing forty pounds. Her answer was to leave the room. She picked up her jacket, stuffed her feet into a pair of boots and headed outside. A throb of tears pulsed behind her eyes but maybe it was long overdue. On impulse and without anyone noticing, she slipped into O'Malley's stable.

She'd found comfort in his warm bulk in the past, and something about Mick's session the previous day had her seek the same simplicity of non-human contact, the warmth of a living being that didn't judge or question. The horse turned his head to look at her, then went back to pulling hay. He flicked one chestnut ear in her direction, as if he were waiting to hear what she had to say, although it was more likely he was staying tuned for the possibility of treats. She pressed her face against his flanks and inhaled the unique scent of horse and damp summer grass. The steady grind of his teeth, the rumblings of his intestines and the rhythm of his heart beneath her face and hands, was undeniably soothing. As was the strength, the power, the grace.

You can give him all your weight, and he'll bear it. He'll carry you.

It was something James had said to a woman who'd lost a leg in a car crash. Now she knew for certain his comment wasn't exclusive to physical disability. She didn't fully understand how or why equine therapies worked, but she was closer to appreciating that sometimes, the facts just didn't matter. It didn't take a huge leap of faith to imagine riding O'Malley up the mountain, sharing the experience in a way that wasn't possible with another human. If only she had the guts and the know-how, she'd do it right now.

Someone slid the bolt back on the stable door, and disturbed their moment. It was Enid, holding a leather halter and a lead rope. They looked at each other with the usual level of discomfort.

'Sorry. I need to get this one out. For the farrier.'

'Yes, of course. A new set again, already.' Laura smiled, moved away and folded her arms. Now she was the spare part.

'Rhian says only his fore shoes,' Enid said, slowly. 'Have you been crying?'

Her mobile buzzed with a text. Maggie: *Have you spoken to Sam?*

No. You're going to have to call Jess and have it out with her. Or take a look at the Twitter feed for Krystal Chandelier.

It felt like she'd cut off her sister as well as her husband. She stood aside to let Enid and O'Malley pass. The girl shot her a sad smile but it was the first time something genuine had passed between them, and Laura felt pathetically grateful for her concern.

The remainder of the week was quiet as the demand for holiday riding began to fall off. Some of this was down to the summer storms, but at least the grass was growing again. Teaching and indoor games took up some of the slack, but the approach of September and thoughts of back to school added to the generally depressed atmosphere on the yard. James remained in a sombre mood, although he had moved back into their bedroom with a fresh supply of painkillers and a new set of exercises from his overdue physio session.

Pete was released from hospital on Friday, so Laura offered to collect Ellie on Sunday. Maggie answered the door in one of her prissy moods.

'Oh. You've just missed him. He's gone for a lie down.'

'How is he?' she asked, following Maggie into the sitting room. There was a makeshift block of wood fastened across the French doors, as if they were barricaded in, but she tried not to focus on that. Her sister closed the door behind them quietly, then placed her hands on her hips.

'We've had a right humdinger.'

'Oh, dear. Not exactly conducive to recuperation. I don't need to ask what about.'

'I had to tell him, I had to tell him *everything*.'

'If it's any consolation, James and I are barely speaking either. I'm sorry I couldn't help, or avert the crisis.'

'I don't think we've actually had the crisis yet.'

Laura was about to probe further, when Ellie burst into the room and killed the conversation.

The day passed in a wet blur, but at least it confirmed the indoor school was a thoroughly worthwhile asset. Mick turned up out of the blue, rain dripping off his baseball cap and glistening in his beard like dew drops clinging to long grass. Laura spotted him hovering by the spectator door, watching James and Ellie. He told her he'd driven over from Liverpool.

'I want to have another go, make it a regular thing.'

'Your session helped?'

'I dunno. But there's… *something*, you know?'

She grinned at his obtuse explanation. 'I do know.'

After a short discussion about dates and times, James entered their agreed appointment onto his diary system – the back of his hand. Mick hung around for a while. He helped Ben lift the paddock gate back onto its hinges, then wandered across the fields, watching the horses graze and tracking buzzards through a small pair of binoculars. Closer to home in the feed store, Laura walked in on a heated discussion between Lucy and Rhian about the rescheduling of Song's work, and how to integrate the mare back into the riding school.

'Yeah, but she isn't yours anymore,' Rhian kept saying. She spat on the pen to get the last bit of ink out of it, before adding Song's name to the whiteboard on the wall. 'Never really was, she was only on loan. She has to earn her keep.'

'But she'll be ruined in the riding school. All that work I've done with her!'

'Don't be so bloody soft. I'm only going to put riders on her, not novices. You can still ride out and use her for comps.'

Rhian was the yard manager and so had the last say. If Laura maintained they were running a business in other matters, then she could hardly intervene and offer to pay. Outright favouritism wouldn't do, but the bond she'd developed with Lucy clouded the issue, and sat closer to her mother-daughter tendencies rather than be firmly controlled within her professional capacity. Given the dissatisfaction with James and Pauline, laying low was the only sensible option, despite the terrible desire she fought to hug the girl and tell her she'd pay for everything, simply to put the smile back on her face. Probably clear evidence she'd make a terrible mother. James had even confirmed as much by his negative reply to her sponsor idea on the occasion she'd been brave enough to mention it.

'Laura, you're not even trading!'

He'd shot her an exasperated look and thrown up his hands, then walked away.

Liz suggested Laura leave the running of it all to Rhian, leave James to his own devices entirely and concentrate on her own plans. She wasn't sure if this was a subtle way of agreeing with her brother, or more about expressing her old frustrations with similar issues. Maybe Liz was half-right and Laura was simply interfering too much in day to day matters.

Carla studied her drawn face. 'Trouble in paradise?' she said, throwing a light rug over Diva. She closed the loose box door, rammed the bolt home and flipped over the kick plate. 'Fancy the pub?'

'Yes. Mine's a double.'

'Mine too. Whoever says mares don't have bitchy cycles, know absolutely nothing.'

They travelled the short distance to the Farmer's Arms in Carla's latest acquisition, a red Audi TT. Rob pulled in at the same time, his face speckled with dung. He was still in his waterproof overalls, the top section rolled down to reveal a dirty jumper. He let out a low whistle at sight of the car.

'Someone's doing well.'

'And that's a problem? Too many liquid assets are never a good idea. I kept telling Derek some spending was in order.'

'That the boss?'

'For the sake of our sanity, we let him think so,' Carla said.

Rob chuckled and pushed open the door, and both women ducked under his arm. It was smoky with a lazy fire in the grate, and the usual group of farmers hugging the bar. Rob was soon swallowed into their midst, caught up in milk yields, the cost of shearing and how much he would charge to treat an abscess on a pig? Carla refused to buy Laura a double orange juice. It had been a long time since she'd allowed herself to relax the pre-pregnancy rules but Carla was persuasive and combined with her ability to listen, soon had her in a better mood over a large glass of red.

When she got round to her concern over Lucy, Carla showed considerable interest in Laura's sponsorship idea, but was typically tough when the actual logistics came into the equation. She never considered emotional cost, which was likely one of the reasons she was so successful in such a male dominated business.

'I just feel I've let her down,' Laura went on.

'How? You gave her a job.'

'It cost her the horse.'

'She needs to prove herself and pass those exams, and once you're making a profit, then that's the time to offer a sponsorship. I think it's a wonderful idea, by the way.'

Rob interrupted and asked them what they were drinking. Presently, he reappeared with two spritzers on a tray and some fancy crisps in a cereal bowl. He straddled a stool and opened a packet of peanuts. 'Something your sister said, Laura. About using a heavy horse on the holiday team, the other week at yours. I know where there's one up for grabs. And this one's *free.*'

'Free? What's the catch?'

'It's only got three legs,' Carla said, nudging Laura's arm.

'Only free to a good home approved by yours truly,' Rob

went on. 'She's been on the college agricultural site. A black Shire cross, called Nancy. Big and strong, but reserved. Like me, in a lot of ways. Everything you'd want in a school horse. Might be a bit heavy on the forehand–'

Carla laughed. 'You mean it's been pulling a plough?'

'Yeah, but you horsey lot can fix that, with a bit of flat work.'

'You'll have to talk to James about it,' Laura said. 'I'm not allowed to mention holidays. It's one of his closed subjects.'

'Nah, I'll just drop her off. You'll fall in love with her when you see her.' He grinned, then took a long swig of ale. 'How is Maggie? I did a quick fix on her patio doors. If I'd caught Armstrong in there, I'd have broken his fucking legs.'

Carla scooped the cherry out of her drink. 'You might be big and strong, Rob, but you're certainly not reserved.'

He ignored this and looked pointedly over his pint at Laura. 'You've got his address, haven't you? Somewhere out Chester way, isn't it?'

All too quickly, they were hurtling into the sort of conversation she didn't want. 'Why do you want his address?'

Rob leant across the table and lowered his voice. 'Because that little runt and his mates nearly killed my best buddy and got away with it. It's been eating away at me for *months*. And he's still a serious threat around people I care about. I can't see that stopping any time soon. Can you?'

Carla looked from Rob to Laura. 'I feel like I've walked into a murder-mystery weekend without a script.'

She felt obliged then, to tell Carla about the resurgence of Armstrong and his connection with the Griffiths.

'Not those prehistoric men who only come down from the hills to find a desperate woman, or to sell dodgy stuff out of the back of a van?' Carla said, looking from Laura, back to Rob. 'I'm sure it's that lot who dabble in souped-up cars and race along the lanes in the dead of night.'

'One and the same. Armstrong got them to do his dirty

work, so there must have been something in it for them.'

'Money? Drugs? But I don't understand, why is this Armstrong character being a nuisance again?'

Laura excused herself and escaped to the Ladies. Rob's anger sometimes fired her own deeply buried resentment. On the face of it, her life looked idyllic. A partially restored farmhouse, the equine business moving slowly forwards. But every day she watched James struggle with his ongoing injuries. He was no longer able to help Ben with the heavy work, let alone ride for any length of time. Fair to say everything was at a halfway house, including their marriage? But nothing was going to change her husband's condition. The sensible part of her brain agreed that beating-up Armstrong – or whatever Rob had in mind – could only serve to perpetuate the current stalemate, and perhaps escalate matters for Pete and Maggie. Neither would it encourage Jess to come home. And if Jess didn't want to be a mother, then she doubted anyone could change her mind.

She returned to the table, but Rob and Carla barely noticed, since they were in a heated discussion about it all.

'No, seriously, Rob. Pete and Maggie need to call the police and let them deal with it,' Carla said, then held up her hand by way of concluding the conversation. Having dated Rob a while ago, she knew all too well how fixated he could be. Carla drained her glass, claiming an early dinner date. She hugged them both goodbye, leaving Rob and Laura staring at each other over the empty glasses.

'The police couldn't pin *anything* on him last time,' he said.

'What about the confession?'

'As a deterrent, it's made no fucking difference, has it? He'll only say we forced it out of him, which we did.'

They travelled back up to the yard in silence, and Laura continued to do battle with the less sensible part of her brain. It was likely hidden within the same emotional vortex which controlled her misplaced mothering system, allowing suppressed fear and a sense of injustice to float to the surface and interfere with all things rational. As they turned into the drive, she spotted James trying to turn out five ponies. They jostled and dragged him across the muddy ground, causing him to let go of the least patient pair so he could at least remain upright. The errant ponies trotted away, trailing lead ropes through the mud. Enid ran to help him, bulky waterproof overalls flapping in the wind. Rob turned to look at Laura and his face registered the same dark anger which flared in her own gut. She slid out of the car, but before slamming the door shut, leant in.

'Bramble Close, that's all I remember. Fifty… something. It's at the end of a cul-de-sac, an apartment.'

He made a zipping motion across his lips.

Nancy arrived the following Sunday. Laura wondered if Rob had engineered it thus, because no sooner had the mare backed out of the trailer, than a dozen admiring teenage girls clustered around her. Nancy was jet black with huge white feathery feet, a big white blaze and a profuse mane and tail, promising many hours of plaiting, grooming and styling. There was little chance of sending her away again. Even a token attempt from James to shove Dorothy into the empty trailer was met with wails of despair from all the children. Several of them even knelt on the muddy ground to embrace the ewe, hugging her sopping wet fleece and feeding her stolen milk pellets.

Laura watched from the bedroom window, not daring to be within a few yards of the horse in case she was forced to admit she'd known about Rob's idea. And then Maggie and Ellie arrived, and soon there was a veritable crowd in the yard, oohing and aahing at Nancy, and laughing at Dorothy. Laura moved back behind the curtains. She certainly didn't want to hang out near Rob and her sister, wondering which way to rearrange her face if either of them said anything inflammatory about Public Enemy Number One, or tried to share a secret look. Other than discuss Pete's progress, Laura had even steered clear of calling round to Hafod House for fear of being initiated into any more heart-to-hearts. Since their respective husbands had both exploded, and since Laura had failed in her mission to speak to Sam, they seemed to have gravitated into a cooling off period, which was no bad thing.

The next time she looked out of the window, James seemed prepared to at least consider Nancy and had Enid turn her out into the small paddock. Enid looked impossibly tiny on the end of the rope, but the mare appeared well-mannered enough to walk at her leader's pace and waited patiently until the girl had opened the gate and removed the travel protection from her legs, before trotting towards the perimeter of her new surroundings, wicking a deep greeting to the other horses over the hedge. The teenagers surged to the gate to watch this interchange along with Enid, and it was good to see their latest recruit becoming fully integrated into the regular gang. Although it was only early days and the missing cash remained missing, Laura couldn't deny that the girl had got under her skin. She smiled a lot more than when she first arrived, even laughed sometimes but they were no closer to discovering her home situation or indeed her real age. Her natural beauty was quite breathtaking, despite being buried beneath a range of ugly, secondhand work outfits. Laura itched to sort out her knotted hair and get rid of the nose stud on a daily basis. James typically didn't seem bothered by any of this, but when it was time to pay the salaries and Laura was sorting through some invoices and the time-sheets, he came to lean on the kitchen table until she looked up.

'Can you pay Enid weekly, in cash?'

'She has no bank account?'

'Just record it as casual labour. Cheaper for us.'

'In that case, do you have any objection to me taking her on a shopping trip this afternoon, to the Outdoor Warehouse?'

'What for?'

'To buy her some clothes.'

His eyes roamed over her face, then broke into a slow smile. 'No.'

'Can she be excused from evening stables, as well?'

A slow consideration at this. 'Yeah.'

Once the accounts were done, she slid Enid's wages into a brown envelope and stepped outside into the mellow September sunshine. It was lunch hour. Rhian, Ben and Lucy would be ensconced in the caravan, but she knew Enid would be more likely wandering about the fields sketching birds. She presumed right, and spotted her astride the fallen tree. At sight of Laura, Enid got to her feet.

'Am I late? Have I done something wrong?'

'Oh, no! No, I've brought your wages, and I've come to take you shopping for some work clothes,' Laura said, handing her the packet. 'If that's alright?'

'I can't afford any, not yet.'

'I'm paying for them. Think of it as company uniform.'

'My brother said we must never owe anyone, anything.'

Crikey but she was hard work! 'You won't owe anything, trust me.'

Conversationally, they made better headway once they were on the road, and once Enid fully understood she wasn't in any trouble, or debt. Laura was careful not to press for too much information for fear of a rapid retreat, so they stuck to talking about her progress with Magenta. Once at the warehouse, a vast store crammed with farm supplies, outdoor clothing and all things equestrian, Enid was putty in her hands. She doubted the girl had ever enjoyed a shopping trip in her life. It was hardly a whirl round the

London boutiques, but it was deeply satisfying in a different way. Laura picked out the basics in order for Enid to survive winter on the yard, including a riding hat which fitted her correctly and a pair of smart boots. Then it was fun to browse the more fashionable outdoor wear, just to see what she gravitated to. Cheap and black, mostly. It was as if she didn't want to push her luck or appear greedy rather than express her genuine, personal choice. As well as this trait being a credit to her integrity, it seemed a lot less likely that she'd taken the forty pounds.

They queued for coffee at a fast food outlet on the same site, and Enid said she could manage a burger. Always hungry.

'So, you live with your brother?'

Again, that cagey look and Laura hoped that the shopping didn't come across as a device, a sort of exchange for personal information, but Enid seemed less cautious.

'My mother passed when I was a baby.'

'Oh. I'm sorry. And your father?'

A shrug and the violet eyes swivelled away from hers. 'Gethin is my legal guardian.'

'And Gethin, he's a farmer?'

'We still have the farm but it needs too much work and there's no money. So he does some labouring, building work. Where he can.'

'I think I've seen his van, does he collect you from work sometimes?'

A nod and a smile, but Laura sensed that was the end of that particular conversation. She agreed to Laura giving her a lift home, but only to the bottom of the drive since the potholed road would wreck her nice car. They gathered up the shopping and headed back to Rowen where Enid directed Laura through the village and then along the increasingly steep single-track road, past the last residential house. After that it was rundown farms, a couple of smart barn conversions, and a youth hostel. Beyond this, they passed through a crooked iron gate and onto open land where it was rough, boulder-strewn and peppered with sheep and ruined stone buildings. Even in the gentle haze of a September afternoon the landscape still managed to look desolate and forgotten. Sagging barbed wire struggled to reinstate the boundaries of tumbling stone walls thick with moss, defeated by the persistence of animals and the unforgiving climate.

There was a brisk wind, flattening the coarse grass and the remains of the browning heather.

When they came to a wide turning area, Enid said she'd get out and walk. Laura spotted a handmade sign nailed to a stake, pointing to Penrhiw Uchaf. She carefully manoeuvred the car round to face Rowen again. Since they were well above sea level, there were far-reaching views along the west coast but Laura's eyes were more drawn to Enid in the rearview mirror, bags of spoils at her feet. She looked forlorn, and it took considerable strength to drive away. What sort of home did her brother make for her, up here in this dilapidated wilderness? The immensity of the Carneddau seemed too close and overpowering. They were of course the mountains where Magenta had been born, and not too many miles from where he'd lost his mother. If anything, this analogy of the respective backgrounds between the pony foal and the girl, only added to Laura's already overburdened emotional responsibilities.

Pregnant. *Not pregnant.* She ripped the cellophane from the packet and studied the contents. How many times had she done this? Too many. But today, she felt strange. She went into the bathroom, peed on the plastic stick and set it down on a slip of tissue.

Through the open bedroom window, hints of autumn floated into the room. Damp, chill air, woodsmoke and soil.

Defying this – visually at least – a soft strawberry blush infused the dawn sky. Mist lay over the fields, suspended like skeins of smoke, and the horses moved as opaque silhouettes. An approaching van pipped its horn, then slowly materialised through the fog. Down in the garden, she watched Washboy leap over the six-foot fence with the grace of a gazelle. Lamby forced herself beneath, scrabbling into the considerable hollow she'd made, before popping up on the other side. So much for keeping them in the garden! Both dogs tore up the drive, barking. James stopped to talk to the postman, leaning in through the window. Laura drank her tea. Another minute passed.

She looked at the result… and her breath hitched.

CHAPTER TEN

Maggie

They argued. First off, about the massive dent in the bumper. Pete spotted it the second she drew alongside him at the hospital collecting area. Then it was the truly gigantic can of worms behind the absence of Jess and Krystal, which went on for most of Friday night. She did her very best to present the facts in as bland a way as possible to save him from getting over-excited, but when it came to Armstrong following them to the airport and entering the house, there were no words she could think of to soften the story or make it seem harmless. The combination of the damage to the Toyota and the wooden brace across the French doors, were clear evidence in themselves that Maggie's report of events was significantly diluted. He listened with a set face and Maggie couldn't be sure if it was anger or crippling sadness behind his silence. It was probably both, coupled with the frustration of not being physically fit enough to properly rant and rave. It was also down in part to Nora and Sid Blake staying in room one. Here they were with the ideal situation in which to elicit a quiet and peaceful haven for their returning guests, when all they really wanted to do was shout.

On the upside, they both slept for nine hours without a single interruption. Ellie was on a sleepover with Willow and the house was unnaturally quiet, in fact Maggie almost forgot the Blakes were in residence and needed breakfast. It was only the sound of Lucy tapping on the front door that alerted her to the fact that she needed to get up. Lucy looked slightly less sparkly than she normally did, but willingly ran up and down stairs with cups of tea and toast for Pete, cleared away all the breakfast pots, collected a miserly three eggs from the hens, and hung out the washing.

The Blakes wanted to book a full week later in the year. Once she'd dealt with all that and sent them on their way to Bodnant Gardens, she helped Pete get dressed and make his awkward progress down the stairs. 'That's good, isn't it?' she said. 'They've booked a full week.'

He went slowly into the sitting room, ignoring her attempt to be bright and cheerful, and landed heavily in his chair. Maggie pushed a footstool under his feet and made sure the remote control and the papers were close to hand, but he put them to one side.

'Tell me again, what Armstrong said. When he was sat *right* here, in my chair.'

Maggie obliged for the second time, and did her best to temper it by not describing Armstrong's facial expressions, his appalling language or the fact he'd made a cup of tea while he waited.

Pete scoffed. 'I've a mind to call the police, Maggie.'

'What about Jess? Where would that leave her?'

'Pass me the phone. And that aspirin. Another bloody tablet to take now.'

'Yes, but you feel alright?'

'I'll feel better once this mess is sorted out.'

'Well, that's not going to happen overnight. And I don't think it's a good idea you getting stressed over it all.'

He took no notice and tried calling Jess, but of course neither of them expected a response since it was the dead of night over there. Then it was Stella. He must have left several less than polite messages on her office phone, and once he'd shuffled over to the computer, an email. And she couldn't be sure but he may have looked at Twitter as well, because all she could hear was tutting and sighing. Then it was the Toyota garage and a quote for the replacement bumper. Maggie could hear him complaining over the cost while she was upstairs, stripping the bed in room one. He was taking it all out on some poor pen-pushing apprentice in the parts department, and it wouldn't make a shred of difference.

In the afternoon, she discovered him asleep in his chair, and that's when Stella called. Maggie managed to snatch up the phone and close the sitting room door before it disturbed Pete.

Stella was loud. 'Maaags! How *are* you?'

It was the kind of hello that befitted a fun event, or the precursor to a happy announcement. 'Not great, as it happens.'

'Pete sounded a bit desperado. So, here I am.'

'He's napping. You'll have to make do with me. We want to know what this adoption idea is all about.'

'Jess hasn't spoken to you about this?'

'Not exactly… no.'

Stella sucked in a deep breath before she exhaled. 'Whoa…'

The gravity she managed to bestow onto that single word, reduced Maggie to an inch tall. This was the bit where Stella needed to say it was all news to her, or something along those lines. And then Maggie would apologise for snapping and they'd have a chat about the ranch. Stella would invite them over for a holiday when Pete was recovered, and she'd promise to get Jess to call her father… blah, blah.

'Look, Mags. Jess was in a real state when she came here a few months ago.'

Maggie felt her hackles rise to another level, as if they didn't care about their own daughter, as if she were a dog from a rescue centre or they were somehow incapable of understanding her needs. *Were they?* She listened to Stella drone on about the counselling and the support they'd given her, all of which Maggie was careful to thank her for, but she wasn't sure how much longer she could keep a lid on it and continue to be civil. Somehow, she'd been relying on Stella to reassure them that it was all nonsense.

'You see, I was in exactly the same situation when I came over here, with Sam.'

'I'm sorry, Stella, but I beg to differ. Not only is Sam's father a wonderful, caring man, but he didn't know of his son's existence for the first ten years. Jess has got herself involved with a criminal and her head's all over the place,' she went on, aware that her voice had risen considerably. 'To assist her in making a decision to give away her baby, and *our grandchild*, is *not* your job!'

'Heeeyyy, just trying to help the girl come to the right–'

Pete snatched the receiver out of her hand. 'Stella? Listen to me.'

Maggie sat on the bottom stair while Pete expressed his feelings on their behalf, although it was more hurt and disappointment masquerading as rage.

'Stop putting ideas into her head,' he kept saying. 'It's a decision she'll regret for the rest of her life! A pretend wedding and giving away the baby, that's your idea of helping, is it? And if Daddy decides to do the dirty and dob you all in, then it's not looking good for Sunshine Sam, either!'

Maggie had to take the phone off him and put the receiver down. Worried for his health, she guided him back to his chair and ordered him to sit.

They ruminated over the facts, but it was looking fairly conclusive that adoption had been duly discussed and considered – without them.

'How *can* she, Maggie?' Pete said.

Maggie didn't know. Somehow, she felt duped. And it was

probably a result of the surgery and Pete feeling vulnerable but when she turned to look at him, she saw a tear in his eye.

The week crawled by. Pete stared at Krystal's Moses basket and the items which had been left behind, soft toys too large to transport and some tiny vests which she'd already outgrown. There was no word from their daughter. On the face of it, everything seemed normal and the workload in the house was calm and ordered. A smattering of guests booked-in over the final summer bank holiday, then Ellie went back to school and Nathan came to stay for a few days. Maggie felt able to escape the house at last.

When she took Ellie riding on Sunday, there was a buzz around some horse in Rob's trailer. It lifted her heart to see the black Shire mare, a sign that the holiday idea was happening? She thought she glimpsed Laura at the bedroom window, but she didn't come down and it was further testament to the splintering of their family relationships — all caused by one, controlling man. Rob kept trying to catch Maggie's eye. Once she'd handed Ellie over to James, Rob followed her to where she'd parked her car.

'Maggie! Any more unwelcome visitors?'

'No. We're still trying to get our heads round Jess' plans to have Krystal adopted.'

'He's fucked-up her life, hasn't he?'

She opened the car door and flung her bag in. 'No one else quite sees it like that. James isn't the only victim, we're all suffering. If we had the money we'd go over there.'

'Fetch them home?'

'Oh, I'm not sure she'd come, not while he's still around to stalk her.'

Rob studied the sky for a moment, then met her eyes. 'I've got his address.'

A shiver of anticipation shot through her gut. She was beginning to see Rob as her one true soulmate in all of this.

His agitation had been palpable when they'd all been sitting around her sister's kitchen table.

'What are you thinking?'

'I'm thinking you could pay him a visit, you know, take the lead instead of letting him call the tune.'

'Not by myself?'

'*Course* not. But I reckon he'd let you in if it was just you he saw standing there. Then the second he opens the door wide, I'll be right behind you and then we can remind him of his obligations.' He gripped the roof of the Toyota and she could see the muscles bulge in his forearms. 'So, are you free tonight?'

Her mouth must have dropped open slightly.

They made arrangements. It felt empowering, like the time she'd marched into Simon's party to demand he gave Laura her share of the cash. How long had her sister been waiting for that money? Simply being proactive had worked to their advantage. These controlling men needed taking down a peg or two! If she could impress on Armstrong that Jess was more likely to rethink everything if he backed off, perhaps send Jess some money for the baby and promise to be reasonable, then at least they'd done everything in their power to try and make it work. It was an option Jess deserved.

And Maggie wanted to see for herself where he'd forced their daughter to live in an emotional prison. She wanted to see who the man was, and possibly where his weakness lay. Her only fear was that Rob might have a different agenda and turn into something of a loose cannon. She'd not be surprised if he produced a couple of black balaclavas and a baseball bat.

She told Pete and Nathan she was going to the new Pilates class in the village, then she'd probably go for a drink after, with the girls. She realised her error straight away because they expected her to leave the house wearing a tracksuit and pumps. But then if she and Rob had to run anywhere, maybe that wasn't such a bad idea. The downside was the lack of fashionable leisurewear in her wardrobe. She laid out her three choices on the bed: a pair of custard yellow trousers with plenty of stretch in them, her compression pants which had replaced the yellow pair for riding, and a pair of Pete's grey jogging bottoms. The yellow were a better fit, and looked half decent with her long line sweater and a pair of old trainers. What she really needed was a sharp suit so Armstrong would take notice of her, but she'd never be able to explain that to Pete and Nathan.

Her son did a double-take. 'Wow, Mum. You'll knock them all dead in that!'

'Yes, well, hopefully it won't go that far,' she said, remembering to smile. 'Don't answer the door to anyone and make sure Ellie gets to bed at a reasonable hour.'

'I know this might be hard to believe, but I am an adult, you know,' he said, hands still in the washing-up.

'Where is Ellie, anyway?'

'Down the road.'

'Again?' She stopped checking the contents of her bag. 'Oh, this has to stop! It's school in the morning and the nights are drawing in.'

'Stop panicking. I'll walk round there and pick her up in a bit.'

She kissed him goodbye, shouted up the stairs to Pete and waited for his mumbled response. It was already dusk which was just as well considering their intended mission, and the distinctive yellow trousers. And then instead of a trendy yoga mat, she had a section of redundant hall carpet to contend with. She hitched it under one arm and prayed she wouldn't bump into any of the neighbours heading in the same direction.

Rob was waiting by the community hall down the side of

Eggy Wilson's poultry farm. She clambered into his vehicle and threw the Axminster in the back.

'What's that, a magic carpet?' Rob said.

'I wish.'

It was disconcerting how quickly they reached the outskirts of Chester, how close Armstrong lived to Rowen. No wonder he was always popping in to the village to spy on them, although it had gone ominously quiet this last week. They pulled into Bramble Close and it looked a decent neighbourhood, but then Jess would never have moved in had it been a dump. Rob crawled the car slowly to the end of the road and stopped in front of a three-storey block of flats. There was a row of garages beneath and on the drive of number 65, Armstrong's Mercedes.

Maggie trotted after Rob as he strode purposefully towards the entrance. Two women, laughing and chattering, were coming out of the building so he shot them a 100-watt smile and caught hold of the door before it swung shut, then indicated Maggie follow him.

'Too easy,' he said, giving the intercom system a cursory glance. 'Lift or stairs?'

'Stairs. I want to go slowly.'

Everything was dated but clean and presentable. It didn't feel like the den of a bad boy, but rather than embolden Maggie she could only think of reverse psychology and the weakness of stereotype. They trudged up two flights then followed the sign for flats 60-66. The corridors were a bit dingy and then her pulse really began to soar when they approached number 65.

Rob stood to the side, well out of view and pressed himself against the wall. 'Go on, ring the bell. I'm right here.'

She rang the bell. There was movement behind the spy hole, then the door was snatched open.

'Well, well... Granny Meddle.'

'Can I come in?' she said, firm but polite, and moved

directly into the hall. Rob was right behind her. Maggie had to duck out of the way as Armstrong shouted and a fist came up, but Rob quickly deflected it and kicked the door shut with his foot.

Armstrong was furious. '*Fuck* off, what you fucking doing here? Get the fuck out!'

'What's the matter? Don't like unwelcome visitors?' Rob said, keeping his grip on Armstrong's wrist, pushing him into the main living area with his arm up his back. The coffee table went over. Armstrong didn't stand much of a chance against Rob's bulk and his efforts were puny really, kicking out at his legs and shouting obscenities. Rob threw him forcefully onto the sofa, then let go of his quarry and straightened himself out.

'Seems you've forgotten the little arrangement we had.'

'I made no *arrangement*. One word from the boys–'

Rob scowled. 'The *boys*? Like some big gangster! What have you got on them, huh?'

'The Griffs? They're just mates. Part of the hunt sabs and stuff.'

'Hunt sabs? Saboteurs, animal rights, that sort of thing?'

'Yeah, what's wrong with that?'

'Nothing. I'm a vet. I'm on your side. Big animal lover me,' he said, banging his chest. Then he leaned in closer and tapped the side of his head. 'Only animal protection is more effective if you've got half a brain. I seem to remember those morons working against us on the Carneddau a lot of the time. Their neck of the woods looked more like a drunken punch-up to me.'

'Yeah, well Hew and Gareth are pissed off with everyone poking their nose in. If there's any funding they should get it, *not you*. They might drive the horses off the Carneddau altogether–'

'Oh, that's a really smart move. Going to manage the welfare and carry out the data by themselves, are they? Stop any rare breed funding in the blink of an eye,' Rob said, snapping his fingers. 'And where are they going to take them? Two hundred worthless wild ponies no one gives a shit about. Winter coming up, what are they going to do with them? Come on, animal lover!'

'They know what they're doing, they're farmers–'

'Don't make me laugh! They're *thugs*. Real farming's too much like hard work.'

'What do you know? Those horses are *nothing* to do with you. Or that teenage bastard heartthrob, *Uncle Jamie–*'

Rob made a lunge for Armstrong, pulling him up off the sofa by his hoodie. It stretched, and he seemed to dangle inside it as the material rode up his back, and the zipper cut across his face.

'You're not fit to speak his fucking name, do you understand?' Rob shouted, unable to let go. '*Understand?*'

The intensity escalated. Maggie could smell it, could almost feel Armstrong's jaw crunching as the thought formed in Rob's mind. This wasn't going to plan, it was about Rob threatening his physical revenge for James. Not that she blamed him, but it had her feel jittery since she was powerless to stop him. She looked around the room, taking everything in. It was impossibly tidy, for a man. Even the books on the shelves were stacked in descending height. There were box files suggesting he kept his paperwork in good order, too. Insurance, pension, mortgage. Everything in alphabetical order. Through the open bedroom door, she could see a suitcase on the bed and several drawers in the chest were half-open.

'Where are you off to?' Maggie said, hoping to swing the situation onto less volatile ground.

'Guess. First job is to sort out Jess, then I'll find that bastard heartthrob's Yankee spawn–'

'Another brilliant master plan, eh?' Rob cut in. 'What you going to do? Take her a bunch of flowers then give her husband a good kicking?'

They began to argue again, Rob reiterating the relevance of the signed confession, poking Armstrong in the chest with each reminder, like a physical bullet point. Armstrong slunk along the sofa, his eyes fixed on Rob's. Maggie looked towards the bedroom and edged her way inside. She glanced over the built-in wardrobes and the pencil pleat curtains. Neat, tidy. She was shocked to see a brand new bottle of Opium – her daughter's favourite perfume, and a box containing a baby mobile. Behind the door there was a passport, a camera, and a set of keys on the bedside table. For a reason known only to her subconscious, she stuffed the passport into her ample sports bra. No, she knew the reason. It was the thought of Sam being hunted down. Photographs taken… the police. Immediately, her face flushed and her pulse began to thump at what she'd done. Smart, or plain stupid?

She moved back into the sitting room, hands swinging by the sides of her pocketless trousers.

Rob exchanged a look with her, a look which said he was already close to the end of his tether. They were both aware that if Rob really lost it, they'd be in trouble. He knew it too, and went to stand at the window, chewing a nail. Maggie moved to the chair but remained standing. If she sat down, there was every chance the passport would crumple up in her bra and poke through her top. She decided to try and get through to Armstrong on a more humane angle, if only to make sense of her being there other than pinching his passport.

'Look, Cal. Can we not work together on this? I'm only here to talk about Krystal. We both want her home, and–'

'Your old man lied to me,' he said. '*Promised* me I could see the kid. Next thing I know she's been fucking kidnapped.'

After five minutes, Maggie deduced that not only was he still insanely jealous of James and Sam in respect of her daughter's attentions, but he struggled to understand how to be a father. Every emotion manifested itself in a desire to be in control. Campaigning for animal rights was the flip-side of his personality. Maybe it was simply the fact that human love was too complicated and demanded too much from him. And like Rob intimated, it also allowed him to be violent and proactive in the name of a good cause. The dangerous aspect was that Armstrong didn't think he had a problem and everyone else was in the wrong. He was a classic victim and everyone owed him something. She wouldn't put it past him to initiate something pointless and perilous just to get the upper hand; as he perceived it.

'I did everything for that girl,' he kept saying. 'Everything. She got everything she ever asked for'

'Except her freedom, and the right to terminate a pregnancy she didn't want.'

'Fucking bullshit!'

Exhausted with the tension and lack of progress, Maggie inclined her eyes to the door. Rob issued another warning to stay away from the village and the second he made to go, Maggie scuttled out after him, her legs shaking as they hurried out. The passport was uncomfortable in her bra. Chafe, chafe, chafe, as they went down the stairs. Rob said he felt like punching a wall. Once inside the car, Maggie flashed a corner of the passport in his direction, and Rob's face creased into a frown, then split into a wide grin. 'You beautiful little sneak.'

'Put your foot down.'

They headed off the estate, Maggie clutching the grab handle. Somewhere around Rhos-on-Sea, Rob pulled over and they got out and walked to where the high tide was slapping right up to the concrete breakers. He ripped the pages from the passport, scrunched them into a pile and set them alight, holding the passport cover over the flames. Then he touched his lighter to the cover and it curled into a husk. The wind caught the remains and blew them into the fathomless swell of the Irish Sea.

Jess called Maggie the following day. Afternoon for Jess, but it was early evening for Maggie. Unusually, she was in the supermarket. Could there be a worse place to try and have a serious conversation, possibly a life-changing conversation? She used to stare at people talking loudly on their phones in public places, everyone listening in to their business. What was so urgent that couldn't wait? But who was she to judge, because as soon as her daughter's name flashed up on the screen, she began pushing the trolley towards the freezers where it was less busy. She pressed the accept symbol, only to fumble and almost drop the phone into the frozen chips and potato products.

'Jess! We've been trying to reach you for days.'

'Why did you call Stella?'

'Why do you think? You left us with no option!' She ignored the challenging silence and pressed on. 'So… it's true then? You're thinking of adoption?'

'You know I am.'

'Why couldn't you talk to us? How do you think this makes us feel?'

It was pointless, the arguing, all the wrong angle. She knew this and yet felt compelled to continue, to get her point across, to hope and pray something would sink in and make Jess think twice. Her daughter listened, punctuating Maggie's tirade with the odd sigh. It was like the old days when she still lived at home, shouting and slamming doors, although this was possibly the biggest door she was ever poised to slam. And it could stay shut forever.

'It might just be that you're not ready to be a mother,' Maggie went on, struggling to find the right words while customers reached round her for bags of peas. 'That's *different* and me and your dad can help! *Please*, Jess, don't do anything you'll regret in a few months' time, maybe in ten years' time… because it's irreversible.'

'You still don't get it, do you? I don't *want* to be a mother, not here, not over there, not anywhere! It's best for Krystal she goes to someone who really wants her. Why can't you see that?'

Someone bumped into her and apologised but at the same time shot Maggie a dirty look. She pushed the trolley further along the freezer section towards the fish, but the signal went altogether and she was forced to end the call. Even so, it was the longest conversation they'd had in a long while. Crazy, and so sad that this had occurred when they were several thousand miles apart, because Jess didn't want to see their faces, their hurt, their disappointment. Maggie didn't remember driving home but she must have left the trolley without going through the checkout because there were no bags of food in the car when she got home.

She let the tailgate clunk shut, dragged herself inside the house and braced herself to tell Pete.

He listened with an expression she'd not seen before; tired resignation, she thought. Then he wanted to go outside, just for a breath of fresh air. Maggie fretted he was overdoing everything, but it was serene in the garden, with weak sunbeams spanning across the recovering lawn. Although they were heading into a chilly autumn with misty mornings, the sun usually burned through to leave the evenings clear and summery.

'Pretty sky tonight,' Maggie said, linking his arm.

'Pink. For a girl.'

She studied his profile more closely. It was out of character for Pete to be fanciful. They walked to the horse chestnut tree which seemed suspended between two seasons. Some of the leaves were green edged with brown, others were more advanced and displayed the full spectrum of autumn colour.

'I imagined us all at Christmas,' Pete said, looking up into the red and golden canopy, the colours of Christmas. 'Funny, isn't it. Whether it's a celebration or a crisis, it's always about the future of Christmas. Do you remember when we first viewed Hafod House? The first thing we did was think about where we'd put the Christmas tree. Stupid, really.'

'No, it's not,' she sighed. 'It's about… love.'

'In the eyes of the world, our grandchild is Krystal Chandelier. As if she's an object. I know we were desperate before, but this feels *more* desperate,' he said, then disengaged himself from her arm, and turned to face her. 'Have we pushed her into this, have we, Maggie?'

'How? And anyway, I always thought the mother and child bond couldn't be broken by anyone.'

A painful face then, because of course it didn't apply to Jess. There wasn't a bond, never had been. They'd refused to face the truth since the day Krystal had been born.

Everything. She got everything she ever asked for.

Not for the first time, Maggie wondered if the entire situation was quite as black and white as it had always seemed. Yes, Armstrong was seriously flawed, but was it realistic to blame him for everything that had gone wrong with Jess? And now that Maggie had witnessed the way he lived, it all needled away at her. He still held down a responsible full-time job, his flat was a respectable home. In his mind, he'd wanted to keep Jess safe in the only way he knew; by control. She dithered about telling Pete about the visit, but concluded that nothing would be gained to ease his suffering.

'What can we *do*?' he said.

She shook her head, flapped her arms against her sides in an admission of total defeat. 'Nothing! We've done everything we can. Jess has made up her mind. We have to carry on with our own lives.'

They carried on, heavy-hearted but busy enough to temper too much prolonged introspection. Bookings increased dramatically, likely down to the unexpected Indian summer but for once, everything ran like clockwork. Lucy continued to turn up each morning. Pete improved. Nathan went back to London, perplexed by Jess, bemused by Ellie and Willow.

'You should see what those girls have made for the rabbits at the doctor's place,' he said, dropping his bags onto the hall floor. 'Automatic feeding stations, tunnels, houses.'

'Really?' she said, absently. 'It's certainly kept them occupied.'

While I've been *pre*occupied, she wanted to add. 'Wouldn't they rather be free, in the garden or something?'

'What, and get eaten by foxes? They don't know how lucky they are.'

He bent to hug her goodbye and she promised they'd think about visiting him and Chris in London, when they had the time and some spare cash. She waved goodbye from the doorstep and decided to walk down to Willow's house later, to see rabbit utopia for herself.

It was true she and Pete had neglected much of what was going on in Ellie's life, which was unforgivable. For such a long time, all the attention had been focused on Jess and Krystal, and she suddenly experienced a severe stab of guilt. This was the way it had often been in Ellie's life, and yet it was Ellie who really needed the most support. Thank God for James and of late, Laura too. She sorted out a clean school uniform for the following day, sewed-up a gym shirt with a frayed collar and several missing buttons, then went through her schoolbag. The rucksack was in a state because she'd been using it to carry chicken wire and God knows what else over to Willow's house throughout the holidays. It needed a good wash. Maggie removed the books and pencil cases, then tipped the bag upside down. Sweet papers, screwed-up paper and odd coins scattered across the table. She went through all the pockets, checking.

Then her eyes fell on something. She snapped the elastic off, and stared. Whichever way she looked at it, the contents on the kitchen table certainly confirmed that she'd taken her eyes off this particular ball for far too long.

CHAPTER ELEVEN

Laura

The second Laura discovered the test was positive, she yelled out of the window. James must have thought the place was on fire. She went quickly but carefully down the stairs to save him labouring up them, and fell into his arms in the hall. He listened, wordlessly, while she waved the pregnancy test and spoke mostly gibberish, but his body language was loud and clear. There was a spark in his eyes which had been missing for a while, something amazingly honest and full of joy. Something which mirrored her own fragile hopes and dreams.

'Maybe this will slow you down,' he said eventually, into her hair. 'Stop mothering the staff and giving them all make-overs.'

She poked him in the ribs. 'I can't believe it. I'm *pregnant.*'

'Promise me, no more yard work or getting stressed over spreadsheets.'

She tipped her head up to look at him. 'You think I don't know all that? I'm terrified something will go wrong.'

'Course it won't.'

'I don't think we should we tell anyone yet, it's far too soon,' she said, then realised she'd have to tell the staff as they'd wonder why she was afraid of lifting anything and she certainly couldn't continue to ride. 'Except the staff… maybe.'

'Up to you. My work here is done,' he said sagely. 'After months of reckless sex, I'm guessing it's going to be a lean time from now on.'

'James, I *can't* take any risks, not with my history–'

He grinned, searched her eyes, almost laughed. 'I *know*.'

She sighed and folded her arms. 'I don't know how you put up with me.'

'It's a conundrum I've learnt to live with. Full on, or all off.'

'Seriously, you are alright with me being pregnant?'

'Anything that gets me out of medical investigation is all good.'

Laura watched him walk back outside into the chilly fog. Instead of signalling the precursor to autumn and winter, the early morning mist had somehow changed its persona to something altogether more dreamlike, with the sun poised to send those magical Jacob's ladders across the fields. When James reached the tack room, he turned to look back at her with his serious smile, and her happiness was complete.

She hooked her phone out of her pocket, eager to log-on to the fertility site and book a doctor's appointment, when a text popped up from Maggie.

Something I need to tell you. Ok to pop round?

What, now?

It can't wait.

Despite it being early, Maggie duly arrived with Ellie in tow. The girl was in her school uniform and her face was smeared with tears. They both entered the house in such hostile silence that Laura could only assume something awful had happened. Ashamedly, she still struggled to disguise the huge grin lingering on her face.

'Ellie has something to say to you,' Maggie said, in her best schoolmarm voice. They both waited, until Ellie stuck out an arm and unfurled her hand. Inside, were two twenty-pound notes folded into grubby squares. Laura listened to the explanation, her eyes flicking from her niece then back to her sister while Ellie apologised for taking the money – blaming Willow, and the heavy financial costs of building an empire.

Laura knelt down to Ellie's level. 'I'm very sad and disappointed about this, but I'm glad you've told me.'

Maggie nodded her approval and told Ellie to go and sit in the car. She tramped back down the hall, school bag bumping along behind her.

'I can't stop,' Maggie said, clutching her car keys. 'I'm on the school run but I just wanted to get this out of the way. She's grounded, and I'm afraid that means no riding for three weeks. Please explain and apologise to James.'

'I will, I understand.'

Laura grabbed her jacket and followed her sister outside but Maggie seemed in a hurry to get away and rammed the Toyota into reverse, then shot forward with a fierce disregard for the gearbox. Combined with the mist, it seemed pointless waving and so Laura wandered over to the menage where James and Rhian were attempting to measure-up Nancy for tack. The rest of the staff watched with interest, making suggestions about the bridle they'd cobbled together, minus a mouthpiece. They had nothing to fit the mare. Not a single girth would meet around her middle. Even Mal's saddle looked like a pea on a mountain and wasn't anywhere near the correct size and shape.

'Have to get something made,' Rhian said, then looked at Ben. 'Go on, give us a leg up, then.'

'It'll cost a bloody fortune in shoes,' James said. 'Look at the size of her feet.'

'My Uncle Bob's a cross-dresser and he can't get decent women's shoes either,' Ben said, and they all groaned, then laughed and pointed at Rhian's boots, barely dangling beyond the top of Nancy's shoulder.

'I reckon three of us could sit up here,' Rhian said.

Ben obliged by assisting Lucy and Enid with energetic leg-ups, to sit behind each other. Rhian clucked Nancy forward, then sent the horse into a trot and they all clung on. Lucy and Enid yelped at the rolling gait and even Rhian raised a smile. The horse was striking with her feathers shimmying at every stride, although Rhian said her head carriage was too low and she didn't use her back end anywhere near enough.

'Basically, she rides like a tractor drives,' Rhian said, with unexpected humour.

Laura didn't understand the equine nuances, but always enjoyed the camaraderie. In her mind's eye, she'd shot forward several years and Jenna was there too, sitting up behind Enid. Something about the mare and the way she related to the past reminded Laura of the old photographs she'd mounted in the hall. And what an odd coincidence that the name Nancy formed part of the word, pregnancy. Combined with Magenta, there was a wonderful poignancy developing in their midst and she visualised the perfect promotional shot where Nancy stood majestically in the paddock, a Carneddau foal gambolling at her feet and the Welsh mountains flushed with autumn colour in the background. She needed to find a photographer!

Business-wise, it summed-up their diversity perfectly.

'I reckon she's a project for you, Rhian,' James said, patting Nancy's mighty shoulder and cutting into Laura's daydream. 'I'll re-mortgage the house and see about ordering some rugs and tack. Get Harry Hoof to come over, will you?'

'But how do we get down?' Lucy said, and Ben made himself into a human mounting block.

As everyone broke away for morning tea-break, Laura filled in James on the missing cash.

'Ellie? You're *kidding?*'

'No. I think I have apologies to make.'

She sucked in a deep breath and walked across to the old caravan. Rhian's previous home sat on bricks since its unfortunate demise into the gorse bushes, but it was warm inside and relatively cosy. The red curtains were still going strong too, although the floor was knee deep in dried mud and straw, and the two cats they employed as hunters were curled-up on the beds. When she tapped on the door and poked her head in, all four staff and both cats looked at her with the same wariness.

Unable to come up with a better idea, Laura told them the missing cash had been her mistake. Other than one of the cats yawning, not one of them responded, although Rhian rarely broke with protocol in terms of facial expression. The real ice breaker was when Laura spoke about her pregnancy, although she was quick to impress that it was very early days and as such, still a secret. Rhian grunted, Ben and Lucy offered more conventional congratulations. Enid looked especially quiet and intense. Laura wondered if the news made her uncomfortable somehow, but later, she discovered a bunch of wild flowers on the doorstep. Yellow poppies, the last of the heather, a variety of ferns, some red campion and a single wild rose.

It must have taken Enid most of her lunch hour to collect them.

September was mellow in every sense of the word. It was a happy time, a period of establishing their marriage, their future and their team spirit. Her pregnancy was confirmed, the due date estimated around the beginning of June. Mild morning sickness kicked-in, gradually increasing to include random times of the day and Laura spent a fair amount of time lying on the bed sipping ginger tea and staring across the landing at the box-room she'd cleared the previous year. Ben painted the walls milk white, just to appease her restless spirit really. She knew James had far more urgent jobs for him elsewhere but she loved James all the more for indulging her love of design. She made a pair of curtains in dove grey. She tried not to browse nursery furniture on the web, but bookmarked everything she came across in milk white, or dove grey. From this, she deduced her accent colour was obviously going to be red, and if James noticed the rug and the gradual assortment of accessories littered across the floor and stacked on the windowsill, he made no comment.

On good days, she worked on the website for the yard and arranged a date for a photographer before light and colours were compromised and the horses were shaggy and covered in mud again. Nancy's saddle and bridle arrived and a substantial new peg was installed in the tack room. Mick continued to appear unannounced, mostly to sit and watch James and any RDA clients, but he wasn't averse to helping Ben either which didn't go unnoticed. James said he was thinking of employing him – on a casual labour basis, which was the only basis James liked to work with. And a new livery horse arrived called Cloud Nine. The irony had her smile, but she chose to believe the dappled grey gelding was a good omen. Then, towards the end of the month, Ellie returned for lessons.

Maggie was still down in the mouth, but seemed reluctant to open up and talk. No doubt she was frightened that if she discussed the adoption conundrum then her sister's fragile mothering obsession would be thrown into another vortex of despair. Laura went along with this, since it made it a lot easier to remain impartial. Christy and Trisha had thrown out an invitation for dinner – the evening before Laura's birthday – at their old Italian haunt in Chester. Laura was mildly surprised that they wanted to reinstate their old routine, but she had to admit she was touched. On impulse, she invited Carla and Maggie along. If Pam Tanner turned up, she wasn't sure how the land might lie, but it wouldn't do any harm to have some personal backup in the form of Carla's quick tongue. Plus, having Carla along dispelled any preconception that Laura had evolved into some sort of quiet country mouse.

'Come on, have a night out. My shout, and I'm driving,' she said to Maggie.

'I've nothing to wear!'

'Not that old chestnut. What about your wedding outfit?'

'Do you think I could? Isn't it a bit formal?'

'Well, you wore it to my wedding and there was nothing remotely formal about that.'

This raised a laugh. 'Go on, then. It's ages since we had a catch up.'

James said he had no objections whatsoever to her driving into Chester for a night out, although he stopped sluicing his boots with the hosepipe so he could look at her. 'Although last time you went out with that lot you came home in a right state.'

Laura shivered and stuffed her hands into her sleeves. 'I know. Down to Pam Tanner. I doubt she'll be there, though. Her allegiance clearly lies with Alice and Simon. You er… you don't want to come along, do you?'

'You are joking? I'm way better at private functions.'

'As in you and me?'

'Exactly. Keep your actual birthday free and we'll have a quiet night in. For a change.'

'Sounds like bliss,' Laura said, and she meant it.

The days might be shorter with dusk closing in rapidly as they headed towards October, but Laura loved lighting a fire in the evenings and curling up with James and the dogs, with something simmering in the Aga. The outside chores extended to bringing in most of the horses at night. Then it was rugging, making up deep straw beds and securing hay nets. Enid made light work of this, and was always finished for six. Her lift home arrived just as she locked the tack room and handed the key to Laura. James switched off the tap and began to brush the water towards the grid, then stopped and leant on the brush. Normally, Enid's brother hovered at the end of the drive in his van. This time, he parked next to the Land Rover and walked purposefully towards them, a hand outstretched.

'Gethin Evans. Enid's brother. Felt it time I introduced myself.'

He looked a lot like Enid with the same dark looks and slight build, but there was a tough wiriness about his frame. He was also ingratiatingly humble and thanked both of them for providing Enid with some sort of stability and a social outlook more suited to a girl of her age. Laura was tempted to pry further, but Gethin didn't give her a chance. 'Thing is, I've got a seven-day contract coming up. The money's too good to turn down. There could be a permanent job in it, you see. Here's the sting. It's, er… it's down in Cornwall. I wanted to ask if you'd look out for Enid. I mean, she's fine by herself for a bit, it's just–'

'You don't need to ask,' Laura said, flicking her eyes onto James, then smiling at Enid. 'Of course we will. Anything she needs.'

His face relaxed. 'That's a weight off, appreciated.'

'He seems a decent sort,' Laura said, watching them head towards the van, Gethin with an arm across Enid's shoulders.

'Yeah. Just a bloody shame he can't make a decent living out of farming.'

A routine card came from Rob's practice to say the annual jabs for the dogs were due sometime in October. On the reverse, he'd scribbled something about not needing an appointment and to turn up towards the end of the day. She told James she wanted to take the dogs herself.

'Washboy'll scarper when he knows where he's going. He'll pull you over.'

'I'll not let him get out of the car. I'll get Rob to handle him.'

She set off late afternoon to travel the couple of miles to Rob's veterinary practice in Tal Y Bont. The dogs knew, somehow, they weren't going on a pleasure trip. James put a rare collar and lead on the lurcher, and tied him to the guard in the back of Laura's car, where he peered back at her through the rearview mirror in abject misery. Lamby was considerably more stoic but she kept her head on her paws, eyes downcast. Laura drove slowly past the primary school, devouring the scene as an after-school club finished and children erupted from the building, spilling outside to shriek and kick at piles of leaves.

The veterinary practice was sandwiched behind the church and an old-fashioned newsagents. When she swung the car into the parking area round the back, she needed several minutes to absorb the possible ramifications of the boarded-up window. There was a handwritten sign fixed to the door. *Open as usual.* She hooked Lamby firmly under one arm. Predictably, it was dingy inside despite it being flooded with electric light. Rob's receptionist alerted him to her arrival, and Laura was immediately waved through to one of the examination rooms, where Rob was scrubbing his hands in a huge sink.

'Be with you in a minute. Five castrations this afternoon, just making sure I'm all clean for you.'

'Anyone I know?'

'Er, let me think… Noodles the whippet, a couple of sex beast rabbits,' he went on, pausing to dry his hands on a strip of paper towel. 'Then Mrs Hopkins' retriever and finally, one I had the greatest of pleasure to perform – post office Tom. That's the cat, not the old guy behind the counter.'

She laughed. 'Really?'

'They don't call him Kitty Killjoy for any old reason.'

Laura set Lamby down on the examination table but the dog trembled so pathetically, she felt compelled to pick her up again. Rob dropped the towel in the bin, then came round the table to plant a kiss on her cheek. He tickled Lamby under the chin, then began to look up the annual records on screen.

'So, both dogs for annual boosters?'

'Please.' She explained that Washboy was cowering in the car.

'Big Wuss. All that's ever happened in here is he's had a tiny pinprick in the back of his neck, quickly followed by a chicken biscuit.'

'He's a boy, what more can I say?'

She watched Rob tap away on the computer system then turn to hunt for something in the cupboard. Lamby began frantically licking Laura's face, sensing impending doom. 'What happened to the window?'

'Ah, you noticed,' he said, and ripped the cellophane off a packet of syringes. 'Some prick lobbed a couple of bricks through it. Still waiting for the glass company to show. Trust us to have a bow-shaped shopfront.'

'Armstrong?'

'More than likely. Amusing really, in that as soon as I said *prick* you made the correct assumption. It's his sort of prank, isn't it?'

'So you went to see him?'

'Sure I did. It was your sister that saved the day, though.'

'*Maggie?* What on earth was Maggie doing there?'

'She's not mentioned it, then?'

'No! I haven't seen her for a while. Ellie... never mind that. Rob?'

He indicated that she should set Lamby down. Laura focused entirely on his face but he gave nothing away and despite his deftness with the syringe, the terrier still looked at Laura as if she'd been sentenced. All over in seconds, Laura scooped the dog back up into her arms. Rob produced the coveted chicken biscuit and suggested he sort out Washboy in-situ, to save stressing him further.

They walked outside and headed towards Laura's car while Rob told her some incredulous story about Maggie stealing Armstrong's passport and secreting it in her bra, then both of them setting fire to said passport on the seafront. The entire exchange sounded closer to a one-sided threatening exercise. It also had a suggestion of farce about it, but mostly it sounded incredibly futile.

'He'll just get a replacement!' Laura said, once she'd got her head around the full story. 'You just wanted to get one over on him.'

'That was a small factor. Look, we tried reasoning. Well, at least your sister did, but it was a no go.'

He reached into the back of her car and made a fuss of Washboy. Not fooled for a second, the lurcher growled and put a leg and his snout through the bars of the grill. 'He really doesn't like me, does he?' Rob said, and plunged the needle into the back of the dog's neck.

'Don't you think there's a chance you may have made everything worse?'

'Not really. It needs to come to a head. And if it carries on, I'll play my trump card.'

'Which is?'

'Sending a copy of the confession to his so-called mates. Let's see how they like being named, might get them off my back once and for all.'

'So, he's hounding you now?'

'Nothing I can't handle.'

'Like what? Rob… *tell* me.'

'Usual teenage antics, trailing me when I'm on an outside job then tailgating me on the downhill sections, or anywhere they perceive is scary.' He waggled his fingers at this and pulled a face. 'Like flying over a cattle grid at sixty.'

She sighed and folded her arms. 'Doesn't he go to work?'

'Oh, it's not just him, this is mostly the Griffiths crowd and their druggie hangers-on. And now the nights are drawing in, the racing's got going again. I had to destroy a couple of ewes up there last week. Left half-dead at the side of the road,' he said, and closed the car door. 'Not a pretty sight. They were some of Gethin Evan's stock.'

'Why aren't the police doing anything?'

He shrugged. 'I don't suppose their nice comfy squad cars can get up there. What they really need is a chopper with thermal imaging. I reckon it'll take a serious accident before anything happens.'

Her gut turned over. She should never have given Rob the address. And to think her sister had gone with him was incomprehensible. The waters were muddied further now by Rob's mutual hate of the Griffiths, and the careless deaths of sheep and ponies. Retribution for James and his concern for Maggie had already mushroomed into something ugly and complicated. The thought that sweet, innocent Enid was in the eye of this storm – albeit mostly in a geographical sense – was something Laura tried not to dwell on.

Dressing-up on Friday night was a flashback to her old life. There was no need to choose something which hid her bump because there wasn't yet one to hide. She applied a dark pink lipstick, stood back from the mirror and smoothed down her black and brown Hobbs dress, taking a moment to rest her hands on her belly. She was almost five weeks pregnant. She tried not to think about her previous miscarriage at ten weeks, when she'd passed out in Strawberry Cottage. James had taken her to hospital. He'd even collected her again, battling through the snow and ice whilst Simon had been in Spain. It might have been the crazy catalyst which had sent her relationships into a different direction, but she really couldn't face a repeat of that. How did women cope when they had one miscarriage after the other? The fertility site had opened her eyes to the endless failure and devastating grief that some women continued to go through.

So far, mild nausea was the only physical proof that something was afoot, although the emotional evidence made itself known on a regular basis. Sometimes, it took her breath away for no good reason. *She was pregnant!* She looked up at the ceiling to stem the familiar overspill of tears then blotted carefully under her eyes with a tissue. A pair of sensible low-heeled boots sat next to her handbag, so she pulled these on and went downstairs. James was asleep on the sofa, partially covered by the sprawling grey form of Washboy. They only stirred when she began to search for her car keys.

'You smell nice,' James said, and struggled to prop himself up on one arm.

'You mean, not of dung?'

'There's nothing wrong with dung. It's only fermented grass.'

'If you say so.'

She bent to kiss him. He caught hold of her hand and threaded his fingers through hers. 'Call me if you need me.'

'I'll always need you.'

'You know what I mean.'

Laura knew what he meant but it was always good to hear him say it, and she released his fingers reluctantly. But then the moment Laura collected Maggie from Hafod House, the euphoria of cosy marriage and impending motherhood vanished as a feeling of unease kicked-in. Silly really, she was overthinking the situation. Checking the rearview mirror every few seconds as if they were a sitting target, was both pointless and exhausting. Rob was probably right and it was all a matter of boys being boys and sooner or later, Armstrong and the Griffiths would overplay their hand, make a mistake and back off.

'I know what you're doing,' Maggie said, staring ahead, bag on her lap. 'And he's not behind us.'

'You can't blame me for checking! Not after your escapade with Rob.'

'Oh. He's told you, then?'

'What were you thinking?'

A long silence. 'I was thinking about Krystal. That's what I was thinking.'

Laura sighed, changed down a gear and took the exit road into Chester. 'I know, and I'm sorry how things have turned out.'

'Pete's inconsolable. And then, Ellie! I'm so disappointed in her.'

'Maggie, I don't want all of this to keep coming between us.'

'I know but it does,' she said, casting Laura a grim smile. 'I'm sorry for my daughters' behaviours, and I'm sorry for being a miserable old bat.'

'There's no need to be sorry.'

They passed the beauty salon where Jess used to work, and Maggie issued another sigh. 'She wanted to stay on the yard, do you remember? We wouldn't let her.'

'I don't think you can keep blaming yourself.'

'No, but she'd never have met Callum Armstrong.'

Laura parked round the back of Nino's and it was like regressing a couple of years, when she'd been pregnant the first time around. Maggie wobbled across the uneven car park in her best shoes then had to resort to holding onto Laura. They were directed to their booked table to find Carla already there, sharing a bottle of wine with Trisha and Christy. No sign of Pam Tanner, thankfully.

Introductions were made and Laura accepted their gifts and cards. It was difficult to keep drinking orange juice and keep the stupid smile off her face, but Laura insisted she was simply sticking to doctor's orders.

'I'm still waiting for my invitation to your barn dance,' Christy said, handing round the garlic bread.

Maggie snorted. 'A barn dance? James won't go for that.'

'They live in North Wales, not Argentina,' Trisha said,

topping up everyone's glass. 'It's the green welly brigade up there in the hills.'

'Well, not *always*,' Carla said, a tad indignantly.

'I think you should do something, though. Maybe a Christmas bash, then? To make up for having no wedding.'

Maggie gave Christy a dirty look and took the largest slice of bread. 'My sister had a beautiful wedding, complete with peacocks and a straw ring. Why does she need to throw everyone a party?'

'I'm with Maggie on this,' Trisha said. 'Such a waste of money.'

'Oh, you're all party poopers,' Christy said. 'I love a cowboy and all that western gear. It's so sexy! I was looking forward to buying a Stetson and a belt with a big buckle on it. And look at my nails! I'm barn ready.'

'Is that the same as oven ready?' Trisha said.

Christy tutted loudly, then fluttered her hands across the table. The nails were bright alternating colours with the head of a horse on each thumb.

'Ellie would love those,' Maggie deadpanned.

'I must bring the children over for some horse riding,' Christy said, fixing Laura with a stare. 'What do I have to do, just turn up?'

Carla laughed. 'Goodness me, no. What you have to do is speak to Laura's yard manager. She'll book the children in and take a deposit from you.'

'What, even for friends?'

'Especially for friends,' Carla said, with a friendly wink. 'Business is business.'

'It's much cheaper if you book a block of six,' Laura offered, but she quickly sensed that Christy had lost interest. It had never occurred to her before that Christy was anything other than a generous soul but Laura began to see something slightly less attractive. Perhaps that was unfair, perhaps it was herself who'd simply changed, moved-on and found a different focus in her life.

The conversation flitted from horses and parties, to work, and then partners. Halfway through the carbonara, Laura experienced a distinct sense of detachment. Staying on soft drinks was probably much of the problem but she did begin to wonder if she had anything in common anymore with Trisha and Christy. Trisha was her usual acerbic self about men and there was some lively banter between her and Carla, but where Trisha used to make Laura laugh with her cutting remarks, now it felt bitter and one-sided. Perhaps this was down to James. There was something intoxicating about being in a relationship which didn't rely on the constant need for validation. They simply didn't have stupid fights. And Carla had a clever, classy restraint which put people in their place without them noticing, whereas Trisha could be aggressive, as hostile as the so-called aggressive men she was often shredding to pieces.

'Some gossip for you, Laura,' Trisha said, tapping a spoon against her glass. 'Alice has *left* Simon.'

'Really? Poor Tara and Cameron. Those children have gone through enough upheaval. Alice had cancer last year, didn't she?'

'Yes, she's in remission now, though. She let Simon look after her, then dumped him when she felt fit enough to cope.'

'Charming,' Laura said.

'I thought you hated Simon?'

'No, I don't hate anyone. We've drawn a line, buried the hatchet or whatever you want to call it.'

'My sister hasn't got a hate bone in her body,' Maggie said, and Carla agreed. 'If she hated him it would mean she had feelings for him.'

Trisha pulled a face. 'I'm still pleased he's got his just deserts; sleeping on Pam's sofa!'

Maggie picked up the menu. 'That's as maybe, but *we've* not had ours. Tiramisu?'

The pudding arrived with two bottles of Prosecco for a

toast, courtesy of Carla. Laura suffered the happy birthday song and took minuscule sips of her drink. When Maggie went to the Ladies, she swapped it with her sister's empty glass even though Maggie was already slurring and getting loud, but at least she'd cheered up.

While they waited for the bill, she opened a text from James: *Look who's flown in.* She scrolled down to see he'd sent her a photo of their resident barn owl, perched on the paddock fence in the dusk. It made her feel horribly homesick and she'd only been away for three hours and twenty-six minutes.

CHAPTER TWELVE

Laura

Diamond Digital arrived mid-morning on a perfect day at the beginning of October. The landscape looked like a messy artist's palette, highlighted with sheep wearing full winter fleece. The whisper of a cool breeze stirred the dry leaves and lifted the horses' manes and tails. Song, Mal, and Nancy had been bathed and brushed to perfection, manes and tails like silk. Everywhere was swept, neat and tidy. The outdoor menage had been raked and all the baskets replanted. A vending machine had arrived just in time and was installed in the spectator area of the indoor school. Their range of show jumps were on full display; the intention being to capture Lucy and Song in action. The stage was set.

The photographer's assistant struggled across the yard with a tripod and a range of lighting equipment, including umbrellas and flapping backdrops.

'I see he's brought plenty of horse-friendly props,' James said. 'Good luck with that.'

Laura's face fell slightly. 'He said he's worked with horses before… James, don't disappear! I need a headshot.'

'I've got a client due.'

'We're supposed to be closed!'

'You might be, but I'm not.'

He managed a cursory nod in acknowledgement of

Diamond Digital, then ambled in the opposite direction.

Mark Diamond came over to shake Laura's hand, and sympathised. 'You know what they say, never work with animals. Or family.'

'I know there's a degree of unpredictability with horses, but it seems my husband is in the same category.'

'Don't worry, he won't escape,' he said, and pulled out some paperwork for her to sign on a clipboard, which he angled in her direction. 'You've sent me a very detailed brief. I hope I can do it justice, given all the unpredictably. Formal indoor shots first I think, while we're all clean and tidy. Then we'll move outside to catch the afternoon light and do some of the more natural, emotive stuff you're after.'

'Sounds perfect.'

Laura looked around for the staff. James was already in deep conversation with a young woman and a grey pony in the round pen. Ben was posing with a yard brush at every turn, looking anything *but* natural. At least Lucy was taking it seriously and looked show-ring smart in her white jods and a black jacket. And although Enid still had a head of snakes in terms of the plaits and matted tendrils, her hair had been gathered up into a presentable ponytail.

More interestingly, she'd removed the nose stud completely.

They moved into the indoor school, and the session went on forever. 'I only need one perfect second,' Diamond kept saying to Lucy. 'Go again, over that triple bar. Without pulling a funny expression on take-off.'

'That's her bricking-it face,' Ben said, unhelpfully.

'It so isn't! I'm concentrating!'

Twenty minutes later they spilled back outside, Lucy and Song bathed in a faint sheen of sweat. Sensing defeat, Rhian emerged reluctantly from her caravan to go through what she clearly perceived as a deeply painful experience. Because she looked so miserable and wooden, Diamond's assistant suggested Rhian walk out of the tack room carrying a saddle.

'Two down, three to go,' he said to Laura, just as Maggie's car swung in. Her sister strode across to the picnic bench where Laura found herself manning the impromptu tea and coffee station and buttering scones.

'What's going on?' Maggie said, helping herself to a mug of tea. 'Where is everyone?'

Laura explained about Diamond Digital and her sister's face brightened. 'Is it for the holiday thing? Are they coming to do Hafod House?'

'Eventually,' she said, then lowered her voice. 'I have to take baby steps with that. And we have got quite a lot on our plates at–'

'Like what? Anything I can do?'

A well-timed distraction occurred when James came into view, talking on his mobile. The conversation ended and he shoved the phone into his back pocket, then came to lean over the paddock rail. Laura looked at him expectantly. 'That was Sam. He wanted to let us know, he's mostly out of reach. On secondment in Alaska. Research… or, something for the Marine Biology Institute I think he said.'

Maggie was practically salivating at this information. Her mouth dropped open slightly, even her eyes bulged and her eyebrows shot up.

'Alaska! How long for? Has he been there a while?'

'A week or so. There for another five,' James said, irritably. 'Is there a problem with that? Jess bored now, is she?'

'No, no not at all. I think that's *wonderful* news!'

He narrowed his eyes, then scrutinised Laura's face for possible clues. She was careful to remain miffed over his snipe about Jess, in the hope it might deflect from Maggie's Miss Marple style enthusiasm.

James rubbed his face. 'Okay. Look, Maggie. If you want to ride Mal sometime, you'd be doing me a favour.'

'I'd love to. First thing Saturday?'

'Fine. Saturday,' he said, then turned to Laura. 'It seems I'm free for an hour, if you still want a mugshot.'

Laura smiled sweetly and passed him a scone.

'What was all that about?' she hissed, once James was out of earshot.

'My delay tactics with the passport came up trumps, that's what,' Maggie said, eyeing a scone. 'Go on, then. Put plenty of butter on.'

Laura pushed a plate towards her sister, with a napkin. 'Help yourself.'

'Rob went round to the flat again, last week.'

'Again? Why?'

'To warn him that since he hadn't backed off, the confession letter had gone in the post.' She paused to slather jam and cream onto her scone. 'This is yummy.'

'Well? *And?*'

'Armstrong wasn't there. Neighbour said he'd gone away. Talk about timing! So… well, I was feeling a bit anxious about Sam, but it seems there's no need now.'

The mention of Armstrong cast a blight on the day for Laura, despite something swinging in their favour by pure fluke. She tried not to imagine how Armstrong might feel once he'd wasted a lot of time and money trailing round Maine, only to discover his quarry was out of town in a seriously inhospitable location, and for several weeks. He'd presume Sam had been tipped off. Laura was just grateful that Maggie hadn't actually put her in that position and expected her to make another secret phone call. Whichever way she looked at it, Rob and Maggie's respective mess with the local bad boys looked set to escalate, while Jess remained in her cocoon.

'And what if he goes over to the ranch?'

'If he can find it!' Maggie scoffed, brushing crumbs off her top. 'Jess said the ranch hands would shoot him if he caused any trouble. They all carry rifles out there, you know.'

Her sister made it sound safe, out of bounds. As if the rifles and the ranch hands operated like British security guards.

'So you've spoken to Jess again?'

'A bit,' Maggie said, then stopped chewing and sighed. 'There's no reasoning with her.'

Laura might have asked her sister to stay and watch the rest of the shoot, had it not been for the cloud of unease she'd brought with her. But as they slipped into the afternoon and the horses were turned out to wander across the fields, Laura relaxed. Diamond changed his shoes for gumboots and worked with a couple of hand-held cameras, his assistant trotting behind with a light meter and a selection of different lenses. The horses were strung out across the misting pasture, the Welsh hills in gentle outline beyond. It was doubtful this background canvas could be improved upon. The trees were especially photogenic, like beacons of light and energy. As well as a magnificent panoramic shot – which hopefully would serve as a header on the website – Diamond seemed especially receptive to finding those small details which expressed their ethos about healing, and their unique diversity through the structured facilities of the riding school, to the equine playground promised by the rugged countryside. And he seemed to enjoy mixing the formal portraits with something creative; finding a dark eye or capturing the light shining through a pale mane. Magenta was a livewire but managed to steal the show a lot of the time, gambolling into shot when they least expected it. Trying to contain Nancy and the foal in the same frame seemed impossible, until it finally happened by accident.

The real surprise was Enid.

She brought something unique to whatever she was asked to do, whether it was running with Mags through the long grass, or standing face to face with Cloud Nine — the images looked haunting, and impossibly beautiful in the mist.

'Striking girl. Complete natural. She could model,' Diamond said, as they walked back up to the yard. 'I'll get these edited and so on and whizz some over for your approval.'

'Can't wait to see them.'

'I think I may have got a bit carried away,' he said, smiling, and loaded the equipment back into the van.

'No matter. I'll probably buy them all.'

The instant Diamond Digital departed, Rhian came out of hiding and the yard filled up again with livery owners and clients for private lessons. Although it still wasn't properly dark after evening chores, Gethin had already left for Cornwall and Laura didn't like the idea of Enid toiling uphill to some cold dilapidated farmhouse to spend the evening alone. But even the offer of cottage pie wouldn't sway her to stay.'I have to get home before dark. For the sheep, and the dogs.'

'Alright, then you can take some with you,' Laura said firmly. 'And I'll drive you home.'

James made them take the Land Rover. Once through the top gate and onto the green lane – which was pitted with skid marks – the vehicle made light work of the uneven ground, and then through the almost leafless trees, Penrhiw Uchaf came into view. It looked as if it belonged to another era, which of course it did. The rear elevation was mostly obscured by a broken barn with a rusting corrugated iron roof. She followed Enid past old pigsties, full of farming clutter and ancient machinery rusted into the ground. The house itself was a typical long Welsh farmhouse, but it was unclear how much of it was habitable. A porch, full of boots, coats and tools, and then a front door with an old-fashioned latch. Enid produced a huge key on a length of string and the lock required a fair bit of negotiation before it would open. There was a faint odour of earth. The low roof and the small windows let in only a modicum of light, and the thick stone walls rendered the interior deathly quiet. Two border collies leapt up to greet them, but other than the dogs and the existence of a wood burner, there was little warmth.

'Would you like some tea?' Enid said.

Laura smiled and nodded, but not because she wanted a drink. She wanted time to absorb Enid. The girl disappeared into a small scullery with a sloping roof. Closer to home, there was a sofa covered in old crocheted shawls and a single modern chair in front of a small television. Through the window, a scrubby patch of vegetable garden ran up to a barn, and then the crumbling stone wall which formed a rough circumference around the entire plot, gradually dispersed onto the open Carneddau. A predatory bird hovered and swooped, and hundreds of crows took flight. It looked impossibly bleak, and yet breathtaking in a way she couldn't clearly define. Maybe it was the overwhelming proximity of life and death. There was certainly a strong resonance with her childhood, and Laura could almost taste the bitter wind and feel the pitiful cries of the ewes lambing in the spring snow. It took her back to a place she thought she'd dealt with, but the evocative mix of distant memories and Enid's isolation – both in a physical and emotional sense – tugged at something buried in her subconscious.

What had James said about her name? *Enid means soul, or life.*

She drew her eyes from the sky. On the wide stone windowsill, there was a pottery vase stuffed with wilting hedgerow flowers, the remnants of a corn dolly, and two photographs. The black and white picture could be the grandparents, both of them young and standing proud at the front door of a brighter looking Penrhiw Uchaf. And then in faded colour, a young woman in the heather with a baby on her hip and a toddler at her feet. Undoubtedly Enid and Gethin with their mother.

She sensed Enid was back in the room. Laura placed the

frame down carefully, and swallowed over her dry throat.

'I lost my mother too, when I was a child,' she said, then turned to take the tea from Enid. 'I grew up in a place just like this.'

'I can't imagine it.'

'What, me on a farm?' she said, grinning. 'I hated it. Then.'

'And now you don't?'

'No, I don't hate it. I've come to understand it, mostly through James.' She hesitated, wondering how to apologise to the girl somehow, for their shaky start. 'He's a better judge of character than me. I make too many presumptions, based on the city life I've led. I think it must dull the senses.'

Enid's face broke into a hesitant smile. 'You're the kindest person I know.'

Early on Friday morning when they were lying spooned together, James reminded her that the annual meeting about the pony round-up was due later, in the pub. It marked almost a year since his accident on the quad bike, and the idea of him repeating the event filled Laura with dread.

'Please tell me you're not-'

'No... no *course* not,' he mumbled into her hair, then moved one hand to rest across her belly. 'Not a chance. I'm going to the meeting tonight, then on the day I'll be there as an advisory. Strictly confined to base camp.'

She covered his hand with hers, mildly anxious at the thought of him even attending the meeting, which was irrational. 'And that's it?'

'That's it,' he said, turning her over slowly to face him, and kissing her.

She groaned, passing a hand across her forehead. 'Feel yuk.'

'You look milk white. Tea?'

'Ginger tea, with sugar, no milk. And a biscuit.'

'Yuk.'

'You do know it's your fault I feel so yuk this morning?'

'I'm a bloke. I'm programmed to realise that everything's my fault in the end.'

'That's complete and utter rubbish,' she said, and threw a pillow in his direction.

He grinned, pulled on a pair of denims and went downstairs and Laura smiled at the ceiling, for no good reason. In a little less than eight months she'd have their child in her arms. Not even morning sickness could spoil the delicious anticipation of that.

It was late afternoon before she ventured out for some air. In the menage, Rhian was teaching Lucy the finer points of lunging a reluctant horse, in preparation for her exam. Ben was oblivious to the world, singing along with his earpieces in as he tidied up the barn. It was stuffed to the rafters with bales of straw and the rich meadow hay cut from their own land. Knowing their winter feed was accounted for always put James in a good mood, especially since the fields had recovered quickly after the dry summer. All the horses were grazing fresh pasture, while the big meadow close to home was being rested before getting treated. She spotted Dorothy nibbling the leftovers in all the most inaccessible areas, while Enid was trying to teach Magenta to walk calmly in his tiny halter. He still had much to learn about taking even-paced steps and not bounding in front of her, or dragging behind if Dorothy moved out of his peripheral vision. James was repairing some of the fencing by the roadside and she could see Mick, breaking-up and shovelling a pile of hardcore around the gate, where it became a sea of mud in the winter months.

She was almost upon them, striding across the soft ground and inhaling the cool air as if it were an elixir, when a manure-splattered Transit van bumped up the grass verge.

The window dropped down, and a man shouted over the hedge.

'Where'd you get that pony foal, Evans?'

Enid stood frozen to the spot, the foal skittish at the end of his lead rope.

James stopped what he was doing. 'What's it got to do with you?'

'My fucking pony, that's what!'

Enid spat on the ground, and James placed a restraining hand on her shoulder. 'Got the papers, have you?'

'Don't need no fucking papers! That's a Carneddau. Don't get clever with me, Jones.'

'You wouldn't understand clever.'

'You send me this, did you?' he said, reaching into his pocket for something. 'Accusing me of fixing some fucking quad bike?'

James reached over the fence and took the single sheet of paper. Laura knew what it was. It was Rob's trump card. Her feet slowed almost to a standstill, and she watched anxiously as James gave the sheet of paper a cursory scan before handing it back.

'No. But I'd watch your back, if I were you.'

'You think I'm scared of a kid and a fucking cripple?'

Mick materialised, carrying a pick axe. His bulk, his sheer menace, was palpable. 'I don't like what I'm hearing.'

'Who the fuck are you?'

'Your worst nightmare. Move on, pal. These good people don't want any trouble.'

Miraculously, the window rolled up, the van skidded off the verge and sped up the lane. She looked to James and his eyes met hers with a hundred questions. He threw the hammer and nails down. They walked back to the house in silence and removed their boots at the door.

'Who was that?' Laura said, reaching for the kettle and making for the sink, her eyes fixed on the garden.

'Who do you think? How did Hew Griffiths get that confession note? There's only me and Rob with a copy, and I know where mine is.'

Laura made the tea and pulled out two mugs on autopilot, staring into them as if the answer might be there. She knew the second she turned to face him her part in his betrayal would be all over her face. And it wasn't the need to purge her own conscience when she decided to tell the truth, it was the growing need to warn him, somehow. It seemed futile to continue to be secretive because none of it had helped bring Krystal home, none of it had stopped Rob's window getting a brick through it, nor had it tempered Armstrong's determination to go after Sam. And now this, the confession letter naming Hew and Gareth Griffiths.

Despite her efforts to the contrary, the story of Rob and Maggie's visit and all the incidentals, came out clouded with emotion and James interrupted her frequently. 'How did Rob know Armstrong's address?'

'I'm sorry,' she whispered. 'I'm sorry, I told him part of it, and he must have worked it out.'

'After *everything* I said? So you, Rob, and your sister have all done the exact opposite to what was discussed in this very room?'

'Rob and I, we-'

'*Unbelievable.*'

He scraped his chair back and left the house. Her heart hammered with shame and frustration. She threw his steaming mug of tea down the sink, then fought back the tears when it splashed everywhere and burnt the back of her hand. She'd wanted a chance to explain how it made her feel to see him struggle when Armstrong still walked free, but he clearly didn't want to hear it. Neither was he interested in Rob's noble sense of retribution, or Maggie's desperation.

She didn't go to find him until almost six in the evening. She'd made a beef stew and opened a bottle of red, but

Mick told her James had gone to drop Enid home, and then he intended to go straight to the pub. If there was any consolation in his behaviour – and she didn't blame him for being angry – then it was the fact that he'd asked Mick to stick around.

'Seems I've got some urgent log chopping to do,' Mick said, grinning at their already towering pyramid of seasoned wood, and Laura heaved a sigh.

'I'm sure I'll be fine if you want to go home.'

'Nah. Nothing at home for me,' he said, leaning on a yard brush. 'The big thing I've learnt about working here with these horses, is this: the pursuit of mastery is destructive to both parties, a bit like war.'

'People are a lot more flawed than horses.'

He doffed his cap. 'True. So, if you need me, I'll be around.'

Laura wanted to hug him, but she wanted to hug her husband more. She dithered on whether to head to the pub but then someone shouted her name and she spun round to see Carla leading her mare in from the field. Diva's foreleg was running with blood.

Laura hurried over, Lamby on her heels. 'What happened?'

'I'm sure it looks worse than it is,' Carla said, struggling to hold the mare by then, who was highly strung at the best of times. 'I don't know how she's done this, but if there's the tiny chance of an accident, Diva will find it. Is James around?'

'No, he's at a meeting.'

'Blast. Rhian?'

Laura hurried over to the caravan and tapped on the door, ignoring Washboy when he peered through the window. The second James left the premises, the dog always decamped to Rhian, although on this occasion it may have been food related too. Rhian always seemed to be halfway

212

through some sort of unhealthy snack. The sense of urgency made little difference and she still managed to eat a sausage sandwich slathered with sauce and onions, while carefully hosing down the mare's leg. A stream of blood-tinted tepid water ran across the concrete and swirled into the sunken grid. Eventually, she hunkered down and peered at the wound in the growing dusk using the light from her phone.

'Needs a stitch in that, might even be arterial. You'll have to get Rob.'

Mick came over to see what the fuss was about. 'Jeeze, what happened here, ladies?'

'Laura, can you give our resident vet a call, please?' Carla said.

'Sure.'

She imagined Rob in the pub, enduring a heated discussion with James, but as it happened he was still at the surgery dealing with an emergency case of theobromine poisoning in a dog. Laura hugged Lamby to her chest, imagining the horrors of weed killer or crop spray.

'What's that?'

'Caused by chocolate, would you believe? I'll be there in ten.'

'Okay. And Rob, I need to talk to you.'

He grunted something in the affirmative, but he sounded tired. 'I'm in serious demand today.'

By the time he arrived, Diva was stabled, highly agitated, and pawing the ground with her good leg. First it was a shot of antibiotics, then a sedative. Once the mare's head began to droop, Mick angled a spotlight into the right position while Rob's big fingers worked at sewing the gash above the mare's knee. During this, Mick whistled tunelessly and studied the cobwebs on the rafters, until his hands began to shake and Rhian had to take over.

Carla sighed and fondled the mare's drooping ears. 'Poor baby. Well, that's our fun on hold for several weeks.'

Rob agreed, and began to repack his medical case. 'I'll call by first thing and check on her.'

'I'm learning some of these aristocratic looking horses can be delicate,' Mick said, stroking his beard. 'All them veins and arteries look too close to the surface to me.'

'That's thoroughbreds for you,' Carla said. 'You can't have speed and elegance without some form of refinement, you see.'

'Which often comes at a price, regardless of species,' Rob quipped, then checked his phone, before pronouncing it dead. He rubbed the back of his neck. 'Been a long day. Anyone coming to the pub?'

Laura's mobile rang and Rob looked up. 'If that's Jamie trying to track me down, tell him I'll be there in ten and to have a pint ready.'

But it wasn't James, it was Enid, sounding very small and far away. 'Hi. It's me.'

'Is everything alright?'

'Not really. They're racing around the farm. Some of them have no lights.'

Laura let herself out of the stable and walked into a fine drizzle and a starless night. Nevertheless, she looked up into the sky and let the rain touch her skin. She began to shiver. 'Enid? Stay inside. I'll come and get you.'

She was loath to end the call but ran inside the house and grabbed a jacket from the hook in the hall, then tried to pull it on and hunt through her bag for car keys as she walked to her car.

Rob blipped his 4x4 open and slung his bag in the back, then frowned. 'Where you shooting off to?'

'I have to fetch Enid. She said they're racing round the farm with-'

'Enid? The Evan's girl? Where's Gethin?'

'Away.'

He immediately stretched an arm across her car door.

'*I'll* take you. You're not going up there on your own.' She thought about this for all of two seconds, then clambered into the passenger seat of his car and pulled the belt across. They headed out and up onto the steep lane, Laura hanging onto the grab handle. She told Rob about the drive-by visit from one of the Griffiths, and the resultant conversation she'd had to have with James. Rob kept glancing at her.

'I'll make it right with Jamie, you don't need to worry on that score.'

'Right now, I just want to get Enid out of there. This has all got too messy and out of control!'

Rob drew his eyes from hers and concentrated on the road ahead, the wipers working hard to clear the greasy windscreen. The murkiness increased the higher they climbed and visibility was reduced to making out the barely distinct shapes of walls and buildings. The mountains bled into the sky, making one dark mass. Fast-moving headlights flashed intermittently through the grey and black like Morse code, only to disappear for several seconds as the track dropped from sight. Then they'd emerge at random, sometimes in convoy, sometimes spaced apart. Rob slowed to a crawl and opened the window. They listened to the guttural sounds of revving engines piercing through the dripping silence. The close proximity of bleating ewes sounded surreal, and especially vulnerable.

'I'm going to kill the headlights before we go through the gate. Don't want to draw attention to ourselves, do we?'

But the gate was wide open. Rob hit the accelerator and the car lurched forwards. Out of nowhere something advanced towards them carrying a single, blinding light. Rob swore and spun the steering wheel into a right-hand lock. The car seemed to stagger sideways and the rough jolting felt like it would never end. Laura shouted out but Rob didn't, or couldn't answer. And then they hit something. The impact was like being thrown against a sheet of granite, hard and uncompromising. The airbags failed to inflate, and the seat belt cut across Laura's throat and seared into her chest. She still clung to it since everything else around her felt out of control, followed by a long moment of disbelief when she realised what had happened. Her body wanted to crumple into a ball but her mind forced her to do something, anything. She fumbled for the door handle but failed to locate it and a sob erupted from her dry throat.

When she dared to look sideways, Rob's inert form was slumped against the driver's door, his face covered in blood.

'Rob! *Rob…*'

There was a commotion outside. Men shouting, arguing, running. Another car on the track above looked to be belching smoke. Someone swung a huge torch round and it flashed through the shattered windscreen, alerting Laura to the fact that they were angled in a ditch and there was a stone wall in front of them. A column of steam rose from beneath the crumpled bonnet. At least, that's what she hoped it was. She began to shake, and then pain like she'd never known coursed through her body and she was gripped in a spasm of fear.

Jenna. Please, God, no. Stay with me.

She closed her eyes.

CHAPTER THIRTEEN

Maggie

Maggie spent a couple of weeks worrying about the visit they'd made to Armstrong's flat, phoning Rob on a regular basis to see if there'd been any repercussions. She'd been disturbed by the damage to his veterinary practice, knowing for a fact that Rob wouldn't accept this behaviour lying down.

'So I went round to his flat, again. I knew he wouldn't let me in a second time, so I hung about outside, waiting for him to come home.'

'Oh?' she said, cautiously.

'Yeah. I wanted to see the little runt squirm when I told him I didn't appreciate getting a brick lobbed through my window, and in view of that I'd sent a copy of his signed confession to his so-called mates.'

'Oh! Have you? And?'

'Neighbour said he'd gone away. Probably running scared. If so, job done.'

At first, this news panicked her. Where had he gone? Had he got another passport or had he gone somewhere else entirely? It niggled away at her until she could bear it no longer and wondered if Laura should perhaps consider calling Sam again. She'd feel happier if he was aware of this development, and not only from a physical point of view, but to ensure he and Jess had a watertight story in case the police looked more closely into their relationship.

On Monday morning, she plucked up courage to go round to test the water with her sister, but there was something going on at the yard with camera equipment and everyone was preoccupied with creating photographs for the new website. As usual, this scenario filled Maggie with yearning. Her ultimate dream for the future saw both families working together. Now that Nancy was in-situ, Maggie felt sure this was a sign and what better use for an unwanted heavy horse to be given a career change, much like herself. Despite her lack of equine knowledge, Laura clearly saw the potential promotional benefits too, and Maggie was itching to ask her sister if she could add Hafod House to their advertising blurb somewhere. Pete kept saying it was too soon and to stop mithering her.

'There's no details worked out. No point in people phoning us if we can't tell them what's on offer and how much it's all going to cost, is there?'

And she'd been forced to agree. That side of things had to come from Laura, but as they headed towards Christmas, Maggie knew they'd be struggling for cash again. They needed another string to their bow! She felt sure James was the stumbling block. It felt frustrating but they all knew he wouldn't be rushed and that he had no real investment in anything overly commercial. It was something they'd have to live with until Laura got up to speed with the horses and worked some magic around his sluggish disinterest. Exactly how she'd do this remained a mystery.

As she tucked into a cream scone, Maggie watched him working with a young woman and a pony that wouldn't load into a trailer. He fixed the problem in around fifteen minutes, then began to show the woman where she was going wrong. Enid watched his technique like a hawk, proper little apprentice she was. And then out of the blue, that phone call from Sam. Knowing that he was well out of danger, the worry over Armstrong's absence faded into insignificance. She even managed to bag a ride on Mal, although she wasn't entirely convinced this offer had arisen from any kind of spontaneous love on James' behalf.

'If it wasn't for this business over Krystal, I reckon we could consider ourselves on the up,' Pete said, as he cooked dinner.

Maggie tentatively agreed. His optimism sprung from bookings coming in for the school holidays, spread over the second half of October depending on which part of the country visitors were travelling from. There were two new reviews on Trip Advisor; a four and a five-star rating, and thankfully, no more bogus one-star disasters complaining about barking dogs in all the rooms or the smell of wee everywhere. Pete was well on the road to full recovery too, although he still didn't fancy driving and so suggested to Ellie that they take the train into Chester on Saturday, by way of some father-daughter bonding. It was something Maggie conceded was long overdue. In fact, they'd made a pact not to mention Jess for a while, at least not in front of their youngest daughter. No wonder Ellie wanted to live with Willow and two dozen rabbits. It wasn't fair to keep inflicting Jess and her problems onto Ellie, and in truth, they could all do with a bit less drama. It helped that the house was calm and ordered, mostly thanks to Lucy, although how long this situation would continue was anyone's guess since the girl looked especially tired under the pressure of two jobs and a looming exam. She was going on holiday at the weekend for a few days with her father, although she'd assured both Laura and Maggie that she'd be back well in time for the school holidays. Pete thought they could manage without her, but Maggie didn't want to preempt anything until they were absolutely sure everything was back on an even keel, but it was certainly looking that way.

On Saturday, Maggie wriggled into the compression pants she always wore for horse riding and ignored Pete's Stan Laurel expression when she had to bounce on the bed as usual, to get them over her hips. Once they were up, she bent her knees to demonstrate their superior stretch and comfort.

'They're a bit tight, aren't they?' Pete said. He even turned her round and looked at her rump as if she were a piece of mutton strung up on a butcher's pole.

'They're supposed to be!'

'Not like that, though. I mean, you know, around your nether regions.'

She put her hands on her hips. 'And who's going to be looking down *there?* Anyway, by the time I've got a coat and boots on and I'm mounted up, no one will see much more than a couple of kneecaps.'

'What if you have to get off, or fall over?'

'Oh, now you're being silly.'

'I'm sure we could run to pair of proper ones. How much are they?'

'Anything from sixty to eighty quid, and beyond.'

'Now *you're* being silly.'

'These were a tenner. Still silly, am I?'

He muttered something about keep-fit in the village hall being cheaper and why hadn't she carried on doing that instead?

She ignored this. Determined nothing was going to spoil the day, she packed a small rucksack and deliberated on whether to ride out to Conwy Mountain. They could pick up the trail from Sychnant. That way, Mal would get a good session of trotting up the lanes first and take a bit of fizz out of him before they hit open land. Pete frowned at her preparations. A bottle of water, a banana and a bar of chocolate went in the bag.

'Be careful, Maggie. We don't want any more accidents. Why don't you ride in that indoor building they've got?'

She scoffed and tutted. 'That's for teaching and schooling. Mal and I want a gallop across the tops! *Stop* worrying.'

Finally, they were ready to go. Maggie blipped open the car, and Pete and Ellie got in. Linda peered over the rhododendron bushes and said hello. Relations had much improved since the wisteria had been replaced, although Maggie noticed it had grown like wildfire round the back of the shed. Pete maintained it was Japanese knotweed.

'Off riding?' Linda said, spotting the hard hat and the gloves under Maggie's arm. 'You should come and try the new Pilates class in the village. The instructor said it was very good for horse riders.'

'Really?' she trilled, and quickly closed the car door. The less Pete thought about that, the better. On the way to the train station, her mobile began to ring. A glance at the screen informed her it was Jess. Odd, because it was the middle of the night in New Hampshire.

'Do you want me to answer it?' Pete said.

'No, no. I'm sure it's nothing that can't *wait*,' she said, implying in no uncertain terms that now wasn't an appropriate time to be talking to Jess.

Conversations with their eldest daughter were more strained by the week and she didn't want anything to blight the day for Ellie. Since they'd given her a little more attention, her communication had improved again and she was seeing less of Willow, although much of that was engineered by themselves to keep her busy. Maggie pulled into the train station on the outskirts of Conwy, and Pete and Ellie said their goodbyes and walked over the bridge to wait on the opposite platform. She waited a moment, in case there was a problem with the Chester train.

Her phone began to ring again and Maggie answered it in a leisurely fashion. 'I can't talk for long, Jess. I'm riding Mal this morning.'

'Bully for you.'

She sighed and opened the window. Damp, salty air seeped into the car and the constant screech of seagulls on the station roof had her wind it back up again.

'Shouldn't you be asleep?'

'Yes! But I've had a phone call from *him*. He only called the fucking ranch – from a US number!'

Maggie pressed the phone closer to her ear in case she misheard anything, and tried to keep her voice steady. 'So… Armstrong's in *America?*'

'Well, he got as far as Maine airport. Where he got *busted* for possession of a class A! He was allowed *one* phone call, and he called *me*, begging for help. Saying he loved me and all that crap. Can you believe it?'

Maggie's mouth dropped open and a huge blob of seagull shit landed on the windscreen. 'I… I didn't know he was on *drugs.*'

An irritated sigh at this. '*No.* He claims he was set up! Look, is there anything going off at your end? Dad said he'd been following you.'

Maggie changed the phone into her other hand and wiped her sweaty palm across her knees. 'Like what? Anyway, what did you say to him?'

'That I couldn't help. He should have called a lawyer! Wait till they check out his UK records. He's got serious form for disturbing the peace, breaking and entering and that. He's been cautioned for all sorts of stuff.'

The fact that Jess had stayed up so late in order to call her, told Maggie she was seriously rattled. She slipped into mother-mode before Jess suspected her stunned silences might mean something else. 'So now's the time to stop with that Chandelier thing, Jess. The police look at everything, you know.'

'It's already gone, ages ago.'

'Oh? Oh, that's a relief. Your dad didn't like that one bit.'

'I was bored with it,' she said, then a huge sigh. 'I really,

really hate the fact Cal's in the same country as me.'

'But if he's in custody he can't bother you.'

'Suppose. What if they come round here, asking questions?'

'Then you answer them truthfully. You say he can't accept you're in love with someone else, and that you and Sam are happily married.'

'Suppose.'

She asked after Krystal, but Jess claimed tiredness and rang off. Maggie stayed sitting in the car park, trying to get her head round the news, mostly to determine whether she and Rob could be implicated in any way. Would they fingerprint Armstrong's flat? What sort of sentence did a class A drug attract? Two years, five years… maybe more? Ironic that the police had never managed to nail him for the quad bike but they'd got him for a crime he perhaps hadn't actually committed, maybe because the evidence was clear cut and made an easy case. Disturbance of the peace and the fact that he must have applied for an emergency passport, would possibly go against him in a way no one could have predicted.

Her phone rang again and in her haste she almost dropped it, but it was only Carla.

'You're my last resort, Maggie!' she said, somewhat indignantly. 'I don't know where everyone is this morning but I'm desperate to speak to Rob.'

'Oh? Why?'

Some story came out about Diva cutting her leg and needing stitches. 'He was meant to be checking on her this morning. And now I'm on the London train and I can't get hold of anyone at the yard, either. I was beginning to think my phone was broken, but maybe there's a line down in the valley, have you any idea?'

'Don't worry, I'm going to both places this morning,' Maggie said, authoritatively. 'I'll report back.'

She quickly started the car and headed back along the valley road, fuelled with a great excuse to actually see Rob and watch his face light up at the juicy news she had to reveal. Was it wrong to feel this smug? Tal Y Bont was a mere ten minutes from the yard so not exactly out of her way, but when she discovered the surgery closed and a long line of disgruntled people standing outside holding dogs and yowling cats, she felt mildly cheated. At least the new window was in. Oh, bugger this, she was meant to be enjoying herself today! She struggled to turn the car round in the awkward turning area with everyone watching, then drove up to the yard which was more than likely exactly where Rob was detained, or else they'd pass each other on the road. But when she trundled down the drive and stopped at her usual parking space, everywhere looked deadly quiet considering it was Saturday morning. There was no sign of Rob's vehicle and her sister's dog was on the farmhouse doorstep, curled-up in a ball. On the upside, she could see O'Malley's handsome head. A quick look over his stable door confirmed he was waiting for her, all clean and trace-clipped. She could whip his rug off, tack up and be off in no time. It was a bit murky and drizzly but she'd borrow one of those reflective tabards from the tack room.

Except that the tack room was still locked.

She spotted Ben with his head down in the field, as if he was scouring the ground. When he saw Maggie, he strolled across to the gate and held up a particularly rusty section of exhaust with several six-inch nails poking out of it, like a piece of abstract art. 'Found this. Some idiot must have lobbed it over the fence in the dark.'

Rhian came out of her caravan, took the incriminating chunk of metal out of Ben's hands and frowned at Maggie's outfit. 'What are you doing here?'

'I've come to ride Mal. Where is everyone?'

She looked at Maggie as if she'd fallen from the sky.

'You've come to ride? Today? Has no one called you?'

'What about?'

'The accident.'

'Oh, yes, that. Carla's trying to track down Rob. You haven't seen him, have you? Only there's a lynch mob outside his surgery this morning!'

Another long pause and a hard look. Rhian pushed her dirty cap to the back of her head. 'No,' she began, slowly. 'I'm talking about the accident with Rob and Laura.'

Maggie studied her face for signs of a hoax, but that wasn't Rhian's style. 'Alright, now you're scaring me.'

Her lips began to move but Maggie barely took it all in. The idea that her sister had been in some sort of car accident and no one had told her, shocked her to the core. Rhian had scant details, only that the police had contacted James the previous evening and he'd been at Bangor hospital ever since. Her legs carried her back to her car where she fumbled with the ignition and the clutch like a learner driver. The self-satisfied glow on hearing of Armstrong's demise, retreated to a dark place full of hissing snakes. The antisocial behaviour directed at Rob and herself might have stopped, but had it started somewhere else? The injury to Carla's horse was despicable. The unknown injuries to Rob and Laura were beyond comprehension and surely beyond anything merely antisocial.

James wasn't answering his phone.

Twenty-five minutes later, Maggie arrived at Bangor. Driving to the hospital was a routine she thought they were done with. She parked-up, pushed her way through the heavy revolving doors and the heat hit her full in the face. Immediately, her clothing felt heavy and furnace hot. The receptionist looked up with a benign smile and Maggie recited Laura's name and address. The woman clacked away at the keyboard.

'Laura Morgan-Jones... yes, she's on the third floor.

Partner's only at the moment, I'm afraid. Visiting is not until this afternoon.'

'But I'm her sister! Surely you can tell me something?'

'I'm sorry, I can't go into details.'

'Is her husband here, then?'

'I'm sorry, I've no idea.'

'Well, is there somewhere I can wait?'

'You can go up to the maternity unit.'

'No, no. That can't be right. She was in a car crash, last night.'

'Yes. She's been on A&E and now they've moved her onto maternity.' Then she stood up and flung her arm to the left. 'End of this corridor and take the lift to floor three. You'll find a waiting room by the cafe.'

Stupid woman. They must be short of beds. Maggie clomped down the over-heated corridor to the lift and hit the button for the third floor. She caught sight of herself in the reflective interior, still carrying her riding hat and gloves under one arm. *Stupid.* Another stupid woman asked if she'd been in a riding accident. She was deliberating on what to say at the intercom when she reached the inevitable locked doors onto the ward, when she saw James. He was sat in the cafe, arms stretched across the plastic table and playing with the salt and pepper. There was a cup of something in front of him but it looked untouched. He looked terrible, bug-eyed and unshaven. She trod heavily across the plastic space between them and pulled out a chair. It made a crude scraping noise across the tiled floor. He chose to ignore her.

'James. How's Laura?' she began, quietly. 'What the hell happened?'

His eyes flicked onto hers then disengaged almost immediately, although he considered her question carefully, as if there was more than one answer.

'I'm not sure I want to speak to you, not right now.'

'Why didn't you tell me Laura had been in an accident? I'm her sister!'

'And I'm her husband, sat here wondering why she's been rushed into a fucking operating theatre!'

Maggie's throat constricted and sweat began to trickle down her cleavage. 'I… Why? I didn't know she was pregnant.'

Just this once, she was desperately hoping he was going to say otherwise but he rose to his feet and leaned across the table. The liquid in the cup slopped over into the saucer and the condiment set fell over. Maggie glanced up at the counter, aware that they were attracting attention. A grey-haired woman in a pink overall stopped arranging cakes and stared right back. She looked ready to *shush* them, a plastic dome suspended in one hand and a pair of tongs in the other.

'Would that have made a difference?' James said. 'I *specifically* asked everyone to stay away from that *mess* initiated by your daughter.'

'That's not entirely fair!'

'Next thing I know, Hew Griffiths is shoving a copy of Armstrong's scrawl at me, and Laura is forced to tell me about some stupid *fucking* stunt you and Rob dreamt up.'

Oh, Lordy. She looked down at her hard hat, where it was jammed up against the table on her lap. Maybe she should have worn it. She had to breathe through her mouth because her nose was restricted and sweat was running down her face. Her thoughts fractured like a swarm of butterflies. She desperately needed to find some common ground, in the hope that James might start opening up to her. She went for her Big News, in the hope they could work backwards from that.

'He's been arrested. Armstrong has.'

He sat down again and searched her face for several intense seconds. '*For?*'

'Drugs. At Maine Airport.'

'Drugs? What about the manslaughter, and all the harassment?'

He had every right to be angry and confused. Maine was one hell of a distance away from Rowen and the current state of affairs, but if it served to remove Jess from his head-space, then at least she could be grateful for that.

'James, please talk to me. Tell me about Laura. What *happened?*'

For a moment he stared right through her, then he stood up and the chair went over backwards. Before she could say another word, he simply walked away from her, claiming he was saving every ounce of his energy for his wife. How could she argue with such logic?

She didn't remember driving home, but she must have done. There was another missed call and a text from Carla, but she had no idea how to respond. To her utter shame, she'd forgotten to enquire after Rob. How could she explain all of this in a text message? Maybe she needed to take a leaf out of James' book and save her energy for Pete and Ellie.

They arrived home by taxi, late afternoon. It took all of Maggie's resolve to pretend she'd had a wonderful ride across Conwy Mountain. Then it was what to have for dinner, although Maggie couldn't swallow anything and Ellie only wanted toast. They'd had a lovely day, Pete said, sailing down the River Dee and shopping in the trendy malls. Then they'd had lunch at the Italian place Maggie had recommended, the place she'd gone for her sister's birthday meal. She had to stifle a sob when she remembered Laura sticking to orange juice and getting ribbed for it, and those silly women prattling on about bloody parties and painting their nails. It reminded Maggie why she rarely went to such girly events. The curious observation had been the polite lack of interest from Laura. It was of course perfectly possible to grow out of people and drift apart but when she thought about it, there'd been something new and different about her for a good while. Not normally given to sentiment or those silly inspirational quotes about life, Maggie surprised herself by coming round time and again to the idea that Laura's serenity was best described as a woman who'd *found* herself. It made her heart bleed to think she may have lost it again. And it was torture not knowing the truth of this. Why wouldn't James talk to her? Was he so doubled-over with grief that he couldn't get the words out? The anger directed towards herself, Rob, and Jess, clouded everything. And it might feel inappropriate to even consider it at such a time, but their joint futures were surely ruined. All those hopes for a double family business that bound them together, had been blown apart.

During the domestic tedium of making cups of tea and finding the right jam for Ellie, Maggie continued to check her phone, put the butter in the oven and drop cutlery.

'Don't worry about feeding us, we're like a stuffed pizza crust, aren't we, Ellie?' Pete said, scrutinising Maggie's face at every opportunity.

She managed to keep grinning until Ellie had gone up to bed, then went about closing all the doors downstairs. Then she burst into tears. Huge, noisy sobs that had been held in for far too long. Pete wasn't at all surprised, and at first he was considerate. 'Is it the baby? It's happened, hasn't it? Has someone come forward for Krystal? Is that what Jess was phoning about?'

She kept shaking her head while he guessed half-a-dozen different scenarios, until he became annoyed with her hiccuping and nose-blowing.

'Spit it out, then!'

She spat it all out. The terrible, twisted truth about Pilates, Rob and Laura's accident, Laura's secret pregnancy, Armstrong's arrest.

Pete didn't interrupt. He seemed mostly speechless for a lot of the time although he did sigh a lot, and finally resorted to looking for the cheap left-over Christmas spirit at the back of the kitchen cupboard. He tipped the last of the cooking brandy into two glasses.

'You don't need me to tell you how stupid you've been, going round there to *talk* to him!'

'I don't care about any of that now. It's Laura I'm worried about,' she hissed. 'I don't even know what happened, Pete! Why didn't she tell me she was pregnant?'

He made a harrumphing noise at this. 'Well, I know what being kept in the bloody dark feels like.'

He fetched the laptop. It took only seconds to find an online report and he angled the screen towards her, so she could read it.

North Wales police were called to an incident during the evening of Friday 7th October, on the green lane connecting the village of Rowen in the Conwy Valley to the upper section of the Carneddau Mountain range. Two vehicles were involved in a collision. A witness said there were no headlights on either vehicle. Two local people were pronounced dead at the scene, and another three have been taken to Bangor hospital, one with serious injuries. Two youths, found running from the scene, were taken in for questioning. The accident followed continued reports of dare-devil driving at night along the single-track roads and bridleways in the area, some of which are highly unsuitable for motor vehicles. A spokesman for the Carneddau Trust said that the situation has become intolerable, causing irreparable damage to livestock and the Eco-system.

CHAPTER FOURTEEN

Laura

The dark pulse of the night bled into the bright nightmare of the day. Her sedated dreams were mostly of Enid. Her face would appear behind a windowpane, invariably crying or shouting and then she'd start banging on the glass or tugging at something Laura couldn't see; an external handle? The sensation of jolting over rough ground came again and again, until she got to the impact, followed by a feeling of floating. Everything hurt along her right side, her shoulder and her neck, even her foot. And Rob... Rob was on her right side too, but he was motionless. She was aware of them cutting him out of the driver's seat and then the passenger door was wrenched off. Someone with a soothing voice fixed an oxygen mask over her face. The landscape was eerie, lit only by the beams from emergency vehicles. The ambulance crew carried her over slippery, moss-covered rocks alongside a deep gully she'd not noticed before, since it was mostly shrouded by hawthorn and dense ivy. Then deep intense pain in her pelvis, so acute she must have passed out.

Enid had held her hand in the ambulance and informed the paramedic she was pregnant.

They still pumped her full of morphine.

A scan revealed that Jenna was ectopic. She was in the wrong place entirely. There was nothing to be done other than remove the microscopic embryo and the partially ruptured fallopian tube she'd been clinging to. The consultant explained the procedure but Laura couldn't comprehend anything. James dealt with all of it. Once they'd fixed her insides with an emergency operation, they set her ankle in a cast, issued her with a stiff surgical collar and set up morphine on a drip. Soon, she was running through the fields at home and Magenta was following her, skipping like a child and tossing his head with exuberance. His limbs looked so fragile and slender she was worried they might break. But it was her heart that was breaking. She invariably stumbled and fell and the pain pooled out of her onto the rough ground. Like pulling a sticking plaster off an internal organ. One grit of the teeth and it was done, gone.

The foal cantered on without her, blending easily into the dark pink of a strawberry sky.

When she stirred from her cocoon of drugged sleep, her eyes slewed drunkenly round the room. James was still there, but rather than find his presence reassuring, it merely reminded her that the last few hours had actually happened. Reality was somewhere she didn't want to be, something she wasn't ready to face. His hand found hers. He'd cried with her, and for her. He blamed Rob, he blamed himself. Enid blamed *her*self. Laura blamed no one.

She understood how exhausted James must be, but it almost added to her burden.

'What day is it?'

'Saturday night.'

'Where's Enid?'

'Her brother came back.'

'Have you seen Rob?'

'No.'

'But he is alright?'

'Concussion and a broken arm. Already discharged.'

'You're angry with him.'

'Dead fucking right I am.'

She sighed and fought back an unexpected rush of tears. 'Why don't you go home?'

He hunkered down. 'Laura, I *can't*. I can't leave you.'

'I want you to.'

She turned over awkwardly, feigning sleep. After a moment, she heard him pull on his jacket. He bent to kiss her, and smoothed back her dirty hair. The softness of his lips traced across her forehead, but she lay like stone. She could hear the mewing of newborn babies down the corridor and they continued to consume her thoughts. Jenna had been in the wrong place and now it seemed, so was she.

A couple of days later, the consultant gynaecologist read her notes and informed both herself and James that her emergency laparotomy had been successful. At first, Laura had no idea what he was talking about. Maybe she ought to have thanked him for saving her life, but any rational thought was suppressed by the overwhelming loss of someone else's life. This was her fault. She'd made a collection of cells into a person, identifying her with a name and a personality. Their unborn baby had quickly metamorphosed into a pretty, energetic child with dark hair. And now she had to grieve for the loss of this entire life and accept that Jenna would never exist, she'd never walk this earth. She'd never sit up on Nancy, she'd never hold Laura's hand or run through the meadows and kick up leaves. The imagery ran through her mind like the trailer to a romantic comedy. It was fanciful, full of feel-good moments which would remain forever out of reach. In her imagination, Laura stubbornly clung to her rose-tinted spectacles.

In reality, she must have looked spaced-out and sweaty, because James passed her a glass of water.

The consultant clipped her notes back onto the end of the bed. 'I'm happy to move you onto a general ward. I'm not expecting any complications, in fact you should be able to go home by the end of the week. You'll be pretty sore for a while, but four to six weeks should see you moving around normally,' he said, then seemed to specifically address James. 'She should be feeling much brighter by Christmas.'

Did he wish to reassure her husband that his Christmas dinner was safe? His choice of words grated; Christmas, brighter, successful. They were words associated with something else entirely and she could barely look at the tall, stooping man who'd ripped out a precious part of her insides and rendered them disposable. But it *was* a relief to leave the maternity unit, although the second she was deemed accessible and out of immediate danger, the police arrived to take a statement. Laura was no use to them. She couldn't remember any specific detail other than her desperate concern for Enid, a smoking car, and men shouting. Their uniformed presence brought a whole host of complicated emotions to play on her already over-burdened system. Her mind was full of unformed questions, her body completely empty. James recharged her phone but when she summoned the energy to look and saw that it was full of text messages from everyone; Rob, Enid, Carla and Lucy, she simply couldn't find the right words or the wherewithal to reply. And then when Maggie materialised in front of her, Laura discovered she was equally devoid of conversation. Her sister tended to encourage stiff upper-lip syndrome at the best of times but on this occasion they were both on unfamiliar territory. It was only towards the end of the week that Laura began to feel marginally less crushed and introspective. On occasion she even managed to be self-depreciating, although she recognised that this hardened attitude was merely a front to what lay beneath the surface. She hadn't shed nearly enough tears to rid her body of the trauma, but she couldn't find the key to release any.

On her second visit Maggie seemed hugely relieved to

see Laura sitting up. This was despite the still agonisingly sore operation site and the removal of the morphine drip. Her broken ankle was itchy beneath the cast and the surgical collar made her feel claustrophobic. She was meant to be back on solids but could still only face liquid nourishment, something she knew Maggie would be desperate to solve with homemade soup and special smoothies.

Her sister pulled up a chair and methodically began to empty a shopping bag containing a homemade lemon cake in a tin, an enormous bag of mint imperials, a book about making curtains, and a sturdy flask. No doubt it contained something blended and pureed.

'Now I've lined it all up it seems an odd collection of stuff,' Maggie said, trying to make room on the already crowded bedside cabinet.

'I can't move my head, so you'll just have to accept that I'm nodding in agreement.'

'I've phoned in every day, asking about you,' she said, then patted Laura's hand awkwardly, partly in admonishment. 'I didn't know you were pregnant.'

'And now I'm not.'

Maggie blanched at the sharpness of her tone. 'Was it a miscarriage, because of the crash?'

'No. It seems I would have imploded, regardless. The pregnancy was ectopic and the tube was partially ruptured. So, I'm down to one ovary and one set of tubes. And before you ask, if I accept defeat and resort to IVF then I risk another torsion down to the fertility drugs,' she said, then paused to draw a shaky breath. 'Are you opening those sweets, or are they just for show?'

Maggie frowned and drew her eyes away. She tugged so erratically at the bag of sweets that it split open and a dozen mints scattered noisily under the bed. While Maggie cursed and scrabbled around the floor, Laura reached for the tissues. Now she'd admitted as much, the steadily increasing odds stacked against her chances of ever conceiving naturally, came home with a violent blow. She wiped her eyes.

'Tell me what's going on,' she said, once Maggie had resurfaced. 'James won't talk about anything he thinks might upset me.'

'James is justifiably upset. And he's angry, especially with me and Rob. And I know you ended up having to spill the beans but I swear I had *no idea* Rob would send that note-'

'Maggie... I really, *honestly* don't *care* about any of that.'

'No. No, I don't suppose you do,' she said quietly, and glanced away with a sigh.

'Well?'

'Well... it's been on the local news. You almost had a head-on.'

'That other car, it came out of nowhere.'

'They were driving without lights and smoking wacky baccy.'

'So... who was in the other car?'

'Five of them altogether. Two dead. One of them was Gethin Griffiths and the other, a young lad from the village. The third fella's in here somewhere, in the hospital.'

'Not... Armstrong, then?'

'No, but he has been arrested.'

It took Laura a while to get her head around it all. Lying down and thinking occupied virtually all of her time when she wasn't trying to eat or sleep. If, in some twisted way, Armstrong had been halted in his tracks and the Griffiths had been halted in theirs, then this was surely the end? Nothing was more final than death, or prison. James couldn't continue to blame anyone for the loss of their child, it would have happened anyway. If she took that out of the equation, then a broken ankle and a strained neck was a small price to pay for peace. The real tragedy was for the mothers of those men who'd given up their lives over such a senseless act. She tried to use this information to give balance to her own grief, but it struggled to register. Nothing did.

James came to collect her on Friday afternoon. There was an overwhelming sense of deja-vu, although this time she'd been prescribed Methotrexate to help her body adjust to the hormonal upheaval. Other than that, she had a paper bag full of ordinary painkillers and the assurance that her stitches would dissolve of their own accord. Getting dressed was a marathon task. A bra was out of the question. James stuffed it back into the bag he'd brought and tried to pull a thick sweater over her head but the neck wouldn't fit over the surgical collar and so they had to abandon that as well. Removing the collar wasn't an option as her neck felt far too fragile to support the weight of her unwieldy head. She told James she felt like a wounded swan might, or the occasion when Alice-in-Wonderland developed a long neck and was mistaken for a serpent by a pigeon trying to protect her eggs.

He shot her a sad smile.

She made do with a shirt and a jacket. James wrapped the sweater untidily round her shoulders. The thought of walking to the hospital entrance assumed the equivalence of climbing Snowdon in a force ten, but James procured a wheelchair from somewhere and she sank into it gratefully. He parked her outside the pick-up area with his coat tucked across her and with a disgusting cap he'd found in the pocket – jammed on her head. It was only mid-October but her teeth began to chatter immediately and she felt nauseous at the thought of getting in and out of a car.

They travelled mostly in silence. Laura fixated on the drab coastal scenery, lit by the occasional splinter of sluggish light where it managed to pierce a grey sky.

She'd imagined the sight of home would at least be uplifting but once out of the car the cold, wide-open space made her feel overwhelmingly vulnerable. Where the colourful trees had once been beacons of light, they now seemed more representative of decay. She clung to James as she made the short painful hobble across to the house and into the sitting room. There was a good fire blazing and he'd made an effort to tidy up although she spotted her best hairbrush had been chewed, partially hidden beneath a bath towel on the floor. Washboy shot her a doleful look but Lamby wanted to jump all over Laura the second James lowered her onto the sofa and the dog had to be restrained.

On the coffee table, there was a pile of cards and a huge spray of expensive flowers, still wrapped in cellophane.

'From Rob,' he explained, then shrugged. 'I didn't get you anything.'

'Why would you?'

She caught hold of his hand and he looked down at her, completely lost.

'I don't need cards and flowers. What I'd really love right now is a soak, and to wash my hair.'

'A bath. Right.'

'I'll need a plastic bag. To put around my foot.'

'Plastic bag. Right.'

He trailed upstairs and presently she heard the thunderous gush of water into the bath. Then he came back down for her and they began the ridiculously slow pilgrimage to the bathroom. He helped remove her clothes. She'd almost stopped bleeding but it was still awkward needing help with such an intimate chore, although she should know better than to think James cared. The hot soapy water was bliss, although her scar was ultra-sensitive and it almost had her eyes watering if she went to twist her torso in any way. The surgical collar was insufferable, worse when it became sopping wet. It didn't help that her broken ankle had to remain completely dry. She propped it on the side of the bath in a heavy-duty carrier bag from the pet shop, strapped on with elastic bands. There was a faint odour of liver and bacon.

'Alice said goodbye to her feet, when her neck became elongated.'

'Then it was the pool of tears,' James said. 'She cried so much she almost drowned.'

'You won't let me drown, will you?'

He stripped off and climbed in. She lay back against him while he gently washed her hair. He remembered the conditioner, combing it through with her wide-toothed comb like he'd seen her do so many times. He rinsed her from head to one foot with the shower head, then helped her back out of the bath and onto a chair where he carefully, tenderly, dabbed her dry. Bundled up in fresh towels, she limped across the landing, noticing that the door to the spare room was firmly closed, then shuffled into the bedroom and found the hairdryer. He dried the surgical collar first which took almost twenty minutes, during which time her hair had exploded into something resembling a dandelion head.

'Curiouser and curiouser,' he said, and although her facial muscles responded to his quip, the core of her spirit lay dormant and brooding.

Finally, James admitted defeat. Laura switched off the drier and they both lay flat on the messy bed.

She felt for his hand. 'I love you. And not just for washing me.'

James sighed and rubbed his face, then stared at the ceiling. 'Last year it was me, and now you and… *this*. I don't know how much more you can take.'

'*We*. We can take. Fifty-percent each.'

'But I'm so tired of this… this *shit*.'

He sounded broken. Then he turned to her and cried.

Ten days later, the funerals took place of Gethin Griffiths and Alun Jones. The village talked of nothing else. The night driving stopped. There was talk of more robust horse-friendly gates and signs to be erected across some of the main bridleways, warning of prosecution to those who misused them. Details of the accident leaked out but people were kind, leaving flowers and gifts on their doorstep. Even Reverend Owen came to see them, wearing a voluminous distinctly non-horse-friendly cloak. James muttered something about Halloween and typically made himself unavailable.

'I'm sorry for your loss,' Owen said, clasping both of Laura's hands in his huge arthritic calloused ones, so there was no escape. 'What a terrible tragedy this has been for the village.'

'Thank you. Yes, it has.'

Eventually, he was defeated by her monosyllabic replies and bid her good day. It was a familiar scenario. Although her physical strength improved on a daily basis, her emotions remained trapped in a membrane. She was able to say the right thing, but she didn't *feel* anything or appear capable of normal mental capacity. Her sense of direction evaporated to the point of staring at the wall if she didn't force herself to think and move. The long-awaited-for photographs from Diamond Digital arrived but she had no motivation to even look at them, let alone suggest changes or choose the best images for the site. She purchased them all, thanked Mark Diamond for his time and expertise, then dropped the whole lot into a folder on her computer, and turned it off. James watched her, knowingly. It was testament to his own strengths that despite his initial grief, he didn't slip into one of his depressions and instead threw himself into work with great temerity on her behalf. This meant showing an active interest in the school, ensuring the local fly-ball team kept their promise on hiring the indoor space, and taking Lucy to her preliminary AI exam in Cheshire. They were gone all day, but returned home triumphant with a clear pass.

'Well done,' Laura said, knowing this reaction was as lame as her broken ankle. Lucy gave her a sad, curious look as if she were frustrated with her, as indeed most of her friends and family were. Liz, Maggie, and Rob, all rang to speak to her on a regular basis, but it was easy to fake normality over the phone. Her sister dropped Ellie at the top of the drive on Sunday afternoons and James always obliged, but Laura hated the estrangement and felt marooned and isolated from not being able to drive. Maggie regularly offered to pick her up so they could maybe go out somewhere. But Laura always declined, more often than not siting tiredness as her number one excuse. A lot of the time this was true, but the world had begun to scare her. Everything felt fraught with danger; the roads, the people, the mountains and the groaning sky.

The staff seemed equally lost. Ben, Lucy and Rhian were kind in their own way, but predictably awkward and distant. Enid was another matter entirely. She seemed upset at the very sight of Laura and offered help with the tiniest of chores. Laura couldn't decide if this was irritating, but then perhaps it was more accurate to say she was irritated with herself. The girl was obviously traumatised by being witness to the accident, and her beautiful eyes were mostly tearful and downcast in Laura's company. She knew Enid desperately needed some sort of reassurance from her, but Laura couldn't find the right balance between her tiny employer hat and the monster hat favoured by her mothering instinct which had grown into a wild, ugly shape.

Enid came out with her news while she was feeding the dogs in the kitchen. 'Gethin's got that job, the one down in Cornwall.'

'Oh?'

'Yes.' She looked round at Laura for a moment as if gauging her reaction, before turning back to scrape out the tin. 'We have to move in December, sometime. Gethin says there's nothing left for us up here.'

'I understand,' Laura said, knowing that her words were not only hurtful but they were woefully inadequate, and what she really wanted to do was to throw her arms around the girl and beg her to stay, *somehow*. It reminded Laura of the moment she'd told her father the exact same thing at the exact same age; that she was leaving the farm. It unearthed a whole host of child-parent issues, painful memories of hopes and dreams scrambled into her current situation, where her befuddled brain tried to make sense of it all. If she knew this, Enid would likely run a mile and think she was demented. As it happened Enid left her alone anyway, sorting through a tangle of saddle clothes and odd socks on the kitchen floor. She should have gone after her, but she simply couldn't face the torturous walk over the rough ground, or maybe this was the first sign that she was developing a phobia about venturing outside her own door. If so, she was in danger of going stir crazy on top of everything else.

Around lunchtime she heard the purr of Carla's Audi. Laura shrugged on a warm coat and braced herself to open the door. She needed to start talking to people. Carla had offered a listening ear or a lift to the pub since the week she'd arrived home, and it was another kindness she'd shamefully ignored. She took a hesitant step. The mild, blustery November air felt good against her skin despite the colourless day. Only black, skeletal trees and a few circling crows remained in sharp relief. The sky was like clotted cream, hanging low over their mud-infested fields and obliterating the Carneddau, land of the ponies. It was a full twelve months since the quad bike accident. This year, the round-up had seemingly gone without a hitch. James hadn't attended.

She progressed slowly, using an old walking stick to prod the sloping ground in advance. By the time she arrived at the loose boxes, Carla had Diva tied up outside and James was inspecting the damaged leg. The accident with the mare was yet another blow for the yard and when Rhian had shown Laura the horrible chunk of metal she'd likely lacerated herself on, her stomach had contracted. She felt terrible that this had happened on their land. To her untrained eye, the mare's knee still looked swollen and the wound continued to bulge and weep. Diva looked as dejected as Laura felt. She touched the warm neck and felt a glimmer of pleasure as the dark bay sheen of her coat rippled beneath her hand, and the mare's delicate muzzle explored her pockets.

'I really don't like the look of it,' Carla said to James, then sighed. 'You may as well know, I've called Rob. His partner doesn't exactly fill me with confidence.'

James shot her a dark look. 'Cancel him. We'll use another practice.'

'No can do,' Carla said, with her usual aplomb, and folded her arms. 'Since I'm paying the bills, I want the expert.'

Laura was less composed. 'James, for goodness' sake! When are you going to forgive Rob for giving me a lift? This feud is so childish.'

'Childish? He nearly fucking killed you!'

'You just want someone to blame.'

'I can think of several someones to blame, including some of your family, and Rob's still high on the list.'

'The bottom line is, I would have suffered a termination in *any* event,' she hissed. 'You *know* that!'

'He was driving without fucking lights!'

'And you know *why*.' She could cry with frustration, in fact she wanted to. 'We've been through this.'

Carla looked at them both with a sort of weary sadness and James turned away, but something stopped him walking. Something dragged his shoulders down and had him look heavenwards. Something had him turn to face them both. 'Alright. I admit this is stupid.'

'You do?' Carla said, as if he were a small child learning a particularly hard lesson.

He rubbed a hand through his hair. 'Yeah.'

Rob duly arrived in a hire car driven by his apprentice.

He gravitated towards Laura and crushed her in an awkward bear hug using one arm. His face bore the scars of several cuts and bruises and his right arm was suspended in a grubby sling.

'Jamie, look, mate… I don't know what to say.'

'See to the mare, will you?'

Rob hunkered down to peer at Diva's leg. 'We've got some granulation tissue building. I know it looks bad, but it is healing. It's amazing what the body can cope with,' he said, and risked a glance at Laura.

Under his instruction, Carla bandaged both forelegs – a support bandage on the mare's good leg – and turned Diva out into the indoor school with Tyler and Dorothy for company, in the hope of alleviating her boredom. James told Ben to keep an eye on them and dole out some hay.

'I'm worried she's going to chase about and tear it,' Carla said.

'With Tyler? Seriously?' James said, then indicated that Rob follow him. They moved towards the tack room, heads down in tense conversation. If she could balance without falling over, Laura might have high-fived Carla. 'Thank you. A small step towards normality, whatever that is and wherever it's gone.'

'It's been a ghastly time. How are you, really?'

'I'm going to try and make cottage pie.'

'Like a proper farmer's wife.'

'Only because James does most of the cooking. Sometimes I feel guilty and so I want to make an effort. It seems I can manage to follow a recipe, if it's simple.'

If Carla thought her response was pure self-pity or borderline snarky, then she chose not to show it. 'I've something I'd like to run past you. You gave me an idea, a while ago. About sponsorship for Lucy?'

'Right.'

'So I pitched it to the board, I hope you don't mind?'

'No.'

'I took the line that it's a show of good will in the local community, and Derek Wilson is always banging on about new promotional tactics. And…well, he said *yes!*'

'Great.'

'I can see the saddle cloths and rugs now… they'd be dark blue, of course, which would go terribly well on that palomino. Lucy Ford and Morning Song, sponsored by Marine Systems of Conwy,' she went on, her eyes sparkling. 'Naturally, I'd insist on gold lettering.'

'Goes without saying.'

'Do you want to tell her?' Carla said, and her face looked full of expectancy. 'She'll be so excited.'

'No, you go ahead. It's your shout.'

Carla narrowed her eyes thoughtfully and Laura trudged back to the house, head down against the breeze.

The removal of her plaster cast at Bangor hospital came as a welcome highlight. She flexed her distinctly smelly foot and wiggled her toes.

'All looks fine,' the consultant said. 'No high heels for a while, though.'

'I don't wear them. I just need to get my boots on.'

After this came an appointment with Doctor Wilson, but Laura managed to evade the critical subject of her mental health. Wilson examined her scar and removed the final stubborn couple of stitches, and then the blessed surgical collar came off. She gently manipulated Laura's head and neck.

'And how are you feeling in yourself?' she said, back at her desk and bringing up her medical records, no doubt reminding herself of Laura's extensive gynaecological history. It was perhaps the perfect cue to talk about her innermost fears, and an opportunity to inquire about IVF and get onto that precious waiting list. But if she talked about her inability to express her emotions about any of these things, she'd no doubt end up on antidepressants and be offered a course of counselling.

'I'm fine.'

Obviously, James was relieved about the physical signs of healing but they didn't talk about the real heart of the matter until they reached home.

Laura moved gingerly around the kitchen, determined to make leek and potato soup.

'Did the doc say what the prognosis is, I mean... long-term?' James began.

'You mean will I ever get pregnant again? I'd say my chances are pretty slim, wouldn't you?'

'So... this... IVF.'

Her pulse began to pound in her ears. 'What of it?' she said, scraping the potato peelings from the work surface and dropping them into the pedal bin. The lid snapped back down like the jaws of a piranha.

'Did you ask? Do you still want to try?'

'Do you?'

'Well, not right *now*... obviously. *Hell*, I don't know! Thing is... I don't know if I can watch you-'

'What? Go through another miscarriage?'

'There is that, yes. IVF's not straightforward, is it? It can be painful and unpredictable.'

'*Life* is painful, and unpredictable.'

'Laura... I'm just trying to talk to you about it, that's all.'

'Like you talk? You're allowed to go off and be quiet and miserable and cut people out of our lives and it's seen as a sign of strength-'

'Now you're talking complete and utter crap,' he said, and left the room.

He was right, of course. She tried desperately to cry, but nothing happened. Her body was a dry husk.

They simply didn't have stupid fights. Well, now they did.

She almost hated James for being so raw and honest and she hated herself for making him feel so obligated to her. Hated her *neediness* to be a mother. She knew what he was really saying. He was unsure if it was worth going through any more potential trauma after the last couple of years they'd endured. He wanted to consolidate their future, make it less uncertain and give her some hope. Remove the expectant pressure. And what did they have to offer a child, exactly? James was in his mid-forties with a spinal injury and she was irretrievably broken inside. She dreaded to think how many attempts she'd need to be successful at IVF. And if she was successful and managed to avoid the torsion problem, then the following nine months would be a living hell of anxiety. And yet she knew if she asked, James would agree to it. But therein lay the rub. He'd be doing it *for* her and not *with* her. If anything could make her feel a total failure, then somehow this did and it drove a wedge between them.

What was happening to them? She knew she had a decision to make, and it was perhaps the biggest decision of her life.

CHAPTER FIFTEEN

Laura

Mick sat opposite Laura at the kitchen table, his hands round a mug of strong black tea. The December rain rattled against the windows as she made out a pay slip for him and pushed the cash across the table. It seemed a pitiful amount of money for a grown man, and considering the time he spent helping them, Laura felt mildly embarrassed. James claimed that most of his wages went on his therapy sessions and that much of the time, Mick was simply hanging around and desensitising himself to the horses, or watching the buzzards.

Laura considered Mick's post-traumatic stress syndrome with more than a passing interest. He told her that the residue of his war experience not only manifested itself in random and inconvenient ways, it could be chronically disabling when he least expected it. The previous afternoon she'd come across him sat on the ground with his hands over his ears, in what looked to be a position of intense defeat. Cutie Pie had inspected the brim of his cap with an outstretched neck and a trembling muzzle, ears working like semaphore. The horse behaved like a parent might reach out to a traumatised child; concerned, but not really understanding the abrupt change of body language. Mick told her that his flashbacks from Afghanistan left him feeling more vulnerable than he had at the actual time of combat. Because he was a hulk of a man, it was difficult to apply the word vulnerable to him in any context.

'Have you found the sessions with James helpful?'

'Sure. I used to think maybe I should just admit to being bat-shit crazy and run with that.'

'And now you don't?'

'I don't know how or why, but the environment you've got here, well, it cuts into something I thought I had no control over, you know?'

She stirred her tea thoughtfully. 'I wish James could help me.'

'Too close? I hit the same wall with my ex.'

'Perhaps. So, tell me, what's the secret to breaking the code and living happily ever after?'

'The equine code? Patience, compassion, strong leadership, respect. All the same things you'd teach your kids, I guess. Your bloke says my connection with the horse needs to work like a conduit. Any anxiety I'm feeling is transferred to him, so I'm doing my darn best to control that and keep him nice and calm. For this to happen I need to show leadership skills. And if I can do that here, I can do it anywhere, right?'

'Right. Vulnerability, whether it's valid or not, is a terrible curse.'

'Pie had a real bad start in life and he's just looking for a safe haven, a buddy to show him the way without getting eaten, or beaten-up.' He considered Laura from beneath his bushy brows. 'My sister fosters kids. Now there's some *real* vulnerability, you know? Abused, abandoned-'

'Like some of our horses?'

'Well, yeah.' He paused to take a slurp of tea. 'Have you ever thought of offering some quality time out for these kids?'

She shot him a wry smile. 'Are you trying to offer me solace, Mick?'

'Would I patronise you? You're one intelligent lady. Both of you, you and Jamie are like one big beating heart. And I reckon real solace works like a conduit. In fact, I *know* it does.'

'That's kind of you, and I hear what you're saying. Truth is, I wouldn't know where to start. I think I've lost my mojo.'

He nodded sagely at this. 'We walked across the fields together the other day, me and that nutty animal. He could have kicked up his heels at any time. I've watched him tear round there like a Grand National winner, bucking like a bronc! But he *didn't*. He chose to walk *with* me,' he said, and curled his fist to punch the air. 'I felt like a fucking king!'

'I saw. You used to be so afraid of him.'

He drained his mug and placed it down, then drew the back of his hand across his mouth. 'Fear stops us from living.'

She thought Mick was partly right, but surely there was a fine line between facing fear for all the right reasons, and simply being delusional or foolhardy. Was it foolhardy to drive her car again? It was getting on for two months since the accident and her termination, but she'd had no real incentive to drive anywhere; until Enid asked Laura to cut her hair. She studied the mass of tangles framing the girl's face.

'I've got a better idea,' Laura said, and began scrolling through her phone. 'You and me, we both need a serious haircut.'

Enid looked mildly panicked at this. 'I've never been to a hairdressers.'

'They can deal with the dreadlocks,' she said, and paused. 'You do want to get rid of them?'

'Yes, but can't you just cut them off?'

'It would look a horrible mess if I did that! My treat, don't worry about the cost.'

She made a double appointment for mid-afternoon. At

the predetermined time, Enid sidled over to Laura's car in the gathering gloom, still wearing her muddy riding gear, although she'd hosed-off her boots. James was moving an enormous pile of used bedding to the manure heap and on seeing them both, stopped in his tracks.

'Where are you going?' he asked, taking in Laura's smart coat and her lipstick. She couldn't decide if he was mildly incredulous at her transformation or the idea that she was going out somewhere.

'The hairdressers.'

'Both of you? Right now?' he said, and dropped the wheelbarrow handles. 'Enid's meant to be working.'

She met his eyes, cross with herself for not taking the obvious into consideration. 'Uh, blast. I didn't think.'

'There's no point setting up all these dog-training sessions and extra lessons if there's no staff to-'

'I'm *sorry!*'

He considered this for all of five seconds and glanced across to Enid, but she continued to stare at the ground and wouldn't make eye contact with either of them.

'Alright,' he said, warily. 'No matter. Drive carefully.'

She did drive carefully, not managing to send the speedometer much above twenty-eight. By the time they reached Llandudno, it was fully dark and manically busy with a constant stream of traffic looking for parking. The wind-blasted decorations and the buskers reminded her of the previous Christmas, when she'd forced herself to shop while James lay in hospital. It felt as if they'd barely moved on, just shifted the cause of depression. She thought about Mick's words, and reminded herself of what she and James had and how rich they were in comparison to millions of other people. She knew all of this for a sure fact, but failed to feel it and nothing would ignite that illusive bubble of happiness which remained buried beneath a cloud of anxiety. She could throw in loss of self-esteem and femininity too, in fact anything that represented negativity could apply for residence in her heavy heart.

They walked in companionable silence for a while, along the blustery promenade to avoid the crowded bustle of the streets. The hotels were dressed for the season, promising Turkey and Tinsel, or Jingle Bells Bingo and half-price drinks. They passed families, couples arm-in-arm, and dog walkers throwing stones across the beach beneath the gentle illumination of the pier. A toddler ran down the narrow jetty and the raging, incoming tide clawed at his feet. For a second Laura thought she might have to run after the boy, but then a man quickly grabbed the back of his coat and swung him into his arms. The knot in her guts subsided, confirming – if only to herself – that she'd be a nervous wreck as a parent and any child of hers would be riddled with phobias in no time.

They left the seafront opposite the bandstand and walked the short distance down a side street. Laura pushed open the heavy glass door of *Waves,* and the junior came to take their coats and fuss with complimentary drinks and mince pies. Enid sat in the chair alongside and thumbed through a glossy magazine while her scalp was slicked with hair relaxant.

One of the stylists tucked a towel around Laura's shoulders and rummaged through a box of scissors. 'I'm Tanya. Is it just a trim, then?'

'Please. Take a good three inches off the length, will you?'

Tanya gently pushed Laura's head forward and began to gauge three inches of wet hair between her fingers. 'Doing anything nice for Christmas?'

'Oh… the usual.'

'Family time?' She inclined her head towards Enid. 'Your daughter is *so* pretty. You're lucky she only went for the dreads, though. My little sister did the works once; tats, nose studs, belly rings. Mum went ballistic.'

'She's not my daughter.'

'Oh, I'm sorry! It's just that you look so alike.'

The salon suddenly felt hot and claustrophobic, but at least the roar of several hairdryers limited conversation from thereon. Her trim took twenty minutes, but Enid was incarcerated for a good couple of hours. A lot of her hair did have to be cut out, but the resultant short bob – albeit still crinkly in part – was a complete transformation. Laura couldn't stop looking at her, and Enid couldn't stop looking at herself.

They travelled back to Rowen in a mildly triumphant mood. Since it was well past Enid's finishing time by then, Laura drove her home. She had mixed motives. Not only did she want to say farewell to Gethin, she wanted to witness his relationship with Enid. Laura hadn't set eyes on the accident site since the day of reckoning and she wasn't sure she ever wanted to, but other than a car-sized impression flattening the gorse and disturbing some rocks, there was little to see in the dark. Despite her initial reservations, it was a tiny step forward and a huge relief to confirm that the area held no catastrophic significance. Her headlights picked out nothing but the rock-strewn bridleway ahead, devoid of life. A splatter of rain hit the windscreen and made them both jump.

'How do the wild ponies survive out here? Our horses are so cosseted in comparison.'

'They've adapted to it,' Enid said, then twisted in her seat to look at her. 'Like, they have a really short cannon bone, shorter than most ponies.'

'Cannon bone?'

'That's the bit from below the knee to the fetlock. They'll never break it cantering over the rocks and stuff. It's how nature let them evolve.'

Maybe that's what she needed to do to survive; evolve. Could she evolve into the sort of childless woman that looked for other, selfless ways to be a mother? It had her in mind of Dorothy and Magenta and their simple need of each other, but Laura wanted more than to simply survive. Mick's incendiary-sized hint about fostering was akin to what everyone liked to suggest. That and adoption. She was unsure how she felt about these options; at the moment it felt desperate rather than a considered decision, and it troubled her that James wouldn't want this burden on top of their existing workload. His commitment to the RDA and the disabled riders who sought his expertise, already stretched him physically and emotionally.

She followed Enid down the muddy track towards the farmhouse, the ferocious wind cutting through her inadequate layers of clothing, although this time, it was considerably warmer inside and there was a welcome smell of something meaty simmering on the Aga. Everywhere looked distinctly spartan and the photographs had gone. The dogs leapt up, barked once, then pushed at her hands for attention. Gethin was surprised to see her, and even more surprised by Enid's appearance.

'Well, well, look at you, chwaer bach,' he said, ruffling her hair, then turning to Laura, 'You spoil her. Have you time for a pannad?'

'It's nothing. And no, no thanks to the tea. I just wanted to say good luck on the move. We'll miss you.'

'Yeah, it's been quite an upheaval,' he said, and began to tell her something of his new job and where they would temporarily live in Falmouth. He looked around the room with only a hint of reservation. 'All the sheep and most of the decent farm stuff has been sold, the tenancy agreement is finished and paid up to the end of the year. Just need to find homes for these two,' he said, indicating the collies. The dogs pressed themselves against his legs and looked up at him adoringly.

Enid glanced away.

The following morning, Laura opened the door to the redundant nursery and recoiled at the odour of trapped paint and varnish. She went to creak open the window and the wind rushed over Tal Y Fan's iced top and forced itself through the tiny gap she'd made. The dove grey curtains billowed frantically. Her mind suitably blank, she focused on packing the smaller items into a box, then sealed it with parcel tape and used it to wedge open the door. It looked very much like a brave, symbolic gesture. Then she logged-on to the fertility site to discover a couple of the women were concerned by her somewhat abrupt absence. She couldn't decide if it was cowardly to remove herself from the site without so much as another word, but she hit the delete key anyway.

Neither of these tasks had her feel especially brave.

Determined to at least be resolute and clear-headed for business, she opened the file for Diamond Digital. It was like browsing through a time capsule, a time when Jenna had still been with her. It took an almost super human effort to put these feelings aside. But then she gasped at the way Mark had captured the iridescent light spanning through the trees, and the shots of Enid and Magenta were simply breathtaking. The way he'd expressed the personalities of his subjects – horses included – was exactly as she'd hoped. Unable to resist then, she experimented with the material on her partly-built website, loving the panoramic header and the black and white shot of James, oblivious to the camera as he worked with a cantering horse. The grey gelding was slightly out of focus, the background blur adding a sense of movement. Lucy and Song looked so full of life and colour. She added the shots of Ben and Rhian to their respective sections, then removed Enid from the copy she'd already written up. It seemed pointless including her as part of the team. This both saddened her and frustrated her ability to move on, and she closed the laptop with a definitive click, but she'd made a start. It was painful, but it was progress.

Outside, it was relatively benign for a December day. Any snow and ice was firmly relegated to the Carneddau summits. James and Rhian had gone on a rare outing to an equestrian supplies show in Chester. Lucy was teaching in the indoor school, leaving Enid to brush the yard, wash-out feed buckets and answer the phone. Ben was changing the oil in the horsebox, although he still managed to distract Enid whenever the opportunity arose.

The majority of the horses were turned out, browsing the sparse pasture. Closer to home, some of the children's ponies were stabled and waiting for after-school lessons, including Peaches, the pony on which Laura had learnt to trot and change direction. It was no mean feat that she'd already outgrown Tyler, and no longer considered herself a complete beginner. She was an *improved* beginner, and this was surely proof that she'd been fearless in the none too distant past. It helped that Peaches didn't take a blind bit of notice of her fumbling ineptitude when she frequently got it wrong. James maintained that if Peaches could talk she'd say, *whatever*, to virtually every question. 'Left here? Oh, you mean *right*? Okay… w*hatever*.'

Laura walked into the tack room and her guts turned over when she looked at the saddle and bridle allotted to the pony.

Without overthinking the idea, she located her riding hat, hooked the tack over one arm and picked up a clean saddle cloth. Moving purposefully, she balanced the saddle on Peaches' stable door, slid back the bolt and moved inside. She got as far as positioning the saddle cloth onto the mare's back and lowering the saddle onto this, when Enid's face appeared over the half-door.

'Laura… what are you doing?'

'Tacking up. Help me with this, will you?'

Enid shuffled inside and shot her a curious look before

repositioning the saddle, then finally securing the girth for her.

'Right. Now, show me how to put the bridle on.'

'Is there someone coming to ride her?' Enid said. 'Only, there's nothing in the book and Lucy's busy with back-to-back lessons till five.'

'No, *I'm* riding her,' she said, fastening her hat on before she bottled out.

They crossed to the mounting block and Enid assisted in holding the pony while Laura hauled herself into the saddle and took up the reins. 'Help me with the stirrups, will you, please?'

Enid adjusted the stirrups to the right length for her and tightened the girth again. 'Do you want me to walk with you?'

'No. No thank you. Could you open the gate, please?'

This was met with a worried frown. 'But where are you going?'

'Probably not very far.'

'She's not used to being ridden out on her own.'

'Neither am I.'

Exasperated, Enid walked over to the gate and held it open. Peaches needed more than a little encouragement to go through it with only Laura in command. Enid passed her a short riding crop and this seemed to reinforce the idea, momentarily. The pony walked forwards along the track for all of three minutes, then stopped dead, head up, ears twitching, testing Laura's mettle. Determined that Peaches wasn't going to beat her, she nudged the pony forwards with her heels, then when this didn't work tapped her lightly with the crop. Peaches grudgingly obliged. They resumed their tentative amble with the mare stumbling over the potholes because she was more interested in looking for an opportunity to turn round and trot back home, or check out anything edible in the hedgerow. Laura shortened her reins, as Lucy had shown her.

When they came to the end of the lane, Peaches obliged by positioning herself by the gate to the bridleway. Laura hesitated, knowing that the horses often cantered there on the soft loam of the forest floor as it climbed gradually towards the foothills of Tal Y Fan, beyond which was miles of open hillside. The alternative was to pass through the other distinctly *non* horse-friendly gate out onto the road, which led through the village. She was undecided which route seemed the least terrifying.

'Okay, so we can talk about this. How about we take the high road, but at a walk?'

Whatever...

She leaned across to pull the handle and the pony moved back obediently as the gate easily swung open. They passed through the narrow entrance calmly, although closing it presented a major conundrum. If she turned Peaches round to face the gate, she might rush back through it and cause an accident. The reins might get caught over the post and Laura might get scraped off, dragged, even! Against her better judgement, she left the gate swinging open and nudged the pony onwards, trying to free her mind of imagining the worst-case scenario at every turn. How could she be this feeble? And she'd already been through the worst possible scenario of her life when she lost Jenna. In a perverse way, this thought emboldened her to carry on.

It was gloomy beneath the trees. The woods were mostly bare tree trunks, ghostly in the dim afternoon light. A flutter of wings and a clucking pheasant suddenly took flight from the undergrowth, startling them both. Peaches pricked her ears and quickened her step, her metal-shod hooves clinking and scraping on hidden rocks. They jogged up a slight incline and the uneven ground had Laura pitch forwards at Peaches' uneven gait, but she grabbed a handful of mane and they reached the modest summit at the viewpoint, more or less in unison. The pony came to a natural halt, blowing slightly. The tops of the fir trees fell away and the Conwy valley stretched before them in a misted blur. Rowen was nestled below, defined by the church spire and several acres of farmland dotted with sheep.

She felt confident enough to put the reins into one hand and pat Peaches' warm neck. 'Result!' It was the sort of comment Simon used to make when they'd secured another deal or made a profit on one of their properties. She'd been full of confidence then; before she'd become pregnant by mistake, changed her mind about an abortion and then suffered a miscarriage anyway. And ever since, she'd tried to reclaim that lost ground, with James. She'd become worn down and worn out and something needed to change, to *evolve*. Riding Peaches might be a small achievement in the grand scheme of things, but it was proof that her body wasn't completely washed-up. And what right did she have to feel sorry for herself if she could do something like this? Her concentration and the physical exertion had removed all thoughts of Jenna from her thoughts for almost half-an-hour, allowing the decision forming in her mind to gather momentum in a way it had struggled to before.

James deserved the best of her.

The moment Laura turned for home, Peaches came to life. Where the previous uphill sections presented themselves as downhills, the pony broke into a fast trot. There was barely time to think. She fumbled to gather up the reins but only succeeded in dropping the crop and losing a stirrup, followed by two seconds of panic before she hit the ground. She may even have shouted out. As falls from moving horses go, slithering off the side of a child's pony was pretty much small fry. Although she clung to this perspective, it still came as a shock to find herself winded, flat on her back and staring at the clouds. A red kite passed between a gap in the tree tops, and screeched. The wet ground, disguised beneath a deep bed of leaves and pine needles – the residue of summer –

soon began to seep through her fleece top. Unconcerned, Peaches watched from a few feet away, chewing frantically.

Laura clambered gingerly to her feet. Other than the accumulation of mud and some deadly brambles, she was pleased to discover herself alive and relatively mobile. She even managed to take hold of the trailing reins as Peaches suddenly flung up her head, startled at the sound of hooves thudding towards them. Hidden at first by the undulating ground, Song's golden coat appeared as a bright flash of colour advancing towards them. Enid slid breathlessly to a halt, then jumped down with the ease of a seasoned jockey. She moved tentatively towards Laura and weighed up her appearance.

'Oh, my God! Did you come off? You did, didn't you? Are you alright?'

'Is it that obvious? I'm *fine*. Other than sustaining a massive dent in my pride, although it's probably not as big as the bruise poised to erupt on my backside,' she said, dusting her hands. 'I'm alright! Come on then, give me a leg up.'

'Are you sure?'

'Well, I'm not walking back.'

Enid looped Song's reins over her arm and did her best, but Laura was a useless pupil and failed several times to get back into the saddle. Enid was soon covered in mud as well from grasping Laura's filthy attire in trying to hitch her back on. They resorted to finding a suitable rock or a sturdy tree trunk for Laura to stand on. These were invariably covered in algae and moss and she slipped off most of them, or Peaches chose to move the second she put her foot in the stirrup. Eventually, the sheer farce of it had them giggling, then laughing until they couldn't see what they were doing for crying. It was a safety valve close to her buried emotions but she kept a handle on it, for Enid's sake.

'Why am I so pathetic?' she said, wiping her eyes.

'You're not. You're really brave.'

They walked, leading their respective mounts back towards the gate, the silence broken only by the pipping of blackbirds signalling the approach of dusk. Cold, and fully sobered by then, Laura found the wherewithal to clamber back onto the mare by utilising a dilapidated picnic bench as a mounting block.

'Thanks for coming after me,' she said, once safely back in the saddle.

Enid studied her solemnly.

As they drew closer to home, she could see James watching their progress as Song and Peaches walked out side by side along the track. It came to her that not only was her escapade similar to the circumstances surrounding the fatal accident that Carys had befallen, but she'd managed to lure Enid away from her chores yet again. By the time they clattered into the yard and Lucy came to take the pony from her, James had moved inside the house and her fragile spirit plummeted. She steeled herself to follow him, her adventure hitting home as her aching joints and several bruises made themselves known. There was even a rock-shaped dent in her hat, although thankfully not in her head.

She kicked off her boots and left them outside before padding down the hallway.

James was in the kitchen, his outline silhouetted against the window.

'I'm sorry I bamboozled the staff again,' she said, irritated by his brooding stance. She took a bottle of wine from the fridge and glugged a third of it into a glass, then waved it around like a belligerent teenager, willing him to challenge her. 'I had some stuff to think about.'

He licked his lips, clearly unsure of her intent. 'Laura, I'm… I'm just worried that-'

'What?' she snapped. 'That I'm losing my mind? That I'm using Enid as a daughter substitute?' she said, then gulped down some of the wine. 'Well, she's leaving soon so you don't need to worry on that score.'

'That's *not* what I wanted to *say!*' he said, loudly and emphatically. She paused to look into his face, and was shocked to see an isolated mirror of her own sadness. She'd willingly taken his love then frozen him out and used him as a mental punchbag for her anger. And then it finally happened. A gushing river of undiluted tears. They streaked through the mud on her face and when she drew a hand across her eyes, discovered there was more mud fringing her eyelashes. James removed the wobbling glass from her hand and pulled her into the sanctuary of his body, her dirty face crushed against his chest.

Eventually, when the tears abated and she'd stopped shaking, he said, 'I was worried you might be heading for a nervous breakdown.'

'And now you're not?'

'Not quite so much. It's just… you wouldn't let go.'

'I *couldn't.*'

He searched her swollen eyes carefully, placed the glass of wine back into her hand, and led her to the sofa in the sitting room. She twisted round to face him, waiting until she had his absolute attention. How could she make him understand that her decision was not the result of any cowardly backlash or foolhardiness, but one of bravery.

'I've come to a decision.'

'About?'

'I'm not sure I want to try again, to conceive. I can't face IVF because… because I'm not sure it's worth the price we *might* have to pay. James, I want to live in the *present*, I want to move on with our plans rather than live in an uncertain future, one which might ultimately destroy everything, destroy *us.*'

His response was slow and considered. 'We need time to think about this, don't we?'

'But I don't *want* to think about it, anymore! I've simply decided to accept it.'

'Accept what?'

She swirled the wine in her glass before meeting his eyes. 'That we'll not be parents without a huge, undefined sacrifice. That I'll probably never be a mother.'

'You don't have to give birth to be a mother.'

The last thing she wanted from James was placatory sentiment, and yet she knew his words spoke the absolute truth. His response was especially indicative of his own true feelings. She risked a direct question, her senses on high alert. 'Is this about Enid?'

'It could be.' He sighed, then sat back against the sofa cushions. 'Her brother's renting two rooms in a B & B and working six days a week on a building site.'

'Yes, I know. What sort of life is that for an eighteen year old?'

'She's *sixteen*, not eighteen.'

'She talks to you.'

'And she looks up to you. Laura, you *need* something from each other.'

'What can we do?'

'That's simple. Ask her to stay here, with us.'

They made love for the first time in months.

Both of you, you and Jamie are like one big beating heart.

CHAPTER SIXTEEN

Laura

Christmas felt poised to happen. Her sister issued an invitation to Christmas dinner, but James wanted their first Christmas together to be at home, and Laura readily agreed. They compromised by negotiating Christmas Eve lunch instead. Pete and Maggie were more than happy to go along with any arrangement since James had given the full go-ahead for the holiday project. He recommended they start after Easter in order to allow plenty of time to work out the logistics and ride the proposed routes. There were several new gates across the Carneddau, prohibiting the use of motor vehicles and improving the safety for those on foot, or riding the bridleways. The possibility of riding for a full day without touching on too many roads turned their idea into a real, viable prospect.

They were to take a trip to Ireland after New Year in order to take in a couple of sales with a view to buying new horses for the holiday venture, and to visit their respective parents. Laura knew that James had partly sanctioned all of this as a means of keeping her occupied and although the sadness buried deep in her core was probably never going to completely heal, it did help that both families were pulling together to make something positive happen out of the ashes. Business was how Laura thrived, and James had finally given her free rein to do that. In respect of this and since her sister's house was beautifully decorated for the season, she'd arranged for Mark Diamond to take some interior shots of Hafod House.

The allotted afternoon was dismal with low cloud and the promise of sleet on the wind, but this time it hardly mattered. Maggie handed round the mulled wine for a second time.

'Are you up for some route planning, Maggie?' James said, swapping his warm wine for a bottle of cold beer.

Her sister looked dumbfounded. 'Me?'

'Yeah. I can't ride for long these days. You and Rhian can go and work out some trails, if you're up for that?'

'Absolutely.'

'We'll be needing a tail-end Charlie, eventually. It'll be a non-paid job, but might you be up for that as well?'

'Try and stop me!'

Laura shot her husband an appreciative smile, and Maggie took Laura to one side.

'I can't believe we're actually doing this! But how about you? Are you fully recovered?'

'Physically, yes, apart from the odd twinge. The rest of it is… calmer. Down to acceptance, I think. How about you?'

'Oh, you know. We've not heard a word from Jess, can you believe it? Pete thinks it's because Krystal's gone, or at least someone's come forward.'

Laura agreed, but refrained from saying as much. 'Is she not coming home for Christmas, not even to visit?'

Maggie pursed her lips. 'Fat chance. I think we must be last on her Christmas list. She probably doesn't want an ear bashing. Last we heard was that Sam wanted to go somewhere hot, so it doesn't take much working out, does it?'

Laura squeezed her sister's arm and they smiled at each other, understanding their respective positions on the art of disappointment. Laura went on to explain their stalled, possibly permanently redundant baby plans, and about Enid. Her sister was only mildly surprised. 'I know it's Christmas but I don't blame you for not wanting to sign up for turkey basting-'

'You mean IVF.'

'Yes, that. And you and James need some time and space to yourselves.'

'And that's what we fully intend, although I can't deny I'm nervous about offering Enid a home. Will she think we're desperate, or just plain crazy? I sometimes think we might be both.'

'If she's any sense she'll snatch your hand off!' Maggie said. 'That brother of hers won't object. Sooner or later, having his little sister along will only cramp his style. She'll be much better off with you.'

Her reasoning was entirely logical but Laura wasn't nearly so confident. Gethin was Enid's only blood relation, and at the end of the day, family was maybe more important to her than anything she and James could offer. They had the weekend to broach the subject before Enid departed for Falmouth. Laura hinted that they should perhaps approach Gethin first but James disagreed; he wanted to gauge Enid's feelings without anyone's influence.

'And if she says no, then we think of other ways to assuage whatever it is we want to do.'

She loved the way he said, *we*.

And she knew it might jinx everything, but she'd already begun forward planning. The old baby room would be her new office space, meaning Enid could take the larger room downstairs. Ben had helped her shift the sofa-bed into there temporarily, just in case. Apparently, there was a send-off party planned in the staff caravan which, according to Ben, consisted of several weeks' supply of junk food and cheap cider. Rather than spoil any fun it was decided between James and herself to let this go ahead before they said anything, because there was every chance Enid *would* actually leave. It was difficult to separate yet another expectation of failure to one of common sense, and she often had to remind herself that Enid was not her child to worry about. Nevertheless, her nerves were frayed. She looked down into her cooling drink and gave the floating slices of fruit a desultory stir.

When she looked up, James caught her eye. He shot her a smile, a real smile that crinkled the corners of his eyes.

He looked especially relaxed and handsome in clean denims and a white shirt, which as far as he was prepared to go in terms of dressing up. But then she hadn't wanted anything too formal for the photographs. Pete provided more than enough gravitas in his full chef whites, and Maggie wore her black and white wedding outfit again, pleased to have yet another occasion to show it off. Laura had opted for smart casual in dark denim and a fitted wool jacket in an effort to balance out their opposing styles.

Mark Diamond ushered them together for a group photo, and they assumed positions on either side of the fireplace. The room looked both opulent and comfortable with the long dining room table set for dinner, and a fire crackling in the grate. A traditional tree bedecked entirely in silver, complimented the dark wood and the powder blue walls. That done, Mark and his assistant carried all the lighting equipment upstairs to the best bedroom. Maggie suggested they toast their combined future success.

They clinked glasses. It was a happy day.

A lot later, when they were lying coupled together in bed, the landline phone rang. They'd been making plans about Ireland and laughing at the lingering bruise on Laura's backside. James persuaded her to leave the phone, and she nestled back into his body.

'Peaches, huh?' he said, head propped on one hand. 'You'll be throwing a saddle on Mal next week and galloping off into the sunset.'

'You're clearly hallucinating.'

The answer machine kicked-in after five rings and Sam's voice boomed out into the hall.

'Hi, Dad, Laura. Just to say, er… well, happy Christmas! I'm er… I'm going to Havana for a couple of weeks. So you can probably expect to receive some cigars in a posh box.'

James murmured, 'Treating Jess to a nice holiday now, is he?' Laura pressed a finger to his lips.

Sam cleared his throat. 'Thing is, I've met someone. Would you believe she's from Cuba?' A huge sigh. 'Look, you may as well know that I'm done and finished with Jess. After *everything* me and Mum have done to try and help her… I can't *believe* what she's…' He trailed to a halt. 'Anyway, I'll try and speak to you both soon, all the best.'

He disconnected. James tried three different contact numbers, but Sam didn't pick up.

Saturday blew in cold and wet. Where once upon a time a lot of their planned riding would have been cancelled, the indoor school was fully booked. It sported an eight-foot spruce decorated with a clashing array of colours and their sound system belted out a medley of festive hits. Lucy and Enid had organised a Christmas gymkhana for the younger regulars and the place was packed to the rafters with children and parents. There was barely room to sit at the spectator end of the school, and the vending machine was out of hot chocolate within the hour. Other than Dorothy letting the side down, there was an appreciative buzz. The ewe had behaved well initially, and some of the children had enjoyed taking selfies with her, but when Dorothy's patience ran out, her revenge was to butt them over like ninepins. Ben eventually persuaded her back outside with a trail of milk pellets.

If only human revenge was so easily diverted and resolved. They talked about Sam's phone call as thoughts occurred to them. Laura's initial reaction had been the need to inform her sister of this development, but James was more cautionary. 'All we *know* is that Sam's come to his senses.'

'No, there's more to it than that. Sam going off to Cuba with another woman is hardly upholding their image of a happy marriage.'

'Yeah, well, that wasn't going to last, was it?' he said. 'My bet is that baby-free Jess has met someone new and has no need for Sam. And Cuba is Sam's reaction to her... I dunno, her usual selfish behaviour.'

'Aren't you tempted to call Stella?'

'Nope. I'm tempted to forget all about it,' he said, then when she frowned in an agony of indecision, gently took hold of her shoulders. 'Laura, there's no point in speculating. Why upset Pete and Maggie when there might be nothing in it? And if it is all about to crumble, then Jess can do her own dirty work.'

She reluctantly agreed. The last thing she wanted to do was spoil what was starting to be a truly happy and settled time between them all.

And overriding everything, filling her every other thought, was Enid.

Laura looked across to where she was busily organising children into teams. Unlike Dorothy, the ponies had little objection to selfies, or being kitted-out with musical antlers and tinsel. Even Nancy stood patiently while all the non-riding brothers and sisters sat on her back, or plaited her tail. Enid had saved Nancy's old shoes, sprayed them silver and threaded heather and other trailing greenery through the nail holes. They'd intended these as booby prizes, but for some reason known only to himself, Ben was wearing them like an African necklace and was now struggling to remove one in order to present Ellie – last in the egg and spoon race – her longed-for prize.

'You *idiot*, why have you put them round your neck?' Lucy said, twisting them every other way.

'Ow! Watch it, Luce! They were getting nicked, that's why. I reckon these kids are all coming in last on purpose.'

Enid rescued the situation by greasing Ben's neck with saddle soap.

Laura watched the scene with amusement and a quiet sense of achievement. She had a notebook to hand, and she'd already made a list of regulations they needed to check, including first-aid training for the staff and how to correctly handle the fire extinguishers. Save old shoes, buy a stock of silver spray paint, and ribbons. If she allowed her mind to drift, she'd fixate on the children and their parents, which was perhaps no bad thing. If Mick needed to desensitise from horses by being with them, then there was no harm in applying the same principle. She spotted Pauline Ford in the crowd. When Lucy and Song won the clear round jump-off against the clock, Laura noticed she got to her feet and clapped. She even lifted a hand in greeting to Laura. No doubt it helped smooth the way that Lucy and Song were fully funded by Marine Systems and wore their new dark blue monogrammed attire with pride. Laura made another note to include the information somewhere on the website.

Carla snapped the red rosette moment on her phone and declared she was sending the photo to all the board members.

'I know it's only a home comp, but if I told them we were at Olympia they'd probably believe me.'

They laughed, congratulated a beaming Lucy and walked outside together, crossing quickly to Diva's loose box in the heavy rain. Rob was making his last visit to assess the mare's torn leg. The laceration looked a lot less angry with new, pink skin forming over the wound, although Rob warned it would leave a scar. Laura couldn't help but compare Rob's inspection to her own current condition.

'A scar? I thought it might.' Carla's shoulders drooped and she wrinkled her nose. 'Is she fit to ride?'

'Yeah, but take it easy.'

'How? She's been flying round the fields like a demon.'

'You know the score. Lunging first, build up those weakened muscles and take some of that silly jinx out of her.'

'Talking of a silly jinx, I guess I need to brace myself for your invoice, now,' she said to Rob. 'I dread to think what two months of visits and all her jabs and dressings have come to.'

'On the house. Call it a Christmas pressie.'

'Are you *serious?*'

'Carla, that chunk of metal got in the field more than likely due to my crude attempt to play the Good, but kind of twisted Cop.'

'And if he hadn't have waived it, I'd have paid it for you,' Laura said. 'I'm so sorry it happened in the first place.'

She stood back and looked at them both, hands crossed on her heart. 'What truly smashing friends I have.'

Despite the extra work created by the gymkhana, the horses were fed and bedded down as usual by six o' clock and their four staff incarcerated in the caravan. The red curtains were closed and a thumping beat sounded across the yard.

Gethin was collecting Enid an hour later, for the last time.

Their evening meal was conducted in silence. Laura finally placed her cutlery down. 'When do you think we should go over?'

'Ten to seven,' James said. 'Bring her to the house and we'll ask her then.'

Ten minutes seemed too short to devote to something so serious, but Laura didn't have a better idea. She pushed her plate away and drained her glass of wine. Enid's final wages were in a packet on the table along with some holiday pay, and a gift; a framed photograph of Enid and Magenta, carefully wrapped in tissue and Christmas paper.

When she did finally run across to the caravan she found Ben and Lucy to be predictably rowdy. As usual, Rhian looked as if she were attending a funeral and Enid appeared to have been crying, as well as laughing. She was certainly bewildered by all the attention. There was a wonky cake, decorated with dark-coloured icing and topped with a plastic foal. It was a hideous concoction, but Enid soaked-up the camaraderie in much the same way Laura always did. Ben and Lucy kissed Enid goodbye and wished her good luck. Rhian raised a hand. Laura's heart leapt in her chest as if it were loose. It beat painfully. It beat for her lost babies and for this sweet, unblemished teenager who walked alongside her, carrying left-over cake.

Once inside, Laura handed over the wages and the present. James asked the question.

Enid looked from one to the other, then began to speak quickly in Welsh. She and James continued to converse in their mother-tongue, while Laura sat glued to her chair, staring at their dirty dinner plates. It was obvious the question overwhelmed the girl, and obvious that the answer was no. It was plain to see in her uncomfortable body language. Her eyes avoided Laura, they may even have flicked to the kitchen clock. And then a pipping horn signalled Gethin's arrival. Enid picked up the present and her packet of cash with a shy smile and they all moved outside, Laura holding a coat over her head against the rain. Enid's brother came out of his van to shake hands and wish them both a happy Christmas. Then they were gone.

She waited until the red tail lights left the end of their drive, before closing the front door. Stupidly, she stared at the letterbox in an effort to compose herself.

'So, tell me,' she said, turning to face James. 'What did she say, exactly?'

'Just that…' He shrugged and ran a hand through his wet hair. 'She had to be with her brother.'

Laura wasn't sure if this was a full account of their conversation, but she really shouldn't have been surprised by the answer. Given her initial speculation and her grown-up sensibility, it hurt more than it should have done. She rested her forehead against his chest and squeezed her eyes shut.

A week later, Christmas Eve rolled in damp and mild with a blustery wind. They decided to close for three days. Along with Rhian, who had no interest in Christmas or its family connotations, they managed the basic yard jobs between themselves. Mucking-out, filling water buckets and stuffing hay nets, gave Laura less time to think about Enid. She'd forced herself to add another consideration to her master list: advertise for more staff, with the proviso she was not to conduct any of the interviews. James was far more astute at gauging what they needed. He looked for something she couldn't possibly see or feel. It was something connected to the Welsh hills, Laura felt sure. Her father called such feelings, *hiraeth*. Whenever he spoke of it, he invariably thumped his chest and stared just beyond her shoulder, as if someone was standing behind her. This had alarmed her as a child and although Laura had looked up the word numerous times, it didn't fully translate into English. Her father maintained it was connected to the mountains and it was about grief, a longing for those who'd gone. Given its pre-Ice Age history the Carneddau represented centuries of grief and hardship, life and death. James said it was a kind of homesickness, a nostalgic yearning for the land in a way that could only be understood by those who'd been touched by its spirit.

Maggie always said it was an ambiguous word and meant whatever you wanted it to, usually something miserable.

Under the guise of last-minute shopping, and very much under the influence of hiraeth, Laura took a detour to Penrhiw Uchaf. She left her car at the usual turning place and climbed out. It was at least two degrees colder than down in the village and she pulled her scarf up across her face and stuffed her hands in her pockets. She stumbled past the pigsties and the broken equipment, to the front of the house where the barn looked ready to collapse. A token glance through the dirty window of the farmhouse confirmed that it was indeed uninhabited. Had she really expected to see Enid camping in there? It was empty. And yet it wasn't, not completely. Something lingered, a sense of something they'd both shared if only for a brief time, something which slipped back a generation to those they'd lost, and beyond. It was embedded in the stones, the peeling wood of the window frames and the blackened fire.

She turned and lifted her eyes to the low clouds obscuring Pen Y Castell and Foel Fras, and the wet ground sucked at her feet.

Life, is painful and unpredictable.

Head down against the wind she trudged back to where she'd parked the car and sat inside for a moment, letting the full force of the crosswinds buffer the vehicle, before turning the key in the ignition. She drove a mile to the local post-office cum off-licence and purchased two more treat-filled stockings for the dogs, a fresh marrow bone, and a bottle of vodka for Rhian. On her arrival home, James cast a shrewd glance across her mud-encrusted boots and her scorched, tear-dashed complexion.

They dressed for lunch. As she looked into the full-length mirror to adjust her dress, James curled an arm around her waist.

'I'm fine,' she said. 'I *will* be. I *know* I will.'

He studied her face, and his olive eyes practically opened her sore heart to look inside.

'You saw yourself, in Enid.'

She nodded and swallowed over a huge lump in her throat. 'Something like that.'

She had on occasion in the past, cursed her husband's almost psychic ability to understand her innermost thoughts better than herself, but there was tremendous comfort in that unity, and they travelled to Hafod House in a lighter mood than she could have hoped for. Pete and Maggie were in good spirits too, although Laura had to stop her sister switching off the radio every time a song came on about the birth of Jesus.

'After last Christmas, I just want everything to be perfect, and I know how sensitive you are.'

'I'm not *that* fragile,' Laura said, and indicated the crate of wines James had lugged in from the car. 'Let's open one of these.'

While Maggie fussed with her best glasses and her Johnny Mathis CD, Laura slid gifts under the tree. They'd bought two pairs of jodhpurs for Maggie, a new riding hat and another one of Nancy's shoes – heavily customised for Ellie – and a coffee grinder for Pete. Maggie told her that Ellie was ensconced in her bedroom with Willow, pizza, and a selection of unsuitable DVD's.

'Why do they always want X-rated films, or something they're not supposed to watch? For two girls who still play with rabbits, I can't fathom it.'

'Sounds good,' James whispered in Laura's ear. 'Can we slip upstairs, do you think?'

They moved into the dining room for their starter of parsnip and apple soup, with Pete's special walnut bread. He still wanted to offer an evening meal to expand the B & B but Maggie was unsure about the extra work involved, especially since Lucy seemed less available these days.

'There must be someone in the village who'd want a few hours' work, why not put a card in the shop?' Laura said. 'Then when we all get really busy with the holidays you'll have someone reliable.'

Pete agreed. 'If we're booked to the rafters and one of us

is out of commission, we'll be in a right old mess.'

'Oh, and you'll need a separate website too,' Laura said, adding another reminder to her ever open notebook. 'Then you can link to Trip Advisor.'

'Ugh, not Trip Despiser,' Maggie said. 'Pete's obsessed with reading those reviews.'

'Funny thing is, all those rotten one-stars have disappeared,' he said, clicking his fingers. 'Just like that, overnight.'

He was about to serve dessert when they all heard the unmistakable turn of a key in the front door.

Maggie stopped stirring the custard, and frowned. 'Who's that?'

'More to the point, who's got a bloody key?' Pete said, then shouted out, 'Is that you, Nate?'

They all turned to look as two pairs of feet advanced down the tiled hall. Sleek, groomed, and bold as brass, Jess poked her head into the room and scanned the remains of their boozy lunch. 'Oh, hello, what's this, then? A welcome home party?'

Hovering just behind her and holding a sleeping Krystal in his arms, was Callum Armstrong.

Their chatter fell away, mouths slackened into wordless shapes. When Laura felt she could draw her eyes away for a second, she threw a horrified glance at James.

'*Un*-fucking believable,' he muttered.

Pete looked mutinous. 'Get. Him. Out. Of. My. House. *Now!*'

'Alright, let's calm down,' Maggie said, her eyes devouring Krystal. 'You'll only upset the baby. Oh, Jess! I can't believe you're both here, you *and Krystal!*'

'Yeah, well, we *thought* it would be a nice surprise,' Jess said, choosing her moment then to carefully lift the baby from Callum's arms and present her to Maggie, who looked as if she'd expire with joy. 'It is, it is! It's a *wonderful* surprise,'

Maggie said, holding out her arms. 'Oh, come to Grandma, sweetheart!'

'What are you playing at?' Pete said.

Jess licked her glossy lips. Her eyes slewed from Armstrong and back to her father. 'Right, look. Don't kick-off, alright? Me and Cal, we've proper decided to give it another go.'

'You proper *what?*'

'Let her speak, Pete,' Maggie said, cradling a plump, eight-month old Krystal. She was beautifully turned-out in a pristine snow-white sleep suit with tiny mittens dangling from the sleeves, and a pink bow in her hair.

Armstrong sighed and looked at the ceiling, then down at the floor. 'I told you this wasn't a good idea, babe.'

'No, come on, we're all interested!' Pete shouted, and stabbed a finger in Armstrong's direction. 'Let's start with *him*, *babe*, and why he isn't locked-up!'

Laura risked another glance at James but he seemed set in stone, his profile inscrutable.

There wasn't much of a story, or at least Jess made it seem that way, explaining away the drug incident as a fuss over nothing. Since the offending item had been a microscopic amount – discovered by a particularly insistent spaniel at Maine airport – and since Armstrong claimed never to have set eyes on it before, the hypothetical jury was still out. His arrest had resulted in five days in a US prison, before being sent back to the UK for further questioning. He was banned from ever re-entering America and due before Chester Crown Court in January for possession of a class A, although it looked likely he'd escape further recrimination down to it being a first offence.

Gaining confidence, Armstrong moved into the room and planted his shiny shoes fair and square on Pete and Maggie's seasoned oak floor. 'And I know who set me up. And if Hew fucking Griffiths steps out of line, I might suddenly remember who might have planted that shit on me in the first place.'

'Calling all the shots now, are you?' James said.

'Dead right.'

Jess laid a manicured hand on the front of Armstrong's designer shirt, and gave him a little push. 'Cal, go and wait in the car.'

Laura sensed James shift in his chair. It was perhaps fortunate that he was firmly trapped behind the table, and although she desperately wanted to leave, she still felt compelled to hear everything Jess had to say.

'I can handle Cal,' Jess said, once he'd gone, dropping Krystal's changing bag to the floor. 'I learnt all sorts of stuff from Stella's therapist.'

Pete scoffed. 'Oh, well, that's alright then! Thanks to Stella, we can all sleep easy in our beds.'

A huge, theatrical sigh at this. 'Dad, *look*. Just give him another chance, will you? He's been through *everything* to get me and the baby back. If it wasn't for Cal, Krystal wouldn't even be here now.'

'She's right about that, Pete,' Maggie said, still swaying to Johnny Mathis as he warbled through his Christmas hits on an unremitting loop. Pete shot them both a weary look and poured himself a large glass of cognac. Jess took the opportunity to cast a sly glance at James from beneath her false eyelashes. Then she began to pull rings from her fingers, leaving a small but significant engagement ring in-situ. She dropped two familiar rings onto the tablecloth. The clogau gold bands spun on their axis for a moment, then lay still amongst the crackers.

Carys had come home.

'Sam's divorcing me,' Jess said, her voice barely above a whisper. 'I thought you'd want the rings back.'

'You thought right.'

'The important thing is,' she said, turning to Maggie, 'I

think I can do it, now. Be a proper mum.'

Laura threw her napkin onto her plate and pushed her chair back. 'I need some air,' she said, and James got to his feet instantly. He pocketed the rings and somehow, they said their goodbyes and left the house, heaping coats and gifts into an untidy jumble on the rear seats of the car. James backed angrily off the drive, just missing the front bumper of Armstrong's Mercedes parked behind the hedge.

'I want to reverse all over him,' James snarled, ramming the car into first gear. But then less than thirty seconds down the road he thumped the steering wheel and stopped abruptly outside the church.

'I need a cigarette,' he said, and rifled through the glove box, then rolled the window down. Cold air filtered into the vehicle, a mix of wet earth and woodsmoke. There was a carol service in full flow, and candles flickered behind the leaded windows. Some of the louder voices were hopelessly out of tune, no thanks to the wheezing organ which seemed to be playing in a different key altogether. The combined lack of musicality managed to lighten her odd, mixed-up mood. Their original wedding day would have been around this time, with blood-red gowns and cream roses. She'd even laboured over a dress for Jess, then ripped it to shreds.

'Well, I didn't see that coming,' James said, after a few moments of intense inhalation.

'No. At least it's made Maggie's Christmas complete, having them both home. And I'm honestly pleased about Krystal. I am.'

James grunted at this and then his phone bleeped. He rummaged through his pockets and checked his messages. A curious smile lit the corners of his mouth and the taut lines on his face fell away. He passed the phone to Laura and she looked down to see a single word on the screen: *Hiraeth*

'I think we should go home,' he said, closing up the window. 'It's time to make our own Christmas.'

She frowned, puzzled by both the message and his cute remark.

It was approaching dusk. A flare of dark red sky above the Carneddau warned that the final hour of daylight was almost upon them. They'd need to bring the horses in soon. As they neared the yard, she saw Mal was already standing by the gate, waiting. And waiting on their doorstep, surrounded by a heap of bags and belongings, sat Enid Evans.

THE END

Jan Ruth writes contemporary fiction about the darker side of the family dynamic with a generous helping of humour, horses and dogs. Her books blend the serenities of rural life with the headaches of city business, exploring the endless complexities of relationships.

For more about Jan Ruth and her books:
visit www.janruth.com

WILD WATER

BY
JAN RUTH

Jack Redman, estate agent to the Cheshire set. An unlikely hero, or someone to break all the rules?

Wild water is the story of forty-something estate agent, Jack, who is stressed out not only by work, bills and the approach of Christmas but by the feeling that he and his wife Patsy are growing apart. His misgivings prove founded when he discovers Patsy is having an affair, and is pregnant.

At the same time as his marriage begins to collapse around him, he becomes reacquainted with his childhood sweetheart, Anna, whom he left for Patsy twenty- five years before. He finds his feelings towards Anna reawaken, but will life and family conflicts conspire to keep them apart again?

WHITE HORIZON

BY
JAN RUTH

Three couples in crisis,
multiple friendships under pressure.

On-off-on lovers Daniel and Tina return to their childhood town near Snowdonia. After twenty-five years together, they marry in typically chaotic fashion, witnessed by old friends, Victoria and Linda who become entangled in the drama, their own lives changing beyond recognition.

However, as all their marriages begin to splinter, and damaged Victoria begins an affair with Daniel, the secret illness that Tina has been hiding emerges. Victoria's crazed and violent ex-husband attempts to kill Daniel and nearly succeeds, in a fire that devastates the community. On the eve of their first wedding anniversary, Tina returns to face her husband - but is it to say goodbye forever, or to stay?

SILVER RAIN

BY
JAN RUTH

Alastair Black has revealed a secret to his wife in a last ditch attempt to save his marriage.

A return to his childhood family home at Chathill Farm is his only respite, although he is far from welcomed back by brother George. Kate, recently widowed and increasingly put upon by daughter, sister and mother, feels her life is over at fifty. Until she meets Alastair. He's everything she isn't, but he's a troubled soul, a sad clown of a man with a shady past.

When his famous mother leaves an unexpected inheritance, Kate is caught up in the unravelling of his life as Al comes to terms with who he really is. Is Alastair Black her true soulmate, or should Sleeping Beauty lie?

Made in the USA
Columbia, SC
16 May 2017